darker angels

BOOK TWO OF
THE BLACK SUN'S DAUGHTER

M.L.N. HANOVER

POCKET BOOKS
New York London Toronto Sydney

Pocket Books
A Division of Simon & Schuster, Inc.
1230 Avenue of the Americas
New York, NY 10020

This book is a work of fiction. Names, characters, places, and incidents either are products of the author's imagination or are used fictitiously. Any resemblance to actual events or locales or persons, living or dead, is entirely coincidental.

First Pocket Books paperback edition October 2009

POCKET and colophon are registered trademarks of Simon & Schuster, Inc.

For information about special discounts for bulk purchases, please contact Simon & Schuster Special Sales at 1-866-506-1949 or business@simonandschuster.com.

The Simon & Schuster Speakers Bureau can bring authors to your live event. For more information or to book an event, contact the Simon & Schuster Speakers Bureau at 1-866-248-3049 or visit our website at www.simonspeakers.com.

Cover design by John Vairo Jr.
Cover illustration by Cliff Nielson

Manufactured in the United States of America

10   9   8   7   6   5   4   3   2   1

ISBN 978-1-4165-7677-8
ISBN 978-1-4165-8432-2 (ebook)

To Anita Blake and Harry Angel

darker angels

introduction

"How long has this been going on?"

The teacher sat on the corner of his desk, a pile of ungraded math worksheets shifting under his thigh, and thought about how best to answer. The woman stood, waiting. She was younger than he was by almost a decade. Pale hair, ice-blue eyes, cream linen suit, shoulder holster. She wasn't how he'd pictured an FBI agent. She was almost small enough to sit at one of the kids' desks, but it took a while to notice that. She seemed bigger.

How long *had* this been going on?

"Maybe six months, more or less," he said, "but

it's not the kind of thing you can be sure. I mean, Daria's always been smart, and this isn't a school system that's been much good with smart kids. Especially smart black kids. She's always had a struggle to find her place here."

The woman smiled and nodded, the implicit message being that she understood. He was free to speak, even about issues of race. The teacher relaxed a little.

"What about the hurricane?" she asked. "She was here when Katrina hit, wasn't she?"

"Yeah, well. There is that," he said. "Her family tried to ride it out. She made it to the Superdome, with her grandmother and her sister. Her brother and mom . . . they didn't make it. I don't know. Maybe it started back then. But the past few months, it's gotten worse. She's late for class half the time, and missing maybe a day every week. Her work's perfect when she does it. I've got the grade book right here. Hundreds and zeros. Nothing but."

The woman stepped forward, looking at the book in his proffered hand. The classroom windows were dirty, the dust and grit softening the late afternoon light. The woman didn't step back, and he found himself uncomfortably aware of her body close to his.

"And the stories?" she asked.

"About six months, like I said. I know all the teachers here. I've talked to them. She never used to lie. Or, you know what I mean. No more than any kid does. Not like this."

"I understand," the woman said, leaning past him to put the grade book back on his desk. Her jacket brushed against his shirt with the soft hushing sound of fabric on fabric. He cleared his throat. The woman strode over to the windows as if lost in thought. He couldn't tell if she was coming on to him or simply didn't recognize the effect she was having.

"Mind if I ask why her?" he said.

The woman turned back, a question in her eyes.

"Daria," he said. "She's a good kid. I like her. But . . . Well, I can say this because I work here. There's a reason we've got so many private schools in New Orleans. The kids I see in here, a lot of them don't always have enough food all the time. Or good clothes. They've got daddies in jail or on the street or missing. This is fourth grade, and some of them are already on drugs. I had a nine-year-old girl last year got pulled out because she was messing around with the boys on school property."

"And you think because Daria's not fucking the other students, she doesn't matter?" the woman said. Her voice didn't give away anything. She might have been amused or offended or curious to see how he reacted to her clear, clean enunciation of the word *fuck*. He felt a twitch of anger, and crossed his arms.

"I'm saying we've got a lot of kids in trouble," he said.

"Not like her, you don't," the woman said.

The slap of small shoes on the tile interrupted them. After classes got out, there were hardly any kids still in the school building. The sound of one child running echoed down the hall, coming closer. The teacher rose. The woman shifted her attention to the doorway, and Daria Glapion skidded through it.

The girl's breath was rushed, her face flushed. The long, tight braids of her hair glowed. She wore a green skirt and a white blouse that looked more like an adult's clothes cut small than something a child would wear. If there was fear in the girl's expression, it was no more than what the teacher expected from a child who'd come late to her appointment. He smiled.

"Daria?" he said. "This is Karen Black. She's the woman who wanted to talk with you."

The FBI agent came forward. Daria swallowed once, then nodded to her and smiled theatrically.

"I do hope you'll forgive my being tardy," Daria said, with an affected formality. Her voice was so adult, she almost sounded British. "I meant to be here before, but my sister was eaten by a snake."

He shot a glance at the woman. *That's the kind of thing we hear all the time.* But the FBI agent was fixed on Daria, the pale eyes suddenly soft and friendly, the smile warm and gentle. She knelt a little to put herself at Daria's height. Daria's smile and posture kept their formality, but he saw the girl's eyes flicker.

"Can I ask you a question, Daria?" the woman said.

"But of course."

"The snake. The one that ate your sister? What color was it?"

The shock on Daria's face was startling. The false air of sophistication vanished; her eyes went round and her skin ashen. The teacher stepped forward with the sense that something dangerous had happened, but didn't know who he should protect or from what. The FBI agent's expression was soft and reassuring and maternal. Her pale eyes had the hint of a smile at the corners.

"It's okay," the woman said. "You're okay. You can tell me."

"It was shiny," Daria said. She sounded terribly young.

The woman nodded, as if the two of them had said aloud something they both already knew. She took a deep breath and let it out slowly, the sound of it loud enough to carry. It was a trick, breathing like that, he thought. She's trying to keep the girl from panicking.

"Okay," the woman said. "I need to ask you something else, honey. And it's very very important that you tell me the truth, all right? It's okay. No one's going to hurt you. It's okay to tell me the truth. You understand?"

There was a pause. He could see Daria's pulse racing in the hollow of her neck. She nodded.

"Do you believe me?" the woman asked gently.

Daria nodded again. The woman reached out and took the girl's small, dark hand in both of her pale ones. Daria's breath was fast, her face bloodless. He almost spoke to break the unbearable tension in the air, but something held him back.

"These things that you're telling me," the woman said. "Have they happened yet?"

The teacher leaned forward.

"No," Daria whispered.

The woman rose to her feet, her expression closed and tight. Where a moment before she had been soft and gentle and welcoming, now she was solid and businesslike. Daria took a step backward, biting her lip as if she could take the word back.

"I have to go," the woman said.

"What—" the teacher began.

"I have to go *right now*."

ONE

"Hey," my dead uncle said. "You've got a call."

I rolled over in bed, disoriented. A dream about meeting Leonard Cohen in a perfume factory was still about as immediate as reality. My previous day's clothes were piled in the corner of the tile floor along with the leather backpack I used as a purse. The pack's side pocket was open and glowing. My uncle Eric's voice came again.

"Hey. You've got a call."

I untangled myself from the sheets and stumbled over, promising myself for the thousandth time that I would change the ringtone. The bedroom was still unfamiliar. The cell phone flashed a number I didn't recognize, but there was a name—Karen Black— associated with it, so she must have been in his contacts list someplace. I accepted the call.

"Unh?" I grunted into the receiver.

"Eric, it's Karen. I've found it!" a woman said. "It's in New Orleans, and I know where it's going next. There's a little girl with Sight, and she says her sister is the next target. I don't know how long I've got. I need you."

It was a lot to take in. I hesitated, and the woman misinterpreted my silence.

"Okay, what's it going to take?" she demanded. "Name your price, Heller."

"Actually," I said. "That's complicated. I'm Jayné. Eric's niece. He's . . . um . . . he passed on last year."

It was Karen Black's turn to be silent. I gave her a moment to let it sink in. I skipped the parts about how he'd been murdered by an evil wizard and how several of Eric's old friends, along with a policeman who owed me a favor and a vampire with a grudge against the same wizard, had teamed up to mete out summary roadside justice. I could get back to that later if I needed to.

"Oh," she said.

"Yeah. He left me pretty much everything. Including the cell phone. So . . . hi. Jayné here. Anything I can do to help out?"

The pause was longer this time. I could guess

pretty well at the debate she was going through. I gave her a hand.

"This is about riders, isn't it?" I asked.

"Yes," she said. "So you know about them?"

"Abstract spiritual parasites. Come in from Next Door or the Pleroma or whatever you want to call it," I said as I walked carefully back to the bed. "Take over people's bodies. Have weird-ass magical powers, kind of like the magic humans can do, but way more effective. Yeah, I've got the For Dummies book, at least."

"All right," she said. "Did Eric . . . did he even mention me?"

"No," I said. "Sorry."

The woman on the other end of the line took a breath as I got back under the covers and pulled the pillow behind my back. I heard Aubrey cough from one of the bedrooms down the hall.

"All right," she said. "My name is Karen Black. I used to be a special agent for the FBI. About ten years ago, I started tracking down what I thought was a fairly standard serial killer. It turned out to be a rider. We caught the horse, a man named Joseph Mfume, but the rider switched bodies."

"So not so easy to track," I said.

"No," she agreed. "My supervisors wanted me to stop. They didn't believe there was anything to it. And . . . well, *X-Files* was still popular back then. There were jokes. I was referred for psychiatric

counseling and taken off active duty. I resigned and
went on with the investigation myself. Eric and I
crossed paths a few times over the years, and I was
impressed with his efficiency. I've found where the
rider is going to strike next, and I need help to stop
it. I thought of Eric."

"Okay," I said.

"Can you help me?"

I rubbed my eyes with my free hand until little
ghosts of false light danced in my vision.

"Hell if I know," I said. "Let me talk to my guys
and call you back."

"Your guys?"

"I kind of have a staff," I said. "Experts."

I could hear her turning that over too. I wondered how much she'd known about Eric's financial
situation. For a man with enough money to buy
a small third-world nation, he hadn't flaunted it; I
hadn't even known until he left me the whole thing.
My guess was Karen hadn't expected Eric to have a
staff.

"I don't know how much time I have," she said.

"I'll get back to you as soon as I can. Promise.
We're in Athens right now, so it may take me a few
days to get to New Orleans."

"I don't mean to be rude, but it's not that long
a flight," Karen said, impatience in her tone. "You
could drive it in eight hours or so."

It took me a second to process that.

"Not Georgia Athens," I said. "Athens Athens. Cradle of civilization."

"Oh," she said, and then, "Oh fuck. What time is it there?"

I snuggled down under my covers and looked at the bedside clock.

"One in the morning," I said.

"I woke you up," she said. "I am *so* sorry . . ."

Amid a flurry of apologies and promises to return calls, Karen and I let each other go. I dropped the phone next to the clock and stared at the ceiling.

The last six months had offered me a wide variety of bedroom ceilings. The first at Eric's house in Denver when I was first thrown into the world of riders and possession and magic. Then the dark wood and vigas of an old ranch outside Santa Fe, then a place in New Haven with honest-to-God mirrors over the bed and red silk sheets, followed by a gray-green retro-seventies number in a rent-controlled apartment building in Manhattan that was so small I got hotel rooms for the guys. There had been a much more civilized beige with a little unprofessional plaster repair near the corner in a townhouse in London, and now the bare white with deep blue notes that said this Greek villa had been a full-on tourist trap rental before Eric bought it.

The guys had been with me the whole time, apart from a couple weeks when Aubrey had gone back to his former job at the University of Colorado to tie up some loose ends on his research. In the long, complex process of inventorying the property and resources Eric had left behind, we hadn't stayed anyplace more than two months running, and most considerably less. None of it seemed like home to me, and from experience, I knew I could stare at the dim white above me for hours and still not sleep.

With a sigh, I got up, pulled on my robe, and made my way downstairs to the kitchen. A newspaper on the cheap yellow Formica table yelled out headlines in an alphabet I didn't understand. I poured myself a bowl of cereal with little bits of dried fruit and added milk that tasted subtly different from the 2% I'd grown up with.

I heard the door of one of the other bedrooms open and soft footsteps come down the stairs. After so many months together, I could differentiate Aubrey from Ex from Chogyi Jake without looking.

"Why do you think it is," I asked, "that someone can on the one hand be talking you into a fight against evil spirits and semi-demonic serial killers, but then on the other get embarrassed when they figure out they woke you up to do it?"

"I don't know," Aubrey said as he sat down across from me. "Maybe he just didn't want to be rude."

"*She* didn't want to be rude," I said. "Sexist."

Aubrey smiled and shrugged. Aubrey was beautiful the way a familiar leather jacket is beautiful. He wasn't all muscles and vanity, he didn't spend hours on his wardrobe and hair. His smile looked lived-in, and his body was comfortable and reassuring and solid. He always reminded me of Sunday mornings and tangled sheets.

We'd been lovers once for about a day before I found out that—point one—he was married and—point two—I have a real hangup about sleeping with married men. I still had uncomfortably pleasant erotic dreams about him sometimes. I also had divorce paperwork in my backpack, filled out by his wife with her signature and everything. I hadn't told him about that. It was one of those things that was so important and central to my life that putting it off had been very easy. Every time a chance came up to talk about it, I'd been able to find a reason not to.

"What's the issue?" he asked, and I startled a little, my still-exhausted mind interpreting the question as being about the divorce papers. I pulled myself together.

"There's an ex-FBI agent in New Orleans. She's on the trail of a rider that's a serial killer," I said, and yawned. "Are there a lot of those?"

"Depends on who you ask," he said. "There are a lot of serial killers who claim to be demons or victims of demonic possession. You remember the BTK killer? His pastor said right through the end that the voice coming out of the guy wasn't the man he knew. There are some people who think that all serial killers are possessed. Serial arsonists, too. Is that the last of the milk?"

"No, there's another whole bottle in the fridge," I said around my spoon. "So is it true? Are they all riders?"

"Probably not," Aubrey said. "I mean some serial killers blame porn or bad parenting or whatever. And you can be mentally ill without there being a rider in your head. But by the same token, I'd bet that some are."

"You'd buy it? This FBI lady has been tracking down a body-hopping serial killer, she's managed to get one step ahead of it, and needs help. Sounds plausible?"

"We've all seen weirder," Aubrey said as he measured out enough coffee for three of us. Chogyi Jake always opted for tea. "Do you have any reason to think it's not on the level?"

"You mean is it the bad guys setting a trap? I don't have any reason to think so," I said. "Also no reason not to, though. I could get a background check on her, I guess."

"Might be wise."

I didn't hear Ex coming. He just breezed in from the hallway. Even the T-shirt and sweats he slept in were black. His hair was loose, a pale blond flow that softened his features. Usually he wore it back.

"Since we apparently aren't sleeping tonight,

what are we talking about?" he asked as he pulled out a chair and sat at the table.

"Serial killers, demonic possession," I said. "Same as always."

"Jayné got us a job," Aubrey said.

I ran down the basics again while I finished eating and Ex and Aubrey started. The coffee smelled good—rich and reassuringly heavy—so I had a mug myself. I had to give it to Greece, the coffee was great. Ex pulled back his hair into a severe ponytail, tying it with a length of leather cord while I talked. The softness left his face.

"Officially, it's one out of seven," Ex said when I finished. "Or that's what Brother Ignatius said back when I was in seminary. A little under fifteen percent of serial killings are the result of possession."

"Creepy," I said.

Aubrey and Ex looked at each other across the table. I could tell there was some kind of subterranean masculine conversation going on, and it annoyed me that I was being left out.

"What?" I said. "It's creepy. What?"

"How are you feeling, Jayné?" Aubrey asked.

"Tired. It's . . ." I checked my watch. "Two in the morning."

"Three weeks ago in London, it would have been midnight," Ex said.

"True," I said. "Point being?"

Aubrey held up his hand.

"We've all been busting hump for . . . well, for months now. We've got six hundred books in the wiki and at least that many artifacts and items, most of which we don't have any kind of provenance for. And we're not a fifth of the way through the list of properties that Eric owned."

I knew all of that, but hearing it said out loud made me want to hang my head.

"I know it's a big project," I said. "But it's necessary. If we don't know what we have to work with . . ."

"I agree completely," Ex said. "The thing is, someone's come to you with a problem. Sounds like it might be a little hairy. Are you . . . are *we* in any condition to take it on? Or do you want to finish the full inventory before we dive back into fieldwork?"

What I wanted was firmly none of the above. I wanted to stop for a while. I wanted to find a lovely alpine village, read trashy romances, play video games, and watch the glaciers melt. And there was nothing to stop me from doing it. I had the money, I had the power.

But this was what Eric did, and he left it to me, and walking away from it meant walking away from him too. I sighed and finished my coffee.

"If this lady's on the level, she needs us. And if we wait until we're totally ready, we'll never do anything," I said. "And I think we could all use a break. So here's the plan. I'll get us tickets to New

Orleans, we'll go save the world from abstract evil, and afterward we'll hang out in the French Quarter for a couple of weeks and blow off steam."

"If we've defeated abstract evil, I'm not sure how much of the French Quarter will still be there," Ex said.

"First things first, padre," I said, standing up and heading for the main rooms. In fairness, the padre part wasn't entirely true. Ex had, in fact, quit being a priest long before I met him. Thus the Ex. *Padre* was what a vampire we both knew had called him, and sometimes the nickname still stuck.

The main room of the villa looked like a dorm room a week before final exams. Books filled cheap metal shelves and covered the tables. Ancient texts with splitting leather bindings, paperbacks from the 1960s· with bright colors and psychedelic designs, medical papers, collections of theological essays, books on game theory, chaos theory. Grimoires of all arcane subjects waiting to be examined, categorized, and entered in the wiki that the four of us were building to support our work as magical problem solvers. Our laptop computers were all closed, but plugged in and glowing.

I sat at mine and opened it. It took me about three minutes to dig up an old e-mail from my lawyer listing all the addresses of Eric's properties, and about thirty seconds from there to confirm that I did indeed own a house in New Orleans listed as being in the Lakeview neighborhood, and valued at eight hundred thousand dollars, so it probably had enough bedrooms for all of us. I wondered what it would look like.

I smiled to myself as I got on the travel site and started shopping for the most convenient and comfortable flights back to the States. The truth was, even as tired as I was, the prospect of going somewhere new, opening a new house or storage unit without having the first clue what we'd find gave me a covert thrill. Yes, it all flowed from the death of my beloved uncle, so there was an aspect of the macabre, but it was also a little like a permanent occult Christmas.

Well, except when evil spirits tried to kill me. I had some scars from those that kept me in one-piece bathing suits. But nothing like that had happened for months, and by the time I had four flights booked from Athens International to the Louis Armstrong International Airport, I was feeling more awake and alive than I had in days. Probably the coffee was kicking in too.

It was four in the morning and still a long way from dawn when I called Karen Black.

"Black here," she said instead of hello.

"Hey. It's Jayné Heller here. We talked a few hours ago?"

"Yes," Karen said.

"I've talked to most of the guys, and it looks like

we can get there in about two days. So Thursday, middle of the morning, but I'll call you as soon as we're in and settled. That sound okay?"

"That's great," she said. I could hear the smile in her tone, and I smiled back. Always good to save the day. Her next words were more sober. "We should talk about the price."

"We can do that once we get there," I said.

"I can do that," she said, and paused. "I don't mean to. . . . When I called before, I was a little scattered. I didn't say how sorry I am to hear about Eric. It was rude of me."

"Don't sweat it," I said. "And thanks. I was . . . I was sorry to lose him. I'm a little thin on family generally speaking, and he was pretty much the good one."

"He was a good man," she said, her voice as soft as flannel. To my surprise, I found myself tearing up a little. We said our good-byes and I killed the connection.

I spent the next hour with the fine folks at Google, reading up on serial killers who had claimed to be demons. I got a little sidetracked on a guy called the Axeman of New Orleans who'd slaughtered a bunch of people almost a century ago. In addition to claiming to be from hell, he said he'd pass by any house where jazz music was playing, which seemed a lot more New Orleans than lamb's blood on the lintel.

Chogyi Jake woke at six, a habit that he maintained in any time zone. His head hadn't been shaved in a few days, and the black halo of stubble was just starting to form around his scalp. He smiled and bowed to me, the movement half joking and half sincere.

"Getting an early start?" he asked, nodding at the dun-colored landscape drawing itself out of darkness outside our windows. The Aegean glowed turquoise and gold in the light of the rising sun.

"More like an early finish," I said. "There's been a change of plans."

TWO

I stood on the street, a rented minivan against the ruined curb behind us. Thick, wet American air pressed in on my skin, indefinably different than the damp of Europe. I looked down at the limp MapQuest printout in my hand, then up at the ruin where the house was supposed to be. The walls were covered in dirt and grit, and they slumped ominously to my right. Grass higher than my hips swallowed the concrete rubble that had been a walkway. The windows were gone, the interior walls all stripped down to water-blackened studs.

I walked up two steps of warped boards. Flecks

of green paint still clung to them. A huge X had been spray-painted on the door, something that looked like a date above it, letters and numbers to the left and right, and a three beneath it. I could watch Chogyi Jake make his way around the side of the house and toward the back, his shadow visible through the holes in the walls. There wasn't enough tissue left on the house's bones to stop the light.

"Are we sure this is the right address?" Aubrey asked.

I put the key the lawyer had express-mailed me into the lock. It felt like I was dragging it through gravel, but the mechanism turned. I pushed the door open to the smell of rotting wood and mold.

"Yeah," I said. "This is the place."

Ex said something obscene in a reverent voice. The rest of the neighborhood, spreading out around us for blocks, was the same. Ruined streets as much pothole as pavement, shells of houses with only a handful restored or in the process of being restored. Tall grass. I was standing in front of an eight-hundred-thousand-dollar wound, and that was just my house. Every ruined house or bare foundation for blocks around was the same thing.

Hurricane Katrina had rolled into New Orleans three years before. I'd been in the long breathless pause between high school and college at the time, waiting tables at Cracker Barrel and screwing up the courage to tell my father that I was going to a secular university whether he liked it or not. I'd seen the pictures on the news, same as everyone else. I'd given some money to someone as part of a relief effort, or I thought I had. I couldn't remember now if I'd really done it or only meant to.

It felt like everything important in my life had happened since then: my whole abortive college career, losing my virginity to an unethical teaching assistant, the explosion of my social circle, losing my first real lover, dropping out, Eric's death, my inheritance, then fighting spiritual parasites and evil wizards. And in all that time, no one had fixed this house. Or knocked it down.

Three years was a long, long time for a twenty-three-year-old woman. It apparently wasn't much for a three-hundred-year-old city.

"Should we go in?" Aubrey asked. "Do you think it would be safe?"

"I wouldn't want to bet on it," Ex said.

"Why didn't the lawyers tell us the place was trashed?" Aubrey said.

"Who would have told them?" I asked. "If Eric didn't come check on it, they might not know."

Chogyi Jake finished his circuit of the house. Yellow-green grass burrs clung to his linen shirt.

"Okay," I said. "New plan. Everyone back in the car."

It took under ten minutes sitting in the backseat with Aubrey beside me on the laptop with the cell connection to find a hilariously pricey hotel, make reservations, and plug the address into the rental's GPS system. Chogyi Jake drove, and Ex rode shot-gun. The jet lag was beginning to lift, my brain start-ing to unfog by slow degrees. The signs of damage that hadn't registered during the ride out from the airport now became clear. The yellow-white-gray high-water mark on the buildings, the broken win-dows made more evident by the few houses where new glass had been installed, the ruined asphalt, the strange and ubiquitous X mark on the houses we passed.

We were moving from water to water. My ruined house was a few blocks south of Lake Pontchar-train, the hotel I'd picked a few north of the Mis-sissippi. But as we headed south on I-10, the signs faded. The water mark fell and went away. The city looked hale and healthy, as if we hadn't just seen a whole neighborhood that had gone necrotic.

"Were you ever here before?" Aubrey asked.

"Are you kidding?" I said. "They have Mardi Gras here. Women get drunk and expose themselves. I'd have been disowned if I'd brought the idea up."

"I don't think the exposing yourself part's re-quired," Ex said from the front. "I've been through a few times, and no one seemed offended when I didn't insist on seeing their breasts."

"Doesn't matter if it's true," I said. "It's all about appearances. Dad thought this place was Gomorrah to San Francisco's Sodom. He'd burst a blood vessel if he knew I was here."

"What does he think of Las Vegas?" Aubrey asked.

"Gibbering hysteria," I said. "Apoplexy. Doesn't have much to say in favor of New York either."

"Forgive the change of subject, but should you consider telling the lawyers that we've changed venues and why?" Chogyi Jake said as he pulled the rental over one lane and got off the highway at Orleans heading toward Vieux Carré.

"Fair point," I said. "I'm on it."

If anyone had asked me, back when I was a college dropout with no friends and a family that wasn't speaking to me, whether it would be harder to deal with an arcane world of possession by bodiless parasites or having a lot of money, I would have guessed wrong. Riders and magic were weird and unnatural, but at least they were expected to be. Money was just as strange, but everyone assumed that if I had that much, I must have some idea how it worked. I felt like half of my day was taken up with doing things that real rich people manage by instinct. Like letting my lawyer back in Denver know where to send things.

The man who answered the phone went from chilly to obsequious as soon as I said my name. Two blocks later, I had my lawyer on the phone, saying she'd get an assessor out to the ruined property as soon as possible. She spoke with careful enunciation so sharp I imagined all the words being relieved that they'd gotten out alive. She was the same lawyer who'd first told me my uncle was dead and that I'd inherited everything. We'd never had a personal conversation, but I secretly liked her.

The hotel was smaller than I'd expected and grander too. A fountain burbled in a low foyer. Dixieland jazz jumped and spun through the air like a company of musical acrobats, each instrument doing something apparently different but all perfectly coordinated. Crystal chandeliers hung from high ceilings. But the bones of the place showed that it had been built before the age of steel infrastructure.

The desk clerk—a black man with perfect skin and a Jamaican accent that could melt butter—handed me my key card. He even got my name right, *zha-nay*. I usually get Jane or Janie. I felt myself blushing a little bit, and wondered how long it had been since I'd been seriously flirted with. The four of us agreed to meet back in the lobby once we were unpacked and settled. I headed to my room.

It wasn't a large room, but it was beautiful. Silk wallpaper, crisp sheets, and wireless Internet. There can be no better. I tipped the guy who'd hauled my bags for me, then popped open my laptop and checked mail for the first time since we'd gotten on the plane in Greece.

The background check of Karen Black was in my inbox, cc'd to all the guys. I settled in to find out what I'd gotten us all into.

Karen Alicia Black was born a little over fifteen years before I was. Her father was a cop, her mother was a mother. No living family now, though. When I was getting out of Mrs. Detwyler's second-grade class at Blackburn Elementary, she was graduating from Oberlin with a double major in criminology and mathematics. She moved to Los Angeles and worked as a cop for two years, then joined the FBI. A note in brackets pointed out that this was an unusually short period of time—the FBI preferred three years of professional experience. I had the impression that whoever was writing the report had developed a little crush on her.

Her record at the FBI was impressive—kidnapping, arson, serial murder—until 1998. The year I'd spent watching *Titanic* fourteen times with Nellie Thompson, a man named Joseph Mfume moved to Eugene, Oregon, from Haiti. In the newspaper clippings that were inserted in the text file, he looked about twenty-five, handsome in a goofy way. During the six months after his arrival, he raped and killed seven women in particularly grotesque ways. Karen Black had been part of the team that brought him down.

After that, her career started going off the rails. Two years later, she quit the FBI under a cloud.

There were suggestions that she'd been asked to resign, but nothing that proved it.

Since then, she'd worked on and off for a private investigator and started her own security consultancy based in Boston. Her addresses were listed with pictures of the offices, and the same contact number that was in my cell phone. Her credit rating was decent, the frequent flyer programs loved her, she'd had a couple of bouts of the flu over the years and treatment for chlamydia eight months ago. She owned a condo in Boston, she had no family, no husband, no kids. She'd been in New Orleans on and off almost since the hurricane.

The last two pages of the report were pictures.

The cool gaze that looked out from my computer screen could have belonged to an actress or a supermodel. Pale blue eyes, straight blond hair, a sly smile at the corner of her mouth that seemed to be part of the permanent architecture of her face. In the first image, she wore a black turtleneck and a leather overcoat that reached her ankles, a gray eastern-seaboard streetscape behind her. The next one was a more candid shot of the same woman outside a nightclub. She was in a low-cut emerald silk blouse and tight leather pants, and she had the figure to make the outfit work. Even without the cut of her clothes, I saw what the report's author was responding to.

She radiated confidence and certainty. It was in

her eyes and the way she held her shoulders. She had tracked criminals and stopped killers, and her success had left its mark on her.

And she had called me for help. I had the uncomfortable feeling I was about to disappoint her.

I closed the laptop and the French doors that opened onto the balcony. The lace curtains shifted in an air-conditioned breeze so slight I couldn't feel it. Behind them, palm trees stood guard before a sky of perfect, almost Caribbean blue. The next thing to do was make the call, tell Karen we'd arrived, where we were staying, arrange to meet. It was what I'd said I would do. And yet, here I was, sitting cross-legged on my rented bed, looking at my cell phone and not reaching for it.

It couldn't hurt to put it off, just for a little bit. The guys were probably settled into their own rooms by now, and talking to them would help take away my feeling of being desperately underprepared.

I took a quick shower, changed into my Pink Martini T-shirt and blue jeans that didn't have the stink of travel on them, shoved my laptop into my backpack, and headed down to the lobby. There was a restaurant where we could grab some coffee and talk. Or, failing that, we were in New Orleans. Rumor had it that the food didn't suck.

Only Chogyi Jake was sitting by the fountain when I got there. He'd changed into a linen suit the color of sand half a shade lighter than his skin. He hadn't shaved his scalp recently, and the stubble was like a shadow. He was looking out the window with his customary air of calm near-amusement. He grinned when he saw me.

"How's your room?" I asked, sitting beside him. The cascade of water gave us a white-noise barrier that meant even though I had to talk a little louder than usual, we still couldn't be easily overheard.

"It's fine. Very comfortable," he said. "What's the matter?"

"I . . . I mean, what makes you think something's . . ."

He tilted his head forward a degree, encouraging me to go on. I sighed.

"Yes, okay. You're very clever," I said, a little more peevishly than I'd meant to. "I'm just feeling out of my depth again. Some more. Maybe coming here wasn't such a great idea."

"Even if this woman needs our help?"

"She doesn't, though. She needs Eric's help. He was better than I am."

"Ah," Chogyi Jake said, nodding. It wouldn't have killed him to disagree.

I knotted my fingers together and looked out through the wide glass window at the narrow street of the French Quarter. Two men in desert-camouflage fatigues walked together, one leaning close to say something in the other man's ear. An older black woman with a wide straw hat and a shining aluminum tripod cane made her careful way across traffic. A girl no more than sixteen with café-au-lait skin and hair in glistening black corn-rows sped by on a racing bike, a parrot perched uneasily on her shoulder.

"You read the report on Black?" I asked, and Chogyi Jake nodded silently, not getting in the way of my words. "She's the real thing. Seriously, even without riders and magic and all the rest, she's a professional. Been doing all this for years. She's trained and experienced. And I'm still faking it. She double majored. I didn't even pick a degree program."

"And yet you were able to take on the Invisible College," Chogyi Jake said as if we were discussing someone else. "Eric wasn't able to accomplish that."

"I know, but it's just that . . . I'm tired. I don't even know why I feel so wrung out."

"We have been traveling constantly for months, working eight- and ten-hour days at a task so over-whelmingly large that even that effort hasn't brought us anywhere near completion," he said.

"Well. Okay, when you put it like that."

"Consider that there may be something more going on within you," Chogyi Jake said.

"Like what?" I asked.

"I don't know. You have chosen the pace we've worked at. You've chosen to come here. And you've said that we'll take a rest when this is resolved, but that isn't the first time you've made that decision."

"What do you mean?"

The front doors swung open, a brief gust of city air cutting through the climate-controlled cool of the lobby. Chogyi Jake counted off fingers as he spoke.

"After Denver, you planned to wait for Ex and Aubrey to close up shop. Aubrey had a career at the university he needed time to step away from. Ex had his own affairs. Instead you went ahead and let them catch up later. In Santa Fe, you talked about taking a week off, but changed your mind when we found the copy of the Antikythera mechanism."

"It could have been dangerous," I said. "I didn't know that—"

He lifted a third finger, cutting me off.

"We arrived in London with the intention to take stock, and then rest for a few days, but those days never came. Instead, it was Athens, and now here. You're exhausted because you're exhausting yourself."

"You're right," I said. "I shouldn't be doing that. It's just . . ."

"I didn't say that you shouldn't. I only pointed out that you are. In order to make that kind of judgment . . ."

I sat forward, looking at my hands while his sentence hung in the silence. I knew what he meant. He couldn't judge what was driving me until he knew what it was. And even I didn't know that. Now that he pointed it out, I could see the pattern, one decision after the next, always pushing a little harder, a little faster. Covering ground.

It was that there was so much to look at. To catalog and discover. But that wasn't it either. Even as I tried out possible answers, I knew I was dancing around something. At the heart of it, the issue was more difficult and more painful.

My hands ached. Without realizing it, I had bunched them into fists so tight my knuckles were white. Chogyi Jake still hadn't broken the silence.

Silence which shouldn't have been there. The fountain, the wild brass band, the street noise. All of it was gone. My head jerked up. The lobby was perfectly still. Chogyi Jake's mouth was half open, caught in the middle of his thought. His eyes were empty as a stuffed bear's. The water from the fountain hung in the air like a thousand glass beads. Outside the window, a pigeon was suspended behind the glass in mid-flap.

A tiny sound—no more than the click of dry lips parting—rang out like a shot. I whirled.

The black woman I'd seen walking across the street stood at the foot of the stairs, leaning against her cane, regarding me sourly. She wore an old dress of brightly colored cotton, flowers blooming on her in red and green and orange. She'd taken off her hat, and gray hair framed her face like a storm cloud. Her lips had the lopsided softness of a stroke victim, but her eyes were bright with rage. When she spoke, her voice had the depth of a church bell and the threat of a power saw. It wasn't the voice of a human being. It was one of them. A rider.

"What the *hell* you think you doing in my city?"

THREE

The last time I'd been in swinging distance of a rider, it tried to throw me off a skyscraper. The adrenaline hit my bloodstream as the first word left the thing's mouth. My body leaped even before I knew I was going to do it, streaming through the unnaturally still air toward the thing in the woman's flesh. I think I screamed. The paralyzed lips opened in what might have been a sneer, and the bright metal of the tripod cane knocked me against the wall like I was a softball.

My head rang. Blood tickled the nape of my neck. The woman was chanting something now, her head bobbing from side to side in a way that was both avian and serpentine. Something brown and gray dangled at the end of her thin hand. The air around me began to writhe. I'd felt this once before; the barriers between Next Door and our world growing thin. The things that lived on the wrong side were coming up toward me to feed. I gathered my will the way Ex and Chogyi had taught me, drawing myself up from the base of my spine, through my heart and throat and out, projecting my qi in a shout.

"Stop!"

The woman staggered, her chant losing its rhythm. The things pressing against reality fell back a little. I moved forward, wary of the reach of her cane. Around us, the world was still as statues. The woman bared her teeth. A vein bulged in her neck, straining with effort. The floor seemed to vibrate against my shoes. The woman raised her fists. Her left hand—the one not holding the cane—was limp, barely able to close.

"I will kill you," she spat. "No sun gonna set on me."

"Bite me," I said.

She screamed, and a play of light came from her mouth, her nose, her eyes. It shimmered like sunlight reflected off the surface of a pool; fire and water made one. Mirrors and crystal chandeliers caught the light, shattered it and made it sharp. Something washed over me, and I staggered. My head was full of cotton, and the blood on the back of my neck burned my skin. Something deep in my belly flipped like a fish on the bottom of a boat. I fell to my knees and retched.

"I am not broken," the thing said. "God himself cut His knuckles against me, but I am not broken. You nothing but a mongrel bitch, coming around here."

I launched myself at her again, my shoulder low. She hadn't expected it, and the cane whistled by my ear, cracking the marble floor where it struck. My shoulder took her in the knees and we tumbled together. She smelled like overheated motor oil, like fish and paprika, like rage. I had my hands around her snakeskin dry throat. She clawed at me, and I felt blood on my arm now too.

Her eyes fluttered and began to close. I was killing her. She was dying. I eased my grip a little, giving her a sip of air. Instead of breathing in, her body shifted under its skin. Bones cracked like a splitting rock as her jaw unhinged, her lower teeth and tongue hanging down almost to her collarbone, and a huge serpent slid out of her skin.

I jumped back, tripping over the bent cane. The snake was easily twelve feet long, thick as a weightlifter's leg, and its scales glowed from within. The woman's skin lay abandoned on the floor behind it, black and ashen within the mocking brightness of its dress. The serpent turned black eyes toward me then flicked its head a degree to my left, its attention drawn by Chogyi Jake still motionless at the edge of the frozen fountain.

"Legba," I said, not sure what I meant by it.

The snake turned back to me, powerful curves forming in its flesh as it gathered itself to strike. The fish in my belly flopped again, banging against my spine. I shook my head once. No.

We were as still as the world around us, statues in a field of statues. I felt my body steeling itself for violence, and the small place in my head where consciousness retreated at times like this noted that either I was about to die or the thing across the lobby was. Even money.

The shriek didn't come from either of us. Grating, wordless, wet, the sound smelled like raw meat and pain. The shining serpent hissed, turned back upon itself, and sped into the fallen skin. The old woman was just beginning to stand when something flashed through the door. I had the impression of knives and pale skin and something soft and organic colored a red so deep it verged on purple.

The black woman turned, and her jaw still had the great snake's needle teeth, her eyes still flat black. The blur spun past her, and I saw the impact on her body without ever seeing the blow. I rolled forward, scissoring my legs against hers, and the black woman stumbled.

I didn't see her elbow twisting around until it

hit my temple and the world went distant and dim.
The snake-toothed mouth came down lightning fast,
flashing toward my bared throat, but something
pushed it aside. An impact like two trucks crashing
head-on. The black woman went sprawling, then
raised her twisted hands, shouted once, and was
gone.

Sound returned, trombone and clarinet blar-
ing with something like joy. In the fountain, water
crashed and splattered. I heard Chogyi Jake say
something like . . . *I would need to understand* . . .
um. An unfamiliar arm was around my shoulders,
strong and gentle. The scent of musk and hyacinth
washed over me. My hair tugged a little at the back
as I sat up, the blood adhering to the marble floor.

She was beautiful. The brightness in her blue
eyes, the careless grace of her hair, the amusement
that waited in the wings behind her smile. She wore
a low-cut white lace blouse and black leather pants.
No one looks good in leather pants, but she did.

"You must be Jayné," she said. "I'm Karen Black."

THE PRODUCTION number that followed
would have been comic if I hadn't ached from head
to foot. The marble floor was broken where the rider
had struck it, and Karen, thinking on her feet, had
pointed to it as the thing that had tripped me. The
concierge fluttered around me, hotel functionaries

bringing wet cloth and hot tea, offering to call a
doctor and fearing I'd call a lawyer.

Chogyi Jake knew better, having seen the flicker
of lost time, but no one else questioned our version
of events. By the time Aubrey and Ex came down,
deep in conversation, the little gash on my head had
stopped bleeding and the hotel management had
dropped down from hyperventilating to concerned.
Everyone got introduced around, but I had the
strong impression that Karen was waiting to talk
until we were someplace less public.

My first impulse was to go back to one of our
rooms, but with all five of us, it seemed like a tight
squeeze. Instead, Karen led us out of the hotel and
into the French Quarter. I could tell the others—Ex
especially—were bursting with questions. Anytime
we got close to the subject of riders or magic, she
steered us away.

We walked down Chartres toward Jackson
Square, which was, Karen said, the center of the
tourist trade. The streets were narrower than I'd
imagined, and the balconies over the sidewalks
made the buildings seem to lean across toward one
another, as if they were greeting each other without
including us. In the middle of a block, Karen steered
us into a dark corridor with ancient wooden stairs
clinging to one wall. We turned into the shadows
under the stairway, walked down another shadowy
corridor with ivy growing up the stucco on the right,

and came out into a wide brick courtyard. Tables and chairs of wrought-iron filigree were scattered under wide, shady trees, and a white man in a soft linen shirt and pressed khakis appeared seemingly from the foliage itself to guide us to a table.

"I hope you don't mind," Karen said as we took our metal seats. "I've used this place before. They're very good about leaving you alone when you want to talk. And the crawfish here are excellent."

"Good to know," Ex said through clenched teeth. "Now would someone tell me what the hell happened back there? Jayné *tripped*?"

"No, I didn't," I said.

"It found her," Karen said. "The rider I've been tracking down. It tried a preemptive strike."

"Okay, hold on," Aubrey said. "What exactly is this thing?"

"Have you ever heard of *loa*?" she asked.

"Afro-Caribbean gods," Chogyi Jake said. "Voodoo spirits."

"And a kind of rider," Karen said. "The sphere of influence between Haiti, Cuba, and the southern coast of the United States is practically alive with them. I've tracked eight hundred cases of people being ridden by *loa* since I started paying attention."

"Eight *hundred*?" Ex said.

"They aren't all confirmed, but yes. That's the ballpark. By which I mean eight hundred in the past ten years."

Karen raised her hand, waving linen-shirt guy over. While the idea of that many riders sank in, she ordered three plates of crawfish and drinks for all of us. The man nodded and vanished. Around us, ferns and tree limbs bobbed gently in a soft breeze.

"Usually, they stick together," she said. "There's something about them that other riders don't seem to like. The one I found in Portland had come from Port-au-Prince. If it hadn't gotten so far out of its home territory, I might not have put it together."

"What was it doing in Portland?" Aubrey asked at the same time I said, "How did it find us?"

Karen smiled and leaned forward. The neck of her blouse gaped a little, showing the curve of her breasts. Ex cleared his throat and looked away but she didn't take notice.

"Just because the *loa* tend to stick together doesn't make them a great big happy family," she said. "There are struggles within the population. They form alliances with each other, they disrupt each other, they fight for power. For horses."

"Horses meaning host bodies," Aubrey said.

"Meaning victims," Karen said. "The one I found had lost some kind of internal power struggle. It had been cast out."

"Voodoo politics," I said. "Sounds like high school. The unpopular demon has to go sit at a different lunch table."

"More like gangs fighting over turf," Karen said.

"They might shoot each other to control some particular street corner, but if an outsider comes into the city, they'll all band together against it. Even with the internal struggles, there's a protection that comes from being part of the community. Exile strips them of it."

"So the loser rode Joseph Mfume out to Portland," Ex said.

"Where it tried to establish territory of its own," Karen said with a nod.

"What can you tell us about how this particular rider behaves?" Aubrey asked, shifting forward in his seat.

Before Karen could answer, the waiter returned, a second man trailing behind him. They carried three wagon-wheel large platters that, when they put them on the table, almost didn't leave room for the drinks. At least a hundred tiny red bodies were curled in each one along with small bowls of red sauce and melted butter. Karen scooped one up, pulled off the tail and sucked at the remaining body chitin. A slow smile spread across her lips as she dropped the empty crustacean back on the plate and started stripping the shell from the tail meat.

"You just don't get these in Boston," she said. "Lobster, yes. Clams. Crab. But there's nothing like Louisiana crawfish."

I picked one up. Its dead eyes reminded me of the shining snake's.

"Pinch the tail off and suck the head," Karen said with a smile.

Well, if she could do it . . .

The hard red shell pressed against my lips, and something hot and salty slid into my mouth. I was prepared to gag, but it tasted good. I considered the small red crustacean skull with pleased surprise.

"You were asking about the rider," Karen said to Aubrey, making the statement an apology. "It's a subtle form. It doesn't kill the horse or displace its soul, just lives in the back of his head and changes him. In this case, it changes him into a serial killer."

"To what end?" Chogyi Jake asked, picking up a crawfish of his own.

"Don't eat that one," Karen said. "If the tails aren't curled, it means they were already dead when they went in the boiler. To what end . . . I think it's a way to enforce isolation. Mfume started with his fiancée, for example. It eliminates the people who are nearest to it. Kills the people the horse loves."

"In order to protect itself from being discovered," Aubrey said.

"Or to break the spirit of the person being ridden," Ex said. "If it doesn't displace the original personality, then Mfume was there. He was watching himself rape and slaughter his lover, and didn't know it wasn't him doing it."

"Exactly," Karen said. "He felt the excitement. The pleasure. He had all the release that a normal human killer has. By the time he understood what was really happening, it was too late. He was crazy."

"Wait a minute," I said. "He figured it out? He *knew*?"

"He did," Karen said. "It's how I knew that it wasn't over. Even after we caught him, we'd only caught the body. The horse. When it left his body, Mfume told me everything. He begged me to find it for him."

"To kill it," I said.

"To bring it back to him," Karen said. "By the time it was over, he was in love with it."

"Okay, huge ick factor," I said.

"I've been tracking this thing for the last decade, one city to another," Karen said. "Six months ago, it finally came back home to the land of voodoo. Something happened within the *loa* that either lifted its exile or made it impossible to enforce."

"Something about the hurricane," I said, thinking of Eric's ruined house and the devastation that surrounded it. The strange X mark on the door. The ring like a dirty bathtub that marked the buildings we'd seen driving in. High water.

"Possibly," Karen said, soberly.

"How did it find Jayné," Ex asked. "She's very difficult to locate magically. This thing must have an angle."

"At a guess?" Karen said. "The same way I found *it*. The little sister. You have to understand that the *loa* have been building voodoo cults in New Orleans for centuries. Things have happened here. Powerful, unnatural things. It's changed the nature of space. The world's thin here.

"There's a girl. Daria Glapion. She has the Sight. Call it limited precognitive ability. Sometimes people know things that there's no particular reason they should know. She told me that her sister was going to be the rider's next victim. Eaten by a snake was what she called it, but I knew what that meant. Maybe better than she did."

"And she spilled the beans about us," Ex said.

"Again, possibly without knowing what she meant," Karen said. "The rider is in her grandmother. Amelie Glapion, self-styled voodoo queen of New Orleans. Glapion has been heading one of the local voodoo cults for years. Her family has a history with the *loa*. When the rider came back, it took her. It was something I suspected, but it's hard to prove. Until I managed to meet the little girl, I wasn't sure."

Karen looked angry. More than angry. Her eyes had a focused, controlled hatred. I remembered how the snake had fled when Karen came to my rescue. Seeing her now, I thought the thing hadn't run fast enough, and if it wasn't still fleeing, it was only from ignorance. That thought sparked another in a little cascade of mental dominoes.

"Hey," I said. "How did *you* know where to find us?"

"I called her," Aubrey said, sounding something between defensive and surprised. "That was the plan wasn't it? We settled in, then we called Karen."

Her contact number had been on the report, it was true. And I'd had the lawyers cc all the guys. I'd assumed that I would be the one to make contact, since I was the one with Eric's cell phone. It wasn't anything I'd explicitly said. It wasn't even something I'd really thought about, and yet something about it unnerved me. Something about Aubrey choosing this moment to take initiative with one of our plans. With seeing those pictures of Karen and being moved to call her.

Karen's perfect blue eyes flickered between me and Aubrey, reading the subtext like it was written in foot-tall flaming letters.

"I should have confirmed with you," Karen said to me. "It was thoughtless of me."

"No," I said, waving it away with a laugh. "No, Aubrey's right. That was absolutely the plan. I just didn't know we'd done it." I picked up another crawfish and snapped its head free. "It's cool."

"Good that he did," Ex said, maybe a little more sharply than was strictly needed. "If Karen hadn't arrived in time to intervene, things could have gotten ugly."

I felt the urge to defend myself, but I wasn't quite sure what from. I wanted to say that I'd been holding my own against the rider. That it was just fine with me that someone else had called Karen and told her where we were. Without telling me. I didn't have a problem with any of it. Chogyi Jake coughed once, then folded his hands on the table. His sweet, enigmatic smile could have meant anything.

"There's more than enough room for ugly still to come," Karen said. "Glapion knows we're here. We don't have a lot of time if we're going to do what we need to do."

We turned toward her like sunflowers on a bright day. Even me.

"The victim is going to be Glapion's other grand-daughter. Not Daria, but Sabine," Karen said. "We can take it as given that Sabine isn't going to accept the idea that her loving grandmother is about to become a soulless killer."

"How do we address that?" Ex asked, and I was a little disturbed by the *we* until Karen smiled. I was being paranoid and territorial and weird. I was tired. None of this was her fault.

"Normally, I'm a strong advocate of people's freedoms and right to self-determination," Karen said. "This is an exception."

"We kidnap Sabine," Chogyi Jake said.

"We do," Karen said. "And when she's safe, we get the grandmother, extract the rider, and kill it."

FOUR

"We need to know where the girl's going to be," Ex said. "When, where. What kind of protection. Does Grandma Glapion have guards on the girl."

"And a van," Aubrey said. "Something like Chogyi Jake's old clunker. No windows. That'll be important, right?"

Karen held up her hand, palm out. The smile at the corner of her mouth deepened slightly.

"We can't just go snatch the girl off the street tonight," she said.

"The more time we take—" Ex began.

"The more prepared we are when it happens,"

Karen said. "Let's say we do the thing right now. Go get the girl, throw her in the back of a rental. Great. Now we've got an angry teenage girl in the car. What exactly do you plan to do with her? And keep in mind, we're actually committing a felony when we do that. The police aren't going to take 'we're protecting her from her demon-ridden family' as a serious defense."

"And," Chogyi Jake said slowly, thinking through the words as he said them, "it isn't as though the rider is without resources. It found Jayné even before she knew where she was going to be."

"The Sight isn't encyclopedic," Karen said. "Daria doesn't see everything, and what she does see, she often won't understand. But yes, we can assume that Glapion will foresee at least some of our plans."

Aubrey leaned forward, brow furrowed. Ex frowned and crossed his arms.

"We need a safe house," I said. "Someplace we can keep her. And we'll want to put wards on it. Like what Eric had on the house in Denver. Something to make us hard to find. Chogyi Jake? You were the one who kept those going. Do you think you could do it again?"

There was a moment's pause. Overhead, a bird rattled and took wing. Chogyi Jake nodded.

"It would take time," he said. "And there is a wooden chest in the London townhouse that would be . . . very useful."

"Okay. So magical stuff from London and a place to use it. Check. Karen? Did you have a place in mind for the safe house?"

"I don't," she said. "I was torn between having something here in or very close to New Orleans and taking Sabine entirely out of the picture."

"Okay," I said, "tell me about that. What are the issues?"

The sly smile bloomed into laughter.

"You *are* Eric's family, aren't you?" she said. "All right. On the one hand, this is Glapion's territory. She knows the city, and the rider has power here. On the other hand, if we send Sabine out of the city, someone has to go to guard her. Also . . . well, I didn't work many kidnapping cases, but the common wisdom at Quantico was that most of the abductees that escape do it when they're in transit. There are a lot of variables in moving people around, especially when they don't want to be moved."

"Yeah, I can see that. Okay, so that's job one."

"And transportation," Ex said. "Aubrey's right. We need something to move the girl in once we have her. Unless we're taking the kid on the bus."

"Do we have a good way to put wards on a van?" I asked.

"I'll look into it," Chogyi Jake said.

"All right," I said. "How about this. Chogyi gets in touch with the property manager in London and gets whatever we need shipped out here. Karen?

You've been local. Can you and Ex arrange the transportation?"

"Sure," Karen said. I had the feeling that her amusement was tempered with respect, and the idea warmed me a little. The truth was I was showing off, taking charge like I was the Godfather. It wasn't how I usually operated.

"If I'm buying something off the lot, I'll need the Darth Vader card," Ex said, meaning my American Express Black.

"Too showy," I said. "We don't really want to be memorable. You guys scout it out. If it's cheap enough to do out of petty cash, just grab it. If we need something new, I'll have the lawyers make the purchase through a shell corporation."

"Right," Ex said. "I'll need a way to go shopping in the first place. Should we take the rental?"

"I'll drive," Karen said. "I know a chop shop that sells a lot of gray-market cars."

I nodded, gratified that Karen was going along with my plan.

"Aubrey and I can hit the real estate sites, do some driving, see what we can find for a safe house."

I pulled my cell phone out of my pack and checked the time. Three thirty, local. In Athens, it was pushing midnight. I felt fine at the moment, but experience suggested that I had maybe four more hours before jet lag kicked in. After that, I'd have about three working neurons, max.

"We don't have a lot of time," I said. "How about we do what we can between now and seven o'clock. Then meet back at the hotel, compare notes?"

Aubrey raised his hand like a kid in a classroom.

"You were attacked by a very powerful rider a little over an hour ago," he said. "Are you sure we should scatter out in all directions?"

I hesitated. The rational, thoughtful part of my mind saw the point, and I had to admit it was a good one. But it also took apart everything I'd just proposed. I was not going to be humiliated in front of Karen.

"I think we can handle ourselves," I said.

"I agree," Karen said. "If a captain's highest aim was to preserve his ship, he'd keep it in port forever."

Ex looked across the table at Karen like he'd just seen her for the first time. I felt an uneasy warmth in my chest that might have been pride or fear or something made from both.

"Okay," I said. "Let's get to it, shall we?"

Back at the hotel, I called the lawyer while Aubrey got online and poked through real estate websites advertising rentals and houses for sale. The best balance of seclusion and proximity we found was a place in Pearl River, about forty-five minutes away. I printed up directions and tossed Aubrey the keys to the minivan. Twenty minutes later, we were on I-10, passing the Irish Bayou Lagoon and heading out over the wide, empty water of Lake Pontchartrain.

I leaned against the window, the vibration of the engine and the road feeling a lot like being in an airplane. I could feel the first soft breezes of jet lag wafting through my mind. My body felt heavy and slightly ill. Outside, a real wind was kicking up tiny whitecap waves.

This was the same water that had swamped the Lakeview house. It looked calm now, silty and greenish in the cool of the coming evening. Hundreds of pilings and wide sections of concrete showed where the damaged southbound bridge was being rebuilt. I wondered if this might be part of the mystery of violence; the way something could look so calm and peaceful, right up until it didn't.

In my hazy state of mind, the thought seemed bigger than this particular water, this particular bridge. I felt like it applied everywhere. A little old lady with a tripod cane who puked out a needle-toothed demon. A favorite uncle who, on his death, turned out to be more than I'd ever known. A simple, physical attraction to a good-looking man with what my mother would have called *a kind mouth* that turned into a night of sex, a mass of guilt, and a set of divorce papers that I still hadn't told Aubrey about.

I must have sighed, because Aubrey looked over at me, concerned.

"Hey," he said. "You doing all right over there?"

"I was just thinking about what Karen said," I lied. "The whole thing with the rider taking over people's minds. About how Mfume loved it by the end. I just don't get that."

"There's a fair amount of precedent," Aubrey said. "Not in vertebrates, particularly. But wasps, caterpillars . . ."

"Ooh," I said, curling up in the seat. "I love it when you talk geeky."

I didn't usually flirt with Aubrey. I didn't usually flirt with anyone. It was the exhaustion, I told myself. And the adrenaline crash from the rider's ambush. It wasn't because I thought Karen Black was smarter and sexier and more competent than I was. Flirting with Aubrey because I didn't measure up to her would have been juvenile and stupid, and I would never do anything like that.

Yeah, whatever.

Still, Aubrey laughed a little, smiled a little, ran his hand through his hair like he was suddenly self-conscious about how he looked.

"There was an example they talked about a lot when I was in grad school," he said. "*Glyptapanteles*. It's a family of wasps that parasitize moths. Well, caterpillars."

"A wasp as a parasite for a caterpillar?" I said. "How do you fit a wasp inside a caterpillar?"

The far shore of the lake was just coming into view. We had almost passed over the water.

"You don't," he said. "The wasps lay eggs in the caterpillar. When the eggs hatch, the larvae live off the host's body. They eat it, but they don't kill it. Eventually, they pop out and pupate."

"*Pupate,*" I said. "Meaning turn into grown-up wasps, right?"

"Yeah," he said. "While they're doing that, they're vulnerable. There are a lot of predators who could just come along and eat them, so there's a lot of evolutionary pressure to keep that from happening. Some wasps, the pupae are cryptic and well hidden. Some of them the larvae get in a really hard-to-reach place before they pupate. *Glyptapanteles* stay right by the caterpillar they came out of. And the whole time that they're turning into wasps, the caterpillar guards them. Anything comes along and tries to eat the pupae, it knocks them away."

"So do they leave a larva behind or something?"

"No," he said. "They all leave. It's not like they're still in there driving the caterpillar's body."

"Then why does it do that?" I asked.

"It's been changed," Aubrey said with a shrug. "We don't know how yet. When you get down to that level of behavior modification, you might just as well say that the caterpillar loves the wasps. It's not like there's a better way to put it."

We passed back onto dry land. The lake faded away behind us in the trees. The sun was off to our left, growing red and heavy in the last few degrees until sunset. Aubrey was a silhouette, the shadows of the roadside trees stuttering like an old movie with its sprockets slipping. I had the uncomfortable sense that I'd done something wrong. I'd sort of been coming on to Aubrey—something I'd tried not to do in these last few months—and the end result was a view of love and parasites that actually left me feeling a little queasy. Normally, Aubrey's biology talks were pretty interesting. That one had felt pointed.

Love is when something's gotten into you, changed who you are, and made you into something not quite whole and entirely self-destructive. My mind kept turning the idea one way and another, like a jigsaw puzzle piece that wouldn't quite fit.

Jet lag, I told myself. Exhaustion and paranoia.

The sun was still up, though only barely, when we turned off the highway and into Pearl River. The streets were almost rural. The trees that lined the roads were thick, and had the haphazard feel of landscape more than landscaping. We twisted down a couple roads, Aubrey squinting against the reddening sunlight while I tried to pick house numbers off the roadside mailboxes.

The place from the Realtor's site was on three acres, and set well back from the road, almost into the woods. We pulled up the long drive. A wide grassy area too feral to be called a lawn. Towering trees, six or seven stories high with wide branches greening with the promise of spring but still bare of leaves. A three-bedroom home, two and a half baths, two-car garage, den, dining room, large shed in the rear yard staring out into the growing twilight, dark windows like unfriendly eyes. A small stone statue of the Virgin Mary lurked near the front door, ivy growing up the side. In context, it looked like a gravestone.

Aubrey stopped the minivan and killed the engine. The quiet wasn't perfect, but it was deeper than I'd expected in a place that was still officially a city. We got out of the minivan. A firefly ignited, floated up in the gloom, and vanished.

"No neighbors to speak of," Aubrey said. "At least not in line of sight."

"Yeah," I said. "Let's go look at that shed in the back."

The shed was bigger than my old dorm room. It was painted red as a rough echo of the barn it almost resembled. There were no windows, but a small, dark vent near the top was choked by a bird's nest. I walked up to it and put my hand on it. Metal siding, but with something more solid under it.

"Would make a decent little prison," Aubrey said.

"I'm always impressed by how much fighting evil feels like committing crime," I said. "But you're right. It's . . . well, if it's not perfect, it's as close as we're going to get on short notice."

"You can afford the place?" he asked. I didn't

answer. He knew as well as I did that I could afford the whole subdivision.

On the way back across the river, I called my lawyer on the cell phone and left her a message with the address of the new house, the listed Realtor, and the instruction that I wanted to take possession as soon as possible. If I stumbled a little over the word *possession*, it was only my unsettled state of mind.

As we sped through the rising darkness, I wondered if this was how Eric would have done things. Everyone I met seemed surprised that he had the money and influence that he did. Apparently, he'd played that close to the vest. The same way he'd played everything. Until he died and left me the keys to the kingdom, I hadn't known that riders existed, much less that he was in the business of opposing them. I still didn't know how he'd amassed the wealth I was spending. All I could say for certain was that it hadn't come from my grandfather, or my own father wouldn't have struggled so hard to keep me, my mother, and my two brothers in good clothes on Sunday.

Would he have come when Karen called? Would he have agreed to her plan, or would he have had a better one? What would he have seen that I was missing? The jet lag paranoia was thick as paste. I told myself that long plane flights always did this to me, and that a night's rest would fix ninety percent of it. Or if not that, at least half.

New Orleans appeared across the water, a glow of light in the dark air. A city half ruined, but still bright.

We got back to the hotel a little bit late. Chogyi Jake, Ex, and Karen Black were already in the restaurant. The afternoon's bright Dixieland had given way to a live jazz band softly playing songs I felt like I knew. The air was thick with humidity, but instead of feeling damp, it seemed lush. Like the whole city had just stepped out of the tub, and hadn't quite gotten its robe on. The table was long enough for six, but set for five. Karen had taken the seat at the head, Ex to her left, Chogyi Jake to her right. Two highball glasses were sweating on the linen in front of Ex and Karen. Chogyi Jake was drinking water. Some things never change.

As Aubrey and I took our seats, Karen waved a greeting, but didn't pause in the story she was telling.

"So there I was, dressed like the world's cheapest hooker, trying to explain to the Secret Service that I hadn't even *known* the vice president was staying there, and that they probably wanted to move him before the rest of the team showed up and arrested half the hotel staff."

Ex chuckled and shook his head. Chogyi Jake smiled his beatific smile and turned to us.

"How was the house hunting?" he asked.

"Decent," Aubrey answered.

"I think we've got a place," I said. "It may be a day or two before we can get keys, though. Money lubricates, but bureaucracy resists."

"It will be at least two days before the package arrives from London," Chogyi Jake said. "But the property manager was quite helpful."

"How long will it take you to get the place ready once all the props are here?" I asked.

"Two or three days," Chogyi Jake said. "Two for certain if Aubrey or Ex can be spared. More likely three if it's only me."

The waiter ghosted up to us, took our drink orders, handed us two leather-bound menus, and vanished again. When Karen went back to the business at hand, she talked directly to me.

"There's reconnaissance work to be done, but I don't know that having four people would actually be an improvement on three. Or two, for that matter. The more people we have, the better the chances of being made."

Ex sipped his drink. I didn't remember ever seeing him with anything stronger than a beer before.

"How about you and me and Aubrey do what we can to track the girl," I said. "Ex? You up for helping Chogyi Jake with the safe house?"

"Sure," Ex said without rancor. I'd expected him to object. I was jumping at shadows.

"What's the deal with the car?" Aubrey asked.

"Ninety-four Ford cargo van," Ex said. "We're

leasing it under a false name, for cash. It'll be here in the morning."

"The gray market's treating us gently," Karen said. "I'll make sure the police aren't looking for it for any other reasons before we take it on the road, but I think we're good."

Aubrey looked suitably impressed. Our drinks arrived.

"We need to switch hotels," I said. "I don't want to try sleeping and worrying that the evil snake woman's going to make another try for me."

"Already done," Karen said. "Ex had the same idea. We even moved your things. We'll go to your new digs after dinner."

I felt a moment's disquiet about other people touching my stuff, but I let it pass.

"So there's just one more thing we need to talk about," I said to Karen. "The price."

Ex, Aubrey, and Chogyi Jake were quiet. Karen's smile deepened slightly, and she looked down at the table. When she looked up at me through her soft, blond hair, her eyes were steeled. It struck me again that she was beautiful. The band shifted into something that I was pretty sure was John Coltrane.

"You're right. I shouldn't have gotten carried away before I knew I could afford all this," she said. "What will it take?"

"Nothing that'll break the bank," I said. "I want you to tell me everything you know about my uncle."

five

The food arrived, a bouillabaisse that smelled rich and oceanic with two side orders of raw oysters for the table. The band took a break between sets, and a recording took their place, muted trumpet and stand-up bass hovering together just under the level of conversation. Karen ate a couple oysters, her eyes focused on nothing in particular, and then, her thoughts gathered, nodded to herself.

"I met Eric in the summer of 2000," she said. "I was still officially working for the bureau, but I'd taken a leave of absence. I was . . . I wasn't well. I don't know how much you know about my history? Do you know about Davis?"

I shook my head.

"Okay," Karen said. "I have to go back a little farther. After we caught Mfume, I wasn't the only one looking for the rider. My partner on the case, Michael Davis, also heard everything Mfume said. We were working on the issue together. The year before I met Eric—July 12, 1999, the rider that had been in Mfume killed my partner. It made it look like an accident, but I knew.

"I went to New York. That was where the rider was. I started looking around. Eric's name kept coming up. Everyone knew him, or knew about him. He was some sort of fixer. The guy you went to when you didn't have anywhere else to go. I made him for a bagman. The public face of something bigger. I was wrong about that. Anyway.

"I found him in a bar on the Upper West Side. He had an apartment, and he was doing business out of it. I tried to lean on him. I don't know exactly what I said. I think I gave him some crap about not having a business license or something," Karen said, and she smiled. "He didn't buy it. I'd meant to go in and roust him, break some heads, find out who his boss was, and if there was any connection to the rider. Instead, we wound up drinking whiskey and . . . and I told him everything. He had a way of listening that made you say things you didn't mean to."

"And he helped you?" I asked.

"He did," Karen said, but her expression was bleak. "We didn't catch the rider, but we cast it out of the body it had taken over. Broke its power a little. Weakened it. Afterward, I was sick for almost a month. It hadn't been . . . it wasn't easy. He let me stay at his apartment. He made me bathe once or twice a week. He kept me eating food."

"He guided you back," Chogyi Jake said. Karen considered for a moment, then nodded.

"He was with me through my breakdown," she said.

"Were you lovers?" I asked.

"Only a couple times toward the end," Karen said. Her voice had taken on a low, throaty amusement. "I wouldn't have been much fun in the sack right at the beginning. But no, we weren't serious about each other. We were just a man and a woman in close proximity for a few weeks. And neither of us had anyone. That's all."

"What was his price?"

"Twenty thousand dollars, and five favors to be named later," she said. "He called in three of the favors. Before I left the bureau, he had me expunge some information from a guy's police record. Then after I left, he needed someone to be a lookout on a job he was doing in Seattle, so I went out and helped with that. The last time I heard from him, he needed me to keep a baby at my apartment for a couple weeks in March of '03."

"A baby?" Aubrey asked.

"Yeah. Little boy," Karen said. "Looked Indian. Subcontinent Indian, I mean. I called him Raja, but I don't know what his real name was. Eric dropped him off, then came and got him again. I didn't ask what it was about."

"March of 2003," Ex said. "I remember that. He said he had to go take care of his mother for a few weeks. In Kentucky."

"Well, he spent at least some of that time with an eight-month-old in Boston," Karen said.

"And Grandma Heller died when I was twelve," I said.

"That was the thing with Eric," Karen said. "I knew a lot of things about him, but I was never sure any of them were true. Maybe he'd been in the military, maybe that was just a story. Maybe he'd gone to Juilliard. Maybe not. He had this way of suggesting things without ever exactly saying them. And then sometimes he was just joking. Or he was protecting me from something."

The muted trumpet rose like a child wailing for her mother and went silent. Karen's structural half-smile softened.

"I'm not helping, am I?" she asked.

"I don't know," I said. "It seems like everyone knew a different version of him. I just wish . . ."

That he'd told me what he was, and what I was

going to become. That he'd taught me. That he'd trusted me.

The Eric Heller I'd known had been the benign uncle, hated by my uber-Christian parents. When I'd gone on the queen mother of all teenage rebellious benders at sixteen and woken up with an honest-to-God lost weekend and a tattoo on the small of my back, Eric had been the guy to cover for me. When my father had informed the family that Eric was an abomination before God, I'd thought it meant he was gay.

And Eric had also been the architect of a secret war against riders. And having an affair with Aubrey's wife, Kim, which was another thing I'd carefully not mentioned. And secreting anonymous babies with former FBI agents.

I ate an oyster, the stony shell feeling unnaturally solid and real.

"I'll tell you what," Karen said. "I'll tell you anything I remember. Any question you want answered about him, I'll do my best. And you can have those last two favors I owed him. And if I happen to win the lottery, I'll pay you back for the house and car."

"Deal," I said, managing a smile.

As we ate, the conversation warmed. Karen was a good storyteller, and Ex, Chogyi Jake, and Aubrey all chimed in. It gave me room to step back and let the fatigue seep in. I wasn't sure what I'd expected, asking Karen to give me information about Eric.

Some handle on him, some indication of whether he would have done what I was doing now. Something. The truth was, I didn't need to charge prices for what I did, and at twenty thousand a throw, Eric didn't either. With the money he'd left me, twenty thousand was pocket change.

But still, he'd taken it from Karen. He'd slept with her, taken her money, nursed her back to health, involved her in his work without explaining anything. I didn't know what to make of any of it, and as the food hit my stomach, my few remaining neurotransmitters seemed to break down. The after-dinner coffee came at nine o'clock. Or five in the morning, Athens time. Fatigue was shaking in my veins.

I paid off the bill just as the band came back for a second set. Five black men in good suits and thin black ties. I wondered if it was a uniform designed to make me think of the Blues Brothers, or maybe it was the other way around. The sax player caught me staring at them and smiled.

"Why don't you guys get the car," Karen said. "Jayné and I can walk it."

I was too tired to object, even though the idea of walking as far as the sidewalk seemed optimistic. Karen tucked my arm in hers and led me out into the thick night air. It was easy to forget how short she was, but as we reached Bourbon Street, she shifted, putting her arm around my waist and looping mine over her shoulder. I was easily four inches taller, and she fit beside me the way I had once fit beside my boyfriend.

The old Sting tune kept floating through my head as we turned north. "Moon Over Bourbon Street." And here I was, walking through the narrow street. Cars moved past us slowly, careful of pedestrians like us. A wide brick courtyard on our left reverberated with a song that was thick and passionate and powerful the way only live music could be. The air was thick with humidity and the smells of gasoline and hot grease and, incongruously, fresh bread. Karen leaned her head against my shoulder, and the intimacy of her body next to mine was unfamiliar and inappropriate, and it was also as comforting as hugging my best friend. Part of me was freaked out by her, and part was grateful she was there. Her perfume was hyacinth and musk. I was surprised she wore anything so feminine.

A girl with café-au-lait skin no older than sixteen skipped up beside us, holding something out in her hand. A silver fleur-de-lis pin.

"Three dollars," she said.

I looked at the pin, then at the girl. Without breaking stride, I pulled my wallet out of my backpack, plucked a five out, and gave it to the girl.

"Keep the change," I said. She grinned and skipped away. I smiled and dropped the pin into my pack along with the wallet. Karen watched it all as if it were happening at a distance.

"How're you doing, kiddo?" she said.

"Everyone keeps asking me that," I said. "I'm fine. I mean, not great, but fine."

"Hope it's okay I sent the boys on ahead," she said.

"Sure," I said, then sighed. "It's kind of nice, actually."

"I wanted a minute with just the two of us. I put you on the spot back there."

"I thought I was doing that to you," I said.

"That too."

A man with a new-looking goatee and a T-shirt that read *I Got Bourbon Faced on Shit Street* lurched in front of us smiling, looked at Karen looking back at him, and scuttled away.

"The things we did today?" she said. "The safe house, the van, the wards. All of it. It would have taken me weeks."

"Nah," I said. "You could have—"

"I couldn't," she said. "You could. I knew Eric maybe as well as anyone, and I barely knew him at all. I can't imagine how hard it would be stepping into his shoes."

I swallowed. If I hadn't been so desperately tired, I probably wouldn't have teared up.

"You're doing great," she said.

The sense of sloppy gratitude was only matched by the embarrassment that I was quite so easy to read. I wiped my cheek with the back of one hand.

"Thank you," I said. "Really. Thanks."

It seemed like we'd hardly started walking when she angled me up and to the left, and the new hotel opened before us. I stopped at the counter and got my key card. The boys weren't anywhere to be seen. Karen took my hand. At that moment, I felt like I'd known her my whole life. The smile at the corner of her mouth snuck up to her eyes.

"Call me when you wake up?" she said.

"I promise," I said. "But it may be early evening. I'm destroyed."

"Whenever," she said, then swooped in and gave me a quick hug. I watched her walk back out onto the street, and I watched the men she passed watch her too. My body felt like overcooked chicken ready to slough off the bone. I made my way to the elevator, up to my floor, to the room number, and into the great, king-size bed, still thinking about Karen without thinking anything in particular.

If there were any justice in the world, I would have gone off like a light and awoken twenty hours later feeling rested and human again. Instead, I lay on the bed and vibrated. The clock at the bedside told me it wasn't ten o'clock yet. My body said I'd been up all night, and I was officially too tired to sleep.

True to their word, Ex and Karen had brought my stuff to the new hotel. I popped open the laptop, checked mail, checked a couple of blogs I followed, and turned to Google.

I got no hits at all for Amelie, Daria, or Sabine Glapion. Not even a MySpace page. I wondered if being a voodoo queen meant being technologically pure or something. I tried *loa* and got a little over eighteen million hits, including things like the Logistics Officer Association, letters of agency, and the Mauna Loa Observatory. I found a Wikipedia article on voodoo gods, and then another three or four references that explicitly disagreed with it without ever agreeing with one another. Damballah was the voodoo spirit of the snake. Or Baron Samedi was. Or Carrefour. Or Legba.

I paused.

Legba.

It was what I had said during the fight in the lobby, the name I had called the old woman and the shining snake. There was a pretty detailed article about Papa Legba on a site Chogyi Jake had shown me, but when I tried to read it, I found myself losing the sense of it. I bookmarked it and promised myself I'd look again when I was functional. I shut down the laptop and stumbled into the shower.

I ran the water cool, and it woke me a little bit. I still felt the exhaustion, but I didn't have the same sense of being caught half in dream, unable to wake up or go down to sleep. I washed my hair twice, just because it felt good to do it. The hotel had a white terrycloth robe with its logo embroidered on the right breast, and I had just wrapped myself in it and stepped out of the bathroom when a knock came at the door. My heart ramped up a little.

"Who's there?" I said.

"It's me," Ex said. His voice sounded odd.

I hesitated, then went to look through the peephole. It was Ex, and he was alone. I gathered my qi, the mystic energy that let me do the little bit of magic I could. I pulled the energy up my spine and into my eyes, using it to see through enemy spells, but Ex was still just Ex. I opened the door.

The stink of alcohol was the last thing I'd expected, but he smelled like the mop at a liquor store. His eyes were red, and he was unsteady on his feet.

"Ex?" I said.

He nodded a half a beat late. He was drunk off his ass. I had never seen Ex drink to excess. I'd never seen him do anything to excess. He pointed at me, his expression almost comically somber.

"You," he said, then paused. "You have nothing to apologize for. Not to me. Not to Aubrey. Not to anyone."

"Are you drunk?"

"No," he said. And then, "Yes, but that's not the point. It's that you are just fine. You don't owe anyone anything. Eric was great, but you don't owe him anything. Or Aubrey."

"What room are you in?" I asked, reaching back for my key card on the dresser. He was on the same floor, but not the same hallway. Key card in the pocket of my robe, feet bare, I took Ex by the elbow and steered him back to his room. An older couple in evening wear passed by us, and I saw myself for a second as they would see us. A young woman with her hair still wet. A slightly older man with his hair coming out of his ponytail. Both of us had to have circles under our eyes dark enough to approach raccoon masks. The woman of the couple smiled at us indulgently.

Scenes like this weren't uncommon in New Orleans, I guessed.

I opened Ex's room with his key card, then stepped him through the threshold, turned him around, and pressed the card into his hand. He looked at it like it was a note from God, written on his flesh. His balance corrected two or three times while I watched.

"Get some sleep," I said.

"You don't owe an apology to anybody," Ex repeated.

"Thank you," I said.

He nodded solemnly, then leaned forward unsteadily and kissed my forehead. Even drunk, he was weirdly paternalistic. Maybe especially drunk. Still, there was something endearing in it. I closed the door.

My experience with alcohol was seriously limited. Apart from my brief sixteen-year-old rebellious phase and two semesters at ASU, all I had were old sermons about poisoning my body and blunting my God-given judgment. Still, as I padded back to my room, I would have put a hefty bet that Ex wasn't going to remember our little conversation in the morning.

In bed for the second time, snuggled deep under the sheets, it struck me that Karen's walk with me and Ex's drunken visit were probably related. The pair had spent the day together, and whatever had prompted Ex to decide I needed reassuring he'd probably shared with Karen. And she had taken the hint. The idea was a little embarrassing, but it was also sweet.

I wondered, sleep soaking my brain, my eyelids heavy as weights, if in the rush and confusion of my new, chaotic life I had maybe found people who really did care. Chogyi Jake and Aubrey and Ex. Maybe Karen Black.

That someone as confident and powerful as Karen might give a rip about my feelings was the most flattering thought I'd had in weeks, and as I lost consciousness, I let myself be comforted by it. It wasn't so bad feeling vulnerable when people had my back. I didn't analyze what Ex had said with any particular care.

If I'd understood what he'd actually been trying to say, it would have saved us both a lot of pain.

SIX

The inside of my new house in Pearl River was pretty in a Spartan way. Without any furniture, the rooms echoed a little, and the space felt bigger than it probably was. It smelled of fresh paint and bleach. The five of us walked through it in the wandering but focused way people get when they're planning a defensive position. There were big picture windows in the front living room and back in the kitchen that looked out on the green grass and trees on the verge of popping out new leaves. Those would be a problem. On the other hand, both front and side doors were solid-core with double dead bolts and interior latches.

The Realtor was an older woman, her hair dyed a soft auburn and her face caked with too much makeup. I thought she looked a little stunned. I tried not to say anything spooky about riders or kidnapping teenagers.

"The former owner was a very dear man," she said. "Lived here for thirty years."

I nodded. There were deep marks in the living room carpet. The couch had gone here, the coffee table there. Something wide and heavy along the wall, the line of crushed nap the only evidence of its passing.

"It looks great," I said. "Do you have the key to the shed too?"

"Of course," she said, fumbling with her purse. Chogyi Jake took the key from her, smiled, and went out the back door toward what would soon be our holding cell. I signed a few papers, shook the Realtor's hand, accepted the bottle of cheap celebratory champagne she'd brought, and ushered her out.

I'd spent two days sleeping, eating, talking to Karen and Aubrey, Ex and Chogyi Jake, and then sleeping some more while my lawyer cut through the red tape, waived the inspections, and sent me the papers I needed to sign. I had inherited dozens of properties around the world, but this was the first one I'd bought myself. It was mine, free and clear.

Ex stood at the front window, watching the Realtor's car wind down the drive, past a stand of trees to the road. His white-blond hair was pulled back in a severe ponytail, his face had the focused, almost angry look that seemed most comfortable on him. I hadn't brought up his drunken visit to my room, and neither had he.

"Well," he said. "I guess we'd better get to work. Aubrey, can you help me haul that box?"

"Sure thing," Aubrey said from the kitchen.

"I need to put this in the fridge," I said, hefting the champagne.

"No fridge," Aubrey said as he walked past.

"What?"

"No fridge," he said over his shoulder. "Range. Oven. Sink. No refrigerator, no freezer."

"Well, little tomato," I said to the small black bottle, "I guess we'll have to drink you warm. That sucks."

Karen Black walked down the narrow stairway from the second floor, the stairs creaking with each step.

"It's not great in a firefight," she said. "Too many windows. And there's no back way off the property except by foot."

"If it gets to a firefight, we'll already have screwed the pooch," I said. "The whole idea is to not get seen."

She nodded, giving me the point. Chogyi Jake came in the back as Aubrey and Ex, black wooden chest between them, came in the front. The chest had arrived at the hotel that morning. Ex and Aubrey put it down, and Aubrey stretched his back with a grunt.

"We're going to need to get some things," Chogyi Jake said. "Fresh salt. Charcoal and oak for ashes. Local honey."

I nodded.

"Can you pick up a couch and refrigerator while you're at it?" Aubrey asked.

"And groceries," Ex said. "Lots of them."

"DVD player and TV," I said. "I don't guess the place has Internet access?"

"The order's in," Aubrey said. "It probably won't be up for a week, though. No phone service either."

"And again with the suck," I said.

We had all spent time in hiding before. The long days besieged in a warded house had taught all of us what we needed. Karen caught the mood. She was wearing dark silk slacks and a pale yellow blouse, but she shoved her hands in her pockets like they were blue jeans.

"I don't think we'll need to stay underground too long," she said. "A week. Ten days at the most. Once the rider's lost its victim, it should be more vulnerable. All this is more for Sabine than for us."

"I don't know," I said. "It seemed pretty butch when it came after me."

"We can take it," Karen said. I bristled a little at her dismissive tone, but I let it pass. She knew what we were up against better than I did.

"Okay," I said. "What's the next step."

Karen leaned against the wall, her hands still in her pockets and twitching restlessly. The rest of us gathered. Aubrey sat on the chest, Chogyi Jake on the floor beside him. Ex stood by the front window, his posture unconsciously mirroring Karen's. I put down the champagne.

"We have to find the girl," Karen said. "The rider knows we're here, and it knows its own vulnerabilities. It's kept Sabine well hidden."

"You got to the little sister through her school," Ex said. "What about trying that with Sabine?"

"She doesn't go to school," Karen said. "Dropped out three years ago. After the hurricane, it was easy to fall between the cracks. As far as the system knows, she might be one of the people that evacuated and never came back. Or she might have died. There were thousands of people reported missing after the storm. No one knows how many were unreported. If the bodies got washed out to sea . . ." She shrugged.

"But someone must be checking up," Aubrey said, though his voice didn't have the weight of conviction. Ex coughed.

"Okay," I said. "How do we find her?"

"We follow her grandmother or the little sister," Karen said. "Daria is still in school, and I've met her so I know what she looks like. The downside of that is that she's precognitive, and the things that affect her directly are going to be easier for her to foresee."

"So the closer we get to her . . ." I said.

"The more likely we are to walk into an ambush," Karen said. "Which leaves the grandmother."

"Hanging out with the evil serial killer lady seems a little problematic," I said.

"It is," Karen said. "But there are advantages. For one thing, we know that in a showdown, the two of us together can beat her. We already have."

"I had a question about that," Chogyi Jake said. His smile might have been apology or accusation or anything in between. "From what Jayné said, I'm not perfectly clear on how the attack at the hotel happened. Or how it was turned aside."

Karen nodded.

"I'll admit that I was surprised at how well Jayné fought," she said.

"Eric put some sort of juju on me," I said. "We haven't found his notes to know all the details."

"But the way the rider seemed to stop time . . ." Chogyi Jake said.

Karen took her hands out of her pockets. Her eyes were focused on the back wall, as if she were reading something there.

"The rider we're fighting is the god of the cross-roads," Karen said.

"Legba. Opener of ways," I said. "I've been read-ing up. It's supposed to belong to a bunch of rela-tively benevolent spirits. Radha?"

Karen shook her head.

"Radha, Petro, Ghede. Who's benevolent and who's evil just depends on who was winning when the propaganda was written," she said. "But what I was coming to was the way Legba gets between things. Between places, between moments. It brought Jayné into that place because it thought they wouldn't be interrupted. I've been working for years to find a way to break through that protection. I can do it again."

"Let's hope you won't need to," Ex said.

"Crossroads," Chogyi Jake said. "I've read something about that. But it wasn't Legba, I thought. Carrefour . . ."

"Carrefour is another *loa* with very similar attributes," Karen said, a little sharply. "Sometimes they're mistaken for each other, but they're different. Legba is Radha, Carrefour is Petro. They aren't on the same team."

"I don't understand," Chogyi Jake said. "They can do the same things . . ."

"It could be like two competitors in the same ecological niche," Aubrey said. "Wolves and hunting cats can have the same prey, and even use the same strategies, but they hate each other. Maybe these Radha and Petro gangs are the same."

Karen blinked, her brow furrowed. She looked at Aubrey and smiled.

"That's a really good metaphor," she said.

"Let's get back to the part where we're following the bad guy," I said.

"Right," Karen said. "My first point was that we can beat her in a fight. The second is that Amelie Glapion is a living woman, and she needs to eat. She's got her voodoo cult, and they have meetings and ceremonies that require her to be out in public. We know where she'll be. And we know that Sabine will be close to her. We do our reconnaissance, find where the girl is, and then we can make a more detailed plan for getting her out."

"But sooner is better than later," I said.

"Absolutely," Karen said. "Time is an issue."

"So how quickly can we do the thing?"

She smiled. The gleam in her eye looked like complicity.

"Funny you should ask," she said.

BETWEEN THE near-apocalypse of places like Lakeview and the Ninth Ward and the undamaged icon of the Vieux Carré, there was a middle ground with no tall grass, no bare foundations. The corpses of the buildings hadn't been washed away in part because they were too large to dispose of. Even if they weren't too big to kill.

Aubrey and Karen and I stood in the empty fourth story of the parking structure as the twilight around us deepened into true night. Across Tulane

Avenue, Charity Hospital still towered, but the hundreds of windows were all dark. Pigeons rose in the dim light, whirled above the street and the traffic and us, and then settled again. We weren't more than ten minutes' drive from the hotel and the restaurants, the music and the tourists, and the life of the French Quarter, and we were in the ruins.

"It's better now," Karen said softly. "Not fixed, better. And not Charity. That's . . . that's never coming back. But the city is better than it was right after."

"I can't believe that," Aubrey said.

"No," Karen said. "What you can't believe is how bad it really was. Come on, kids. Let's suit up."

We turned back to the minivan. Karen had known where to get the things we needed. The right props and clothes were as important to what we were doing here as the ritual unguents and incense that Chogyi Jake and Ex were using back at the house were to their work. Only instead of looking like weird occult freaks in the suburbs, we looked like weird ninja wannabes in the city. I pulled black surgical scrubs over my jeans, a soft black windbreaker over my T-shirt. Karen stuffed her pale hair into a tight black cap.

"They've been meeting here almost since it was abandoned," Karen said as she strapped leathersheathed knives to her forearms and plucked the sleeves of her windbreaker over them. "Amelie's always in attendance."

"And the girl with the Sight?" Aubrey said. "She's here too?"

"Sometimes," Karen said.

I tested the little blue LED flashlight, then stuffed it in my pocket.

"So if she tipped them off, we could be going into a huge building filled with crazed, armed rider cultists," I said.

"It's a risk," Karen said with a grin. "Come on. Who wants to live forever, right?"

She walked away fast. Aubrey and I trotted to catch up.

"Me," I said low enough I didn't think either of them would hear. "I would very *much* like to live forever, thanks."

Aubrey turned his head and chuckled, but neither of us stopped.

Karen led us down a side street, walking with her hands loose at her sides and a bounce in her step. When she ducked in close to the building itself, the motion was perfectly graceful and natural. Aubrey and I followed. Karen helped us through an empty window frame, then slid through herself without making a sound louder than breathing. I felt like a kitten on its first mouse hunt.

The hallways were darker than night. The emergency lights had died years before. I took out my little flashlight, and the hall lit up in dim monochrome blue. Graffiti sprawled along the walls and

debris covered the floor; old plastic chairs, bits of
desiccated shrubbery, a wide, clear plastic box that
reminded me of the incubators they kept premature
babies alive in. The stink of mold was overpowering.
Karen slunk along the passage like a cat, her hands
out before her, fingertips touching each obstacle,
and then moving on. Aubrey and I followed as best
we could. I felt the adrenaline seeping into my blood
even before we heard the drums.

The bass carried through first, a throb so low it
almost wasn't sound. Like the building had a heartbeat. Karen grinned and picked up the pace. Aubrey
and I struggled to keep up. Higher tones started to
join the beat—bells, tambourines, bongos. At the
corner of two wide hallways, Karen lifted her hand
and pointed to the flashlight. I turned it off. Far
away on our left, a dim light danced, red and gold
and flickering like flames. I saw Karen's silhouette
as she moved toward it. When she reached a pair of
double doors with AUTHORIZED PERSONNEL ONLY in fading red, she gestured to the thin gap between them
with her chin. I snuck over and peeked through.

The cultists had taken over what might have
been an emergency room or some kind of intensive-
care ward. There was room for twenty or thirty
beds, though the space had been cleared of them. A
curved desk squatted in the middle of the room like
an altar. Ruined curtains hung like cobwebs from
rusting metal tracks. On the far side of the room,

half a dozen men drummed, their eyes a perfect, pupilless white.

The light wasn't fire, but a collection of orange and red lamps. The flickering came from twenty or thirty dancing bodies. Men and women. Old, young. Mostly black or brown skinned, but I saw at least one woman as pale as me. All of them were naked.

They writhed and leaped and called out. If there were words, I didn't catch them. My vestigial fear of being discovered eased. These people wouldn't have noticed if I'd led a riot squad through the door. I felt Karen lean over me, squinting through the same crack. She tapped my shoulder and pointed to the far corner of the space.

Between the bodies, I caught a glimpse of what she meant. The old woman from the hotel—Amelie, Legba, whatever we were calling her—walked through the crowd toward the altar. She wore a thin, shifting gown that might have been white, but glowed gold in the light. And behind her was a girl no more than sixteen years old in a matching outfit. The girl's face was as serene as her grandmother's, her skin darker, her hair in shining plaits. She was stunning. I touched Karen's arm and nodded. I saw her.

Sabine Glapion. The girl we were supposed to abduct. The girl we were trying to save.

Legba rose to the desktop, but I didn't see quite how she got there. Her head was moving to the lush rhythm of the drums, but awkwardly. She shouted and raised her hands. Her left arm was noticeably thinner than her right, and rose more slowly. The drums quieted, but did not cease. The dancers stood in place, swaying. Their faces were ecstatic and empty.

"Children!" the old woman said. "My children, we are set upon! We are attacked! *Comprenez-vous?*"

The dancers shouted something with one voice, but I couldn't make out the word. When the old woman spoke again, her voice was a low growl, her hands stretched before her like claws.

"We are weak, my children. Weak! But we shall be *strong*! We are fallen, but we shall rise *up*! The spirits hear us, and they will not be *denied*!"

The crowd shouted again, and the the old woman clenched her fists. Sabine was behind her, almost directly across from me, swaying in the same oceanic flow as the dancers. As her grandmother's claws clenched into fists, her eyes fluttered closed.

"*Louvri!*" the old woman cried. "*Legba! Legba! Ki sa ou vlé! Louvri les pót!*"

The air around me flashed with something that wasn't sound or heat, but something of both. For the space of a heartbeat, I saw the serpent where Amelie Glapion stood, its black eyes glowing in the lights, its skin shining like sunset on the ocean. I was backing away from the door even before I knew I intended to, but I was too late.

I had felt the abstract, other-reality of the

Pleroma—what Aubrey called Next Door—come close to me before. I had seen things, felt things. Now, like I had been hit with a brick, the two worlds fused. I saw things all around me, bodiless and aware and hungry.

Something pressed at my belly, looking for a way in. A powerful rush of heat blazed in my spine, pushing the rider back, keeping my flesh my own. Karen staggered, her mouth gaping open like she'd been gut-punched. The shouting beyond the closed double doors changed to screaming, and the drumbeats stopped.

"We have to go," Karen said. "We have to get out."

I nodded, turned, and stumbled into the darkness. Karen was at my side. I didn't realize Aubrey hadn't followed us until we had gone twenty, maybe thirty feet. I could see him standing by the double doors, ruddy light flickering on his face. The shrieking rose in a crescendo. "Aubrey!" I shouted. "Come on!"

Aubrey turned. In the dim light filtering through the crack between doors, I saw his eyes. I saw him see me, and the slow, feral grin that came afterward. Things moved in the shadows behind him like smoke, and the fear hit me like stepping into a freezer.

He was being ridden.

SEVEN

"Jayné!" Karen called from the darkness behind me. The thing in Aubrey's body howled and leaped forward, vanishing as it left the thin strip of light. I tried to backpedal, but the hallway was thick with debris that caught at my ankles. Without the flashlight, I might as well have been blind. I hunched, hands out before me, and braced myself for impact. It wasn't enough.

Something hit me hard across the chest, and I fell back. The ancient linoleum flooring was gritty and slick, like sand and motor oil. I heard the rider step close.

"Aubrey! Fight it," I yelled, and his foot slammed down into my ribs. I thought I heard something crack. My breath went out of me, and a terrible calm came in. I swung my arm up, closed fist driving hard into Aubrey's crotch. He doubled over with a groan, and my legs swept out. I felt them hit the backs of his knees, heard him fall.

The rider cried out words I didn't recognize, but the tone of its voice was enough; rage and pain and fear. I rose to my fingertips and the balls of my feet, knees bent and ready to spring. It was like I had been pushed to a small, observing part of myself while my body took on the fight. I closed my eyes, the raw spiritual energy of my qi bringing my ears, my nose, my skin to a terrible sensitivity. The shadows brushed against me like small, dry hands. I could smell something sweet and fatty, like burning pork.

"You are mine, little girl," the rider said. Its voice was inhuman; feminine and raw and powerful. My head shifted a degree, homing in on the sound. "I will taste your soul. Your blood will spill from my mouth. *Fear me!*"

Something washed over me. Its will, its power. The greatest magic a human being can summon is nothing compared to what riders command, and at its word, the quiet, observing part of me started bouncing around the interior of my skull, screeching like a monkey. My body remained still as stone.

It shifted its weight, and I jumped. The flesh I slammed into wasn't like Aubrey's. It was thin as a starving woman but solid. My shoulder took it in the belly, and we both fell down. Skeletal hands wrapped around my throat, but I shifted, pushed, and got on top of the writhing, killing thing.

"Who are you?" it shrieked. My fist buried itself deep in the gristle of its throat.

It's also Aubrey, I thought. *It's his body. I can't kill it.*

The momentary hesitation was all it needed. With a shout, it arched, throwing me into the air. In the black, I didn't know where the wall was until I hit it. My head rang and brightness filled my peripheral vision. I fell to the floor. My feet slipped under me as I tried to stand. Something—fists, foot, club— hit me in the right kidney, and I went down again.

Red light flooded the hallway. The double doors had opened, and naked men and women were running silently into the hallway toward us. I saw Amelie Glapion—Legba—limping in the middle of the crowd, her paralyzed face lit with rage. I turned to what had been Aubrey.

His flesh had been turned to the rider's will. His shirt had ripped in the fight, exposing a shrunken chest, ribs black and red as a burn victim. Small, flaccid breasts hung, black nipples pointing to the ground. The face was still partly his. The angle of its jaw was familiar, the shape of the eyes. It was also a woman's death's-head grin. The rider shifted its gaze to the coming cultists, and rose an inch, as if preparing for an attack from them too.

With a shout, I brought up both fists under its chin. It felt like punching cinderblock, but the thing's head snapped back, and it fell like a marionette with its strings cut. I rolled to my feet.

The cultists came forward. Their naked bodies had no sense of vulnerability. At least two of the men had huge erections. At least one of the women had a machete. I stood up. None of them spoke. The first of them stopped no more than thirty feet from me. Another half dozen came out from the doors, their shadows stretching ahead of them. One of them was Sabine. There were too many.

And Karen flew past me like a wind.

She stood between me and the oncoming mob, knives in both hands.

"Go!" she yelled over her shoulder.

My throat felt stiff. The words had to fight their way out of me.

"Can't leave Aubrey."

"Take him and *go!*" Karen said and turned back to the cultists. At my feet, the body was turning back into the familiar shape, the face filling out, and the burns fading. I scooped the unconscious Aubrey up like he was a child and ran. The shrieks of battle sounded behind me.

Without Karen to lead me, the hospital was

a labyrinth. Doors splintered by water damage refused to open. Hallways seemed to lead in circles. After the first couple of turns, I had to stop, fumble with the LED flashlight, and then stumble on. The smell of mold and death nauseated me. As the adrenaline faded, Aubrey grew heavier. I wasn't looking for the way we'd come. Any way out would do.

It seemed like forever before I hauled Aubrey into a room with an ancient couch decomposing against the wall, and a window wide enough to crawl through. A thin network of rusted wire held the remains of the safety glass in place. I put Aubrey on the couch while I kicked the dead wire free.

Somewhere in my flight, I'd started crying. Small, slow tears that didn't mean sorrow or fear. They didn't mean anything in particular, except that as I tried to lift Aubrey's dead weight to the open window, they shifted into sobs. I ignored myself, pushing his limp arms and legs out into the night air, then crawling after him.

The clean night air tasted wonderful. I let myself pause, my back against the rotting concrete wall, my breath labored. Aubrey lay beside me. His chest rose and fell deep and slow, as if he were only sleeping. As if he were the only one in his body. My hands were shaking with fatigue and the aftereffects of battle, but I couldn't stop. At any second, Legba's followers could pour out of the building. Or worse, the thing in Aubrey could wake up.

I fireman-carried Aubrey across the street, shuffling as quickly as I could to get across before a pickup truck ran me down. No one stopped to help, but no one stopped to ask me what the hell I was doing. At the base of the parking structure's stairway, I paused again, gasping for breath. I was still weeping a little, and I hated myself for that.

Karen was back there, in the hospital. She was probably dead by now. Between one breath and the next, it had all gone to hell, and there'd been nothing I could do. And the elevator was broken, meaning four long flights of stairs to the car. I couldn't carry him that far. I sank down to the steps, pressed my palms to my eyes, and trembled.

"Okay," I said. "Get it together. Come on, Heller. Get it together."

I swallowed my tears, looked up the twisting metal and concrete stairway, then back at Aubrey's still-inert form. I couldn't carry him. I just couldn't.

"Fine," I said. "You stay here, okay?"

Aubrey didn't answer, of course. I took a deep breath, nodded, and ran up the stairs by myself. Yes, someone might come by and find Aubrey passed out in the stairwell. Yes, the rider might come awake, and greet me with a renewed attack. But I needed the car, it was on the fourth level, and so I was going to go get it.

Driving slowly down the empty parking structure grounded me. By the time I got back to Aubrey, I'd almost stopped shaking. Karen's black duffel bag was still in the backseat. I thought I'd remembered seeing a roll of duct tape in it. Not quite as good as handcuffs, but what the hell.

As cars passed by on the street, I wrapped Aubrey's arms behind him, taping them together with almost half a roll. The rest, I put around his ankles and knees. He murmured once as I moved him, the voice not his own. I debated for a minute between the backseat and the trunk and opted for the backseat. I got him in, pushed the doors closed, and found my cell phone. Ex answered on the third ring.

"Where are you?" I asked.

"At the house," he said. "We've finished the first cycle of wards. I was thinking we could go pick up a refrigerator."

"Stay there," I said.

"What's wrong?" he said. I could see his face, the hardness of his eyes, the cold fury.

"The reconnaissance went south," I said. "Just . . . just stay there."

I dropped the cell onto the passenger's seat, turned on the engine, and started to pull out to the street. The cell lit up.

"Hey," it said. "You've got a call."

The display said it was Karen Black.

"Hello?" I said.

"Where are you?" Karen asked.

What if she'd been taken captive? What if it wasn't really her?

"In the car," I said, not lying, but not giving away anything.

"Great," she said. "Take La Salle south. Toward the Superdome. Turn left at Perdido. I'll watch for you."

"How do I know this isn't a trap?" I said.

There was a pause. I thought she was laughing, but she might only have been out of breath.

"You don't, really," she said. "But it's not."

In the backseat, Aubrey muttered angrily and shifted his weight. I wondered what I was going to do if the rider came to before I got back to the house. Was it a bigger risk to get Karen, who might be the free cheese in the mousetrap, or drive alone with a demon in the backseat? I thought about how I would have felt if she'd been the one to reach the car.

There wasn't really a choice.

"Okay," I said. "I'll be right there."

The traffic was light. I took La Salle down a long city block. Perdido was a one-way, and I slowed the car to a crawl. City hall was creeping up on my right when Karen stepped out of the shadows, opened the passenger door, and got in without my stopping the car.

She looked spent. Her face was spattered with blood, and a long rip along the side of her shirt showed a deepening bruise. She'd lost her hat, and her hair was pale and wild as hay.

"How's our friend?" she said.

"Possessed by evil. Wrapped in duct tape," I said.

She muttered something obscene.

"What about the others?" I asked. "Legba? The cult?"

"I held them off as long as I could, then rabbited. Nothing slows down a naked man like an angry woman with a knife. We're clear. For now."

"What happened?"

"I don't know," Karen said. Her voice was low and tired.

I got on I-10, heading north. Heading toward help. Aubrey growled low in his throat, but didn't sit up or try to kill us. I was reconsidering the wisdom of picking the backseat over the trunk. We passed the edge of the land, black water on either side.

We could take care of Aubrey, I told myself. We could pry the rider out of him. He'd be okay. I told myself he would be okay, and hunched over the wheel, and drove too fast.

We were five miles over the river when Karen said, "Not doing that next time," at the same moment I said, "That could have gone better." She turned and looked at me. I glanced at her. I couldn't say who started laughing first. The panic and the danger and the violence spilled out of us in shared, wordless hilarity. For the rest of our passage across the lake, we were sisters. Travelers on the same dark road.

"MARINETTE," Ex said. "From what it looked like, I'm thinking definitely Marinette."

The shed was lit by the white, unforgiving light of a Coleman lantern. The air smelled like turned earth and burning fuel. Darkness pressed in at the windows. The lights of the city were a glow on the underside of scattered, low clouds. The first crickets of spring were singing.

I felt like I was waiting for a doctor to tell me whether the lump was malignant.

Aubrey sat in the center of the space, looking at each of us—Ex, Chogyi Jake, Karen, me—with a pure, black hatred. A double circle of salt with careful designs in brightly colored chalk dust between them kept the rider bound.

"It's supposed to be kind of an ambassador figure between *loupines* and the *loa*," Ex went on. "And it's apparently a queen bitch to keep confined, so we need to move fast."

"You've been reading up," Karen said.

Ex scowled at her, but a heartbeat later allowed himself a little smile. Chogyi Jake nodded to Aubrey. Or to the thing inside of him.

"It isn't in the same clan as Legba," he said. "Legba is supposed to be Radha *loa*. Marinette is Petro."

"And when you're a Jet, you're a Jet all the way?" I asked. Both men turned to look at me. I shrugged. "What does it matter what team the thing's supposed to be on?"

"I'm wondering why Legba, an exiled spirit making its toehold for a forced return to unfriendly territory, would be working with its traditional enemy," Chogyi Jake said. "Perhaps this isn't Marinette. Karen mentioned how difficult it could be to tell one *loa* from another."

"Or maybe the local spirits are attacking the exile, and we just got in the way," Karen said, her voice oddly sorrowful. "Maybe they all still hate it."

"Okay, but if it's after Legba, why attack *us*?" I said.

"You have no place here," the rider said. "You have *fallen*."

"Be quiet," Karen said, and I could feel the force of her will in the air like the draft of a truck speeding past. Aubrey made a strangled sound.

"Karen's right. Don't listen to it," Ex said. "The only power it has right now is to confuse us. You three go. This is my job."

"You're an exorcist?" Karen said.

"I've managed before," Ex said.

She smiled at him a little more warmly.

"I've known others," she said. "It's hard work. Painful."

"But you can do it, right?" I said. "You can get it out of him? You can get Aubrey back?"

Ex turned to look at me. The lantern threw shadows on his cheek and in the hollow of his eyes. There was something in the way he held his body that I couldn't understand, like he was guarding himself. It reminded me of a man with broken ribs steeling himself for a blow.

"I can," he said.

Karen put a hand on my arm. I nodded, and we walked out of the shed into the darkness of the yard. The house squatted before us, light blazing from the windows. The bareness of the kitchen was like a particularly depressing movie. Bare bulb, no furnishings, old paint. I half expected a film student in a black turtleneck to come out with a handheld camera and tell us to start improvising dialogue. Chogyi Jake followed us, and the shed door closed behind him.

"I'll stay with them," Chogyi Jake said. "You should go back to the hotel. There's no food here. No beds."

"We could sleep on the floor," Karen said.

"It wouldn't help," he said.

"Ex can do this," I said. "He's done worse before. And he's really good."

Chogyi Jake didn't answer one way or the other.

I could have stood some reassurance. In the shed, something popped and I heard Ex's voice in a rising chant. Aubrey screamed. I wanted to go in. I wanted to stop it or help or something. Anything.

"This will take hours," Chogyi Jake said. "Go. Rest. Only . . . be careful."

"It's going to be all right," I said. I didn't sound convincing, even to myself.

I crawled back into the car and aimed us south again, for the French Quarter. Karen, in the passenger's seat, had grown quiet. I went through my leather pack with one hand while I drove, found a Pink Martini mix disk I'd burned, and popped it in the CD player. Their soft, eerie version of "Qué Será Será" started up. *What will be, will be,* I thought, *whether I like it or not.* I skipped ahead to "Cante E Dance."

When Karen sighed, I knew it was a preface. I expected her to apologize. This was her fault, she'd led us into danger, and so on. It was what I'd have been saying in her place, and I had my response all planned out. We were big boys and girls, we knew the risks, and we'd come of our own free will. All the things I'd have wanted to hear.

She surprised me.

"They care about you," she said. "Those three. You call them your staff, but they care about you."

"Yeah," I said. "I mean. Sure. I guess so."

"Must be nice," she said, and that was all.

eight

The hotel room was soaked in class and a little light starch. Crisp, white linen on the bed, a glass French press to make my morning coffee, a gold foil fleur-de-lis chocolate on the pillow. The building was old enough that I could open the window and look out on the street. A couple dozen people walked and shouted and laughed. There was music playing, but I couldn't tell where it was coming from. It was barely midnight in New Orleans. In Athens, I would have been finishing breakfast. In London, I would still have been asleep.

And so would Aubrey.

I had offered to drop Karen at her place or to have her stay there with us, but she'd turned me down. I wasn't sure whether I was sorry or relieved that she wasn't there. I stepped away from the window and turned on the television. I turned off the television and booted up my laptop. I left the laptop on standby and pulled my backpack onto the bed. Sitting cross-legged, I took out the wide manila envelope I'd been carrying since Denver. I drew out the note.

Jayné:

I suppose it's a failure of nerve leaving like this. I hope you can forgive me. I've struggled with this more than you know.

I had dreamed of the day when I could come back to the life I left behind. Now that the obstacles that held me apart from Aubrey and Denver are gone, I find that there are more reasons to stay away than I had realized.

I care for Aubrey very deeply, but as I look back at the manner in which he and I fell away from each other, I can't in all honesty say I'm sure it would be different now. I know that if I stayed, if I saw him, I would be tempted to try. The rational part of my mind says that would be a mistake. And so I'm taking the coward's way out.

Tell him that I wish him well. Tell him that I

blame him for nothing, and that I forgive him as I
hope he will forgive me.

Take care of yourself.

Kim hadn't signed the note, but she had signed
the divorce papers that went with it. She'd left them
in my care, to do with as I saw fit. At first it had
seemed like a gesture of trust and intimacy, and for
weeks I'd put off telling Aubrey about them because
I needed to decide what I thought and felt and
wanted. Then after that, I hadn't told him because
I would have had to explain why I hadn't told him
earlier. Now, a thick Gulf breeze stirring the sheer
curtains, my laptop fan whirring quietly to itself, the
Vieux Carré outside leading its subversive, rich, wild
tourist honey trap, her decision seemed monstrous.
Why was this my business? Why did I have to be the
one to decide whether Aubrey and Kim could learn
to love each other again? It wasn't fair to pull me in
this way. It wasn't right.

And anyway, if I did give him the papers, what
would he do?

Kim had known all that. She'd apologized. And,
honest to God, she wasn't the one I was angry with.
I promised myself that if Aubrey came back, I would
tell him everything. I caught myself.

When. *When* Aubrey came back.

I took a shower, watched the talking heads on
Fox News yell at each other, and waited for time to

pass. Every five minutes, I reached for the phone to call Chogyi Jake and ask for a report. Every time, I restrained myself and tried to pull my attention back to something small and innocuous. Aubrey would be fine. It wasn't my fault he'd been taken. Just because he would never have been there except for me . . .

I picked up the phone and called Chogyi Jake.

He answered on the third ring.

"Jayné. I hoped you'd be asleep."

"Short on Ambien," I said. "What's the word?"

"I'm on my way back to the hotel now," he said. "It went . . . well enough."

"Okay," I said. "You need to explain that comment."

I could hear the smile in his voice when he spoke.

"Aubrey is himself again. But Marinette was very strong, and there was some violence. Ex doesn't need stitches, but he will need at least a day or two of rest. I suspect Aubrey will too. They're both asleep now. The house isn't fully warded."

"And we don't know where the kid is," I said. "And the bad guys have the little girl who sees through time or whatever. We're not in the best position. Check. But Aubrey's back?"

There was a hesitation, but it might only have been Chogyi Jake changing lanes.

"Yes," he said. "Aubrey's back."

"Okay," I said and the knot in my chest loosened. "Okay. I might be able to sleep after all."

"Try," Chogyi Jake said. "I'll stop by your room in the morning."

I looked at the bedside clock: 3:41.

"Not early," I said.

"*Not* early," he agreed. I dropped the connection and fell back into bed. I felt like shouting. By any rational, objective standard, we'd gotten our asses handed to us. Right then, it still felt like victory.

I closed my eyes for a second, and when I opened them, there was sunlight shining through the window and a Vietnamese maid apologizing in a voice that suggested it was my own fault for not putting up the DO NOT DISTURB sign. The lady had a point. I made some apologies of my own, which were much more sincere, hung the appropriate sign on the door, and made coffee. Until I saw the manila envelope where it had slipped to the floor in the night, I'd forgotten my little vow to the universe.

Aubrey was back. It was time.

Instantly, I came up with several excellent reasons not to. He'd just been through an ordeal; adding to it would upset him. There wasn't anything pressing about the divorce; I'd had the papers for months now, so what difference would a few more days make? Chogyi Jake was going to come and meet me, and it made more sense to wait until I had the straight skinny on the night's events.

I told myself that it made more sense to wait. Until it was easier. Until he was ready or I was ready or some cosmic alignment made everything easy. Until the mythical perfect time that never quite seemed to be *today*.

I looked into the coffee cup, as if it might have an opinion. The French press left a bright layer of oil on top of the darkness that seemed lush and decadent, but not particularly eloquent.

"Just go," I said. "Put it in your pack, and go to his room. If he's too blasted, you can chicken out then."

I still didn't move.

And then I did.

Aubrey's room was a floor down from mine, and I took the stairs rather than waiting on the elevator. My knock seemed intrusive and loud. I was already regretting having come. He was probably asleep. I was probably waking him up. I sucked. No sound came from the other side of the door, and I shifted from side to side wanting to knock again and also not wanting to.

The door opened an inch, Aubrey's bloodshot eye made an appearance, then the door closed again and I heard the security bar they use in place of a chain being fumbled aside. When the door opened again, it opened wide.

Aubrey leaned against the doorframe. His bathrobe was the white hotel terry-cloth from his shoulders to his knees, then more familiar soft gray sweatpants under that. His sandy hair stood at a hundred different angles, and the whites of his eyes were full-on pink.

"Hey," he said. His voice was hoarse and careful. "Hell of a night, wasn't it?"

"Yeah. Not strictly according to plan," I said. "Look, if you're crashed out . . ."

"No, no. Come in. I was just staring at the ceiling waiting for my brain to start working again."

I walked in slowly, my heart in my mouth.

His room was a little smaller than mine, the view out the window a little worse. It was still pretty nice, though. His laptop was on the desk, the screensaver scrolling a quote from Voltaire about not believing in absurdities. I tried not to take it as an omen.

Aubrey sat at the head of the bed, stuffing a pillow behind the small of his back and groaning. I perched at the foot, my leather pack stowed discreetly on the floor. We were silent for a few awkward seconds.

"So," I said. "How are you doing?"

"Honestly?" Aubrey said. "I don't know. I feel . . . I don't know how I feel. I keep surprising myself. One minute, I'm thinking, *Ah hell, that wasn't too bad,* and the next my heart's racing and I'm sweating like a pig. Ex said it'd be like this for a while. Didn't say how long, though. Seems kind of stupid, really. I mean, it's over. It feels like it should be over when it's over. You know?"

"Intellectually," I said. "But I think Ex is right. It was a bad night. You have to respect that."

He shook his head and leaned forward, the bed creaking under him.

"I've never had one of them inside me," he said. "All the time I worked with Eric, I saw maybe a dozen people all told. Some of them had things in them. Some of them had been kicked out of their bodies."

"Aaron," I said. He was a cop in Denver who'd been living in his girlfriend's German shepherd while a *haugtrold* ran his original body. Nice guy.

"Aaron," Aubrey agreed. "I never really thought about what it's like for them. Having something else in their body with them."

"Only now you've been there," I said.

He started to speak, then only nodded. His robe gaped open at the neck. Raw red gouges started at his collarbone and ran down and to his left. Claw marks.

"It was . . . intense," he said. "I was still in there. The whole time, I was aware of everything. Well, until you knocked me out, at least."

"Yeah, well," I said. "Sorry about that."

"No. Don't be. I knew you might have to kill me. When we were in the hallway, in the dark, I knew that the only way to really stop the rider was going to mean breaking my body bad enough that . . . I was rooting for you. I wanted you to."

"I wouldn't hurt you," I said. "If there was any way not to, I would never hurt you."

"It didn't give you a lot of choice," he said. "I could feel it too. The thing. Marinette. It was like my mind and its mind were hooked up at the back."

"You knew what it was thinking?"

"What it was feeling, more like. It had this energy. Wild and angry and . . . I don't know how to say this. Confident? I was standing there, peeking in at the ritual with you two, and then it was like someone had thrown me in a prison cell about five inches behind my eyes. But I could feel the anger. It hates Amelie Glapion—I mean *hates* her—but it hates Karen worse."

"I guess it would," I said. "Karen's like the kick-ass rider hunter, right? The thing in Glapion's a rival and an exile and all, but at least it's one of their kind."

"Yeah, I suppose," Aubrey said. He swallowed, the delicate mechanism of his throat shifting under the skin. "I think I tried to kill Ex. After the exorcism part started up, I get a little fuzzy. But I think I hurt him."

"Nothing he can't come back from," I said. "Chogyi promised that a little rest, and the padre will be right as rain, whatever that means."

Aubrey smiled. It was the first time that morning I'd seen him smile, and it looked like it hurt.

"I see why they do it," Aubrey said. "The rider

cults? The ones like Glapion's where people actually invite things into them? I get it now."

"I don't."

"There's this amazing sense of power. Marinette could have done . . . well, not anything, but almost. More than I could ever dream of. She was invulnerable and wild. Feral. I could feel it. I participated in it in a way I can't exactly explain. The only thing I didn't do was control it."

"Power without responsibility," I said. "Every girl's dream."

"If I had been there as part of the cult. If it had been something I *wanted*," Aubrey said, then took a long, slow, shaking breath. "I don't think I know how to talk about this."

"You're doing fine," I said.

"No, I'm not," he said. "The words don't fit around it."

"Of course they don't," I said. "That's all right."

"I couldn't stop it. I couldn't stop it from killing you," he said. "And it was *inside* of me. My body . . . I just couldn't . . ."

There had been a time, no doubt months or years before, when I'd thought that Kim and the divorce papers were the most important issue between me and Aubrey. It couldn't have only been minutes. I would never be that shallow. Just then, watching Aubrey start to weep, the wife and legal proceedings didn't matter at all. I leaned forward and took his hand in mine. His knuckles were skinned. Eyes closed, he wrapped his fingers with mine. He looked up at me.

I had seen Aubrey naked. I had seen him in the throes of orgasm. I had seen him unconscious and helpless as a baby. I had never seen him as vulnerable as he was at that moment. I moved up the bed, pulling his arm around my shoulder, and held him as he rocked gently forward and back. There was blood on his robe. His body smelled like musk and clean sweat and the peculiar almost-pepper that was just him. He cried like he'd lost something precious, his arms tight around me.

I wept too. And I rocked him.

And I kissed him.

Here's the thing about sex. It's like music or language or anything really human and complicated. It can express anything; love or lust or anger, loss or sorrow. I kissed Aubrey, and he kissed me back. He was gentle at first, and then it was hard and rough and desperate. And I met him, pressure for pressure and power for power. Grief for grief. I pulled open his robe, my fingertips tracing wounds that hadn't fully stopped bleeding. He pulled off my shirt, his hand resting on my side where my old scars had almost turned white.

"Aubrey," I said.

"Please," he whispered.

I put my hands in his hair, holding him. I didn't

remember moving in to straddle his lap, but I was there now, and it felt perfectly right. His breath was deep as if he'd been running. Mine was too. I leaned to the side, rolling onto the bed with him still locked between my knees.

"Yes," I said.

There were a hundred things to say. Sane, rational, responsible things. You're still married. You're vulnerable. We don't really know what we are to each other. We should be careful.

I didn't even manage *Do you have a condom?*

The last time I'd had sex, it had been with Aubrey. He had been gentle and giving and funny and beautiful. Now we were different people, and our bodies were saying something else to each other. He was strong and selfish, angry and rough. Once, we had made love; now, we were fucking. And even as I pulled him into me, even when I crawled on top of him, I was there as witness to his pain.

We ended the way we began, locked in each other's arms, crying. I had cataloged all the injuries on his flesh. The scrapes, the scratches, the bruises and cuts. I had kissed them all. He tried to thank me, but I pressed my fingers to his lips until he gave up the effort.

He fell asleep first, his skin glowing a little in the soft sunlight of early afternoon. His breathing became slower, deeper. More peaceful. I pulled the blanket up over us both. Once again, things hadn't gone to plan. I wondered lazily if they ever would. I appeared to really suck at planning. I let my eyes flutter closed.

In my dream, I stood alone and naked in the desert. A gentle wind was blowing across the stones and sand. I knew with the logic of dreams that this austere, lifeless landscape was my home and that it was sacred. There was something I was supposed to do there, and I didn't remember what precisely it was. I knew I was in time, but that a moment would come—and sooner rather than later—when I would have to act. I tried to remember what exactly I had agreed to do.

Far above, a hawk that was also Chogyi Jake cried out. When I looked up, there were two suns in the sky. One was the burning disk I was used to, and the other was darker. Instead of radiating light and heat, it was radiating purification. I opened my arms to it, recalling that this was what I'd been meant to do. Something bigger than mountains whispered my name, and I woke up.

The knock came again. Hard pounding at the door. I lifted myself up. Aubrey muttered in his sleep as I fished his robe off the floor. I heard a voice I recognized. Ex.

"Aubrey!" he said, words muffled by the closed door between us. "Get up! Jayné's missing!"

I fumbled the security bar off and opened the

door. Ex looked ill. His skin was gray, his eyes red-rimmed, his pale blond hair hung to his shoulders. He opened his mouth to further announce my absence, went pale, and then blushed a deep scarlet.

"Yeah," I said. "Could you maybe give us just a minute?"

nine

We held the postmortem in the back of a French Quarter bar. We had the room to ourselves, and for a couple hundreds, I made sure it stayed that way. Having normal people walk in on the conversation seemed graceless. The sound system in our room was turned off, but Louis Armstrong rolled in from the front, his voice like a cheerful landslide. The chairs were all wooden and worn, three different layers of paint showing in carefully calculated decrepitude. A waitress brought us a bowl of salted peanuts and drinks. Light lagers for me and Aubrey, water for Chogyi Jake, Guinness for Ex. Karen got something hard; a bottle of bourbon and a tall glass.

"Okay," Karen said when the waitress had gone, "time to reassess."

She leaned forward in her chair, one hand brushing a stray lock of hair from her eyes. She was in jeans, a white T-shirt, and a tight-fitting leather jacket that she didn't take off when she came inside.

"I don't think Glapion knew we were there before the *loa* possessed Aubrey," Karen said. "If Daria's Sight had tipped them off, they would have been prepared."

"Prepared?" Aubrey said.

"Possession is bad," Karen said. "Shot in the face is worse. It didn't go the way we planned, but it could have been much worse."

Aubrey bristled, and I changed the subject before things could degenerate.

"Do we know anything we didn't know before?" I asked. "We saw Sabine. That counts for something, right?"

"Yes," Karen said. "We didn't get to follow her, and I don't think there's much chance that they'll go back to Charity now that they know it's compromised. But we have confirmed that Sabine is in the city."

Ex cleared his throat. If Aubrey looked like the victim of violent crime, Ex looked like someone fighting cancer. The exorcism had left him wasted, dark circles under red-rimmed eyes, a sense of weariness that verged on melancholy on him like an illness. He didn't look at us, his eyes focused on the center of the table.

"What about the time frame?" he asked. "We're here to stop a murder, and the killer knows we're coming close."

"What about it?" I said, specifically to Karen. "You're the resident expert on this thing. Did we spook it? Will it move up the schedule, kill the girl sooner?"

"I don't think it can," Karen said. "When I was chasing it, there were . . . gaps. Normally when you see a serial killer, they start off needing a lot of time between victims, then slowly ramp up. They need more and more, faster and faster. This one didn't do that."

"Because it's stuck on a timetable?" I asked.

Karen took a deep breath and let it out slowly, giving herself time to think.

"More that the thing is in a new host body," she said. "When the murderer's just a human being, the first kill is the hardest. There are inhibitions to overcome. The second time, it's easier, and so on. With the rider, it's in a new person. There are fresh inhibitions that come with the new personality. Whoever it was in before could have killed twenty people, but Amelie Glapion hasn't killed anyone she loves. Not yet."

"Didn't seem to make much difference for me," Aubrey said. There was an edge to his voice.

"It did," Karen said. "I don't care what kind of wards and cantrips Eric put on her, Marinette would have killed Jayné if you hadn't been holding it back."

Aubrey blinked, sat back in his chair, and drank his lager. I felt a rush of profound gratitude to Karen for pulling even a little of the poison back out of him. He hadn't been able to overcome the rider, but he hadn't been thoroughly ineffective. Fighting a losing battle isn't the same as being powerless.

He caught my eyes and smiled. I felt a little blush rising in my cheeks and turned away. When I looked back up, he was still smiling a little. Ex coughed.

"Then the question is," Chogyi Jake said, "when did Legba take Amelie Glapion?"

"Yes, how long ago did it take her," Karen said. "And how strong-willed is Glapion. And how much power has it regained. There are a lot of variables, and there isn't a way to get good information."

"What would we do with it anyway?" I said. "It's not like we can get the wards up on the new house any faster than we're doing. The only thing I was thinking . . . can we skip grabbing Sabine and head straight for Amelie Glapion?"

"No," Karen said. "If we go straight for the rider, it *will* spook and kill the girl, and it won't matter how much Grandma wants to stop it. I can promise you that."

"That's happened before?" Ex asked.

"Close enough," Karen said.

A fast tapping sound came from the tabletop, almost like a phone set to vibrate. I was a little surprised to see that my fingers were making it. I considered my hand. *Yeah*, I thought. *The smell of this ain't quite right.* But Karen's certainty carried me. This was her show, after all. She was the expert. We were just the hired help.

"From here, we have several options to pick the trail back up," Karen said. "None of them are great. Unfortunately, I don't have access to the tools I had when I was with the bureau."

"Tools?" I said, latching onto the word.

"Databases. Surveillance teams. Numbnut beat cops to go canvass neighborhoods," Karen said. "Running solo, or even with a small team, just doesn't have the same range, but we'll do the best we can."

Chogyi Jake, Aubrey, Ex, and I all exchanged glances. Karen frowned.

"Am I missing something?" she asked.

"We may have some other resources," I said.

IT MIGHT have been petty of me, it might have been small, but the surprise and pleasure on Karen's face made me feel like I was worth something.

"Let me read this back, dear. Sabine Glapion," my lawyer said from the other end of the cell connection. She spelled out both names, then went on. "Granddaughter of Amelie, sister of Daria. Approximately sixteen years of age, but not attending school."

"I know she was in New Orleans last night, and I have reason to think she's still here."

"All right. Just whereabouts? You don't want her contacted?"

"Just where she is," I said. "I'll take it from there. But sooner would be good."

There was a small, sharp sound on the other end of the connection. It had a finality to it, like something being closed.

"I'll get back to you as soon as I have something, dear," she said. "If anything else comes up, you'll let me know?"

"Absolutely," I said, then dropped the connection.

"You think that's actually going to work?" Karen said. I could hear in her voice that she wanted to believe, but didn't quite dare to.

"Pretty confident," Aubrey said. Either he was sharing some of my smug, or I just wanted to see it in him. "Jayné's lawyer isn't someone I'd cross."

"Well," Karen said. Then, a moment later, "All right, then."

"We still need the wards up on the safe house,"

Ex said. "And the van. And we need a refrigerator and some food at that place. I don't think we're going to want to order delivery pizza with a girl tied up in the back."

"It will take longer, working alone," Chogyi Jake said. "Two more days, perhaps?"

Ex took a long drink, the last of the black stout sliding past his teeth.

"We don't have time," Ex said. "I can help with it."

"After last night . . ." I said.

Ex looked up at me, his eyes hard as stone.

"This is what I do," he said. "I can handle it."

"I'll help out too," Aubrey said.

"It's a two-man job," Ex said.

"Then I'll get the fridge."

"Okay, but food first," I said. "We're getting snappish, and that always means low blood sugar. Karen. Is the food any good here?"

"You're in New Orleans," Karen said. "The food isn't bad anywhere."

"We'll get burgers or something on the way," Ex said as he stood. "Aubrey. Jake. Shall we?"

The others rose, and half a beat later, I stood up too. Karen's bright eyes shifted between Ex and Aubrey, then to me. There was a question in her gaze, so the sudden, inexplicable appearance of a stick up Ex's ass might not have been entirely my imagination.

We walked back to the hotel in three groups; Ex and Chogyi Jake at the front, Aubrey by himself close behind them, Karen and I bringing up the rear. My cell phone said it was a little bit after five, but the sun was already hidden. I'd barely started my day, and the darkness was coming on.

I'd had sex with Aubrey. Again. Months of keeping myself at arm's length and agonizing about the divorce papers that were still in my pack had turned irrelevant. The thought alone was surreal, then add in that he was walking two strides ahead of me, his hands in his pockets, and his shoulders tensed up around his ears. Part of me wanted to skip up beside him, pull his arm around my shoulder, and lean my head against him or his against me. The rest of me thought that would be a hilariously bad idea, and kept walking with a scowl through the French Quarter.

It wasn't a big deal, I told myself. It wasn't like sex was entirely new territory for us. I remembered the things Karen had said about the rider overcoming inhibitions. The first time out, it took a lot of work to get past the fear and uncertainty and resistance. The time after that, not so much. He was shocked and vulnerable and hurt, and he'd needed that reassurance.

And still, it wouldn't have killed him to walk beside me.

"And what about you?" Karen asked.

I blinked. For half a second, I thought she was

asking how my needs and feelings fit in with Aubrey's renewed sex life. She went on.

"With the boys tied up with the safe house, what were your plans for the evening? Dinner and an early night?"

I laughed.

"Early night isn't really an option," I said. "Right now, I'm barely up to late morning. I was figuring I'd hang at the hotel, do some research."

"Research?"

"More about the *loa*, and Legba. More about the serial killer thing, and what the rider does. Ever since I took over the gig from Eric, I feel like I'm cramming for the big test."

Karen made a noncommittal grunt. Her expression went blank.

"Why?" I asked.

Karen glanced at me, her eyes almost apologetic.

"I'm feeling a little keyed up," she said. "Whenever I was on a case and we saw some action, we'd have to stop and file reports afterward. I hated that part. It always broke my stride. This part where we have to wait on the safe house and your lawyer feels a lot like that."

"Sorry," I said.

"Oh, no," Karen said, her hand touching my elbow. "That sounded like criticism. I didn't mean it that way. I just need to get my mind off of things for a couple hours. Blow off some steam."

"That would be nice," I said wistfully. Not thinking about Aubrey's hot-and-cold or Glapion's attacks or Ex's moralistic disapproval sounded like a little dark-chocolate slice of heaven.

"We're on then?" Karen asked. The sly smile looked playful now. "Change into something slutty, I'll take you dancing?"

My first response was surprise, my second was resistance, and my third was an almost defiant resolve. All in all, I didn't think about it for a minute.

"Sounds like a plan," I said.

KAREN AND I got to The Dungeon just after nine o'clock; it was still early for the nightlife. The club wasn't entirely open yet, but we could get in the front room, which was good enough for a couple beers and some coin-operated pool tables. Karen was in a small green skirt with seamed stockings, a halter top that made her look considerably more stacked than I'd thought she was, and lipstick the color of fresh blood. I was in my most outré outfit: tight black blouse with a neckline down toward my cleavage and matching skirt slit up the side. I'd done my best with the makeup, but I didn't usually wear more than a little light eyeliner and lipstick for special occasions. Beside her, I looked like I was in a school uniform.

All the colors in her outfit were saturated and

bright and confident. Her body was closer to magazine-cover perfect than mine had ever been. She looked like a 1950s pinup girl come to life, but what made her beautiful were the scars: the white line at her collarbone, the barely visible pucker on her right arm, the ancient star-shape that made me think of bullet wounds on her ribs just at the hem of her top. Karen's flesh bore witness to a lifetime of risk and violence, and her acceptance of them—her lack of shame or apology—drew my eye more than admiration or envy.

I had one set of finger-marks where a rider had stabbed me with its claws, and that alone was enough to keep me in a one-piece bathing suit.

"So how did you get into the business?" Karen asked me as she racked up a game of eight-ball. "All Eric's doing? You break."

I chose the stick that seemed least warped and took my place at the table. Karen leaned on the side, a bottle of Dos Equis in her hand. I knew the rules, but I'd never played pool before. I wasn't about to admit it.

"More or less," I said. "He left me everything when he died, and I kind of pieced it all together from there. The boys all know more about it than I do, really. Aubrey got into it because he's really a parasitologist, and Eric thought maybe there was something there."

"And Ex?"

I chalked the end of the stick, lined up the cue ball, and did my best. The report was loud and satisfying, and through blind luck two balls dropped into pockets, one solid and one striped. I figured that meant I could pick which one I wanted.

"Ex and Chogyi Jake had both worked with Eric, one time or another. I got in over my head, and I called Aubrey. Aubrey got the others," I said, lining up what looked like a plausible shot on the nine. "The rest is history."

Karen shook her head.

"I never pictured Eric as the kind of guy with a family," she said.

"Everyone comes from someplace. He and my dad . . . didn't get along. I was really glad to have Eric as an uncle, though," I said. The nine went in its pocket too. I thought maybe the fifteen next. It would mean bouncing it off one of the sides, but it looked possible. "What about you? What does your family think about the whole combating abstract evil thing?"

"Nothing," Karen said. "I was an only child, and my parents are both dead. There was a fire a couple years ago."

"Jesus. I'm sorry," I said.

Karen smiled gently and shook her head; she didn't say anything. I took my shot as a way to avoid the increasingly awkward silence.

"Nice," Karen said.

"Thanks," I said. "So I don't want to pry or anything . . ."

"Pry away."

"How do you do it?" I asked, leaning on my stick. "I've been running around for the last six or seven months doing nothing but cataloging and studying and practicing little cantrips, and I don't feel like I've got a clue what I'm doing. You know?"

"I do," Karen said. "That never stops. You get better, you know more, but that feeling that you're a fraud? You never get over it. At least I haven't."

A thick-wristed man with fading tattoos came up to the table, nodded politely, and put two quarters down on the rail. I realized how rude it was of me to hold up the game talking, lined up the twelve, and sank it.

"You have friends," she said. "That counts for a lot. I miss having someone I could work with. Davis was a good man."

It took me a second to remember that Michael Davis was the partner that Legba had killed, but Karen hadn't noticed my momentary confusion. She kept talking, her voice taking on a distance.

"I sure as hell never meant to get here. I started out trying to stop bad guys. Drug smugglers, kidnappers, terrorists. And honest to God, I think I did some good. After Mfume, I figured out there was a whole class of bad guys I couldn't even touch. And because I wouldn't let it go, I lost the bureau. Except Davis. And then I lost him too.

"We do what we have to," she went on. "It's not about whether we like it or not. Whether we're particularly suited to it. We are what we are."

"What doesn't kill you, defines you," I said and sank another ball. Pool was easier than it looked if I didn't overthink it. Karen laughed.

"I hadn't heard that version."

"It's from my ex-boyfriend's favorite movie," I said. "But I never bought that whole *makes you stronger* thing. Doesn't leave room for *cripples and maims you horribly*."

"Does it define you, Jayné?" Karen asked.

"What?"

"Fighting riders. Doing the things we do," Karen said. "I wonder sometimes if this is really all that we are."

"Well," I said, "I'm not doing anything else these days. And before this, I was a college dropout with no family left who'd speak to me. By comparison, this is a pretty good gig."

"It's lonely, though," Karen said. I looked up at her. Her pale blue eyes were locked on the distance. Her hair caught the neon of the signs and the flicker of the television. There were no lines on her face. She looked as young as me. Younger.

I thought of the last six months. Of being with Ex and Chogyi Jake and Aubrey. Of traveling the world with my best and only friends. Of the power I had now to pluck out a credit card and buy a car or a house or an airplane. And I thought about how my life had been before. I took another shot, then stood up with only a vague satisfaction. I'd almost run the table.

"It really is," I said.

The inner doors of the club swung open, and the sound of the televisions was suddenly competing with old-school Nine Inch Nails remixed—brilliantly, hilariously—with Pat Benatar's "Hell Is for Children." I started laughing. Karen's eyes lit, her mischievous smile returned, and she dropped her cue stick on the table.

"Come on," she said, taking my hand. "At least let's show the bastards we can go down dancing."

TEN

The house had been transformed. Where once it had seemed empty and maybe a little sad, our best efforts had made it downright creepy. Chogyi and Ex had gone through the place, carving sigils and symbols around every doorway, every window. Even the electrical outlets bore arcane markings in black ink and knife scratch. We hadn't gotten beds, but futon mattresses lay on the floors of the bedrooms. A black leather couch squatted in the living room. We didn't have a television or DVD player yet, so it was facing a bare wall.

Out back, the shed had been converted into a

prison cell. Security bars had been installed on the outside of the door, and an extra layer of two-by-fours encircled the structure, making it impossible to kick out a wall. On the inside, manacles were set in a deep hole of still-curing cement. Egg cartons and old rugs lined the walls and ceiling, swallowing sound.

On the upside, we had a refrigerator.

"Once we have Sabine here, it will be important not to go between the shed and the main house too often," Ex said. His voice was thick and phlegmy. He sat on the couch with his hands between his knees and nodded to the back door. "The pathway itself isn't warded. But, as long as Jayné is the one going to her, the risk is minimal."

"Why's that?" Karen said.

"She's very difficult to see," Chogyi Jake said. "Part of Eric's protection of her."

Karen nodded. Perhaps alone among us, the morning found her looking rested and ready for action. God knew I still felt pounded. We'd been out until sometime after four AM. That alone didn't bother me; my circadian rhythms had resigned in disgust days before. But I'd had a little too much to drink, gotten a little dehydrated, and danced to Goth and industrial music more or less nonstop when I wasn't drinking. Three men and two women had hit on me that I noticed. I'd had to give one guy a fake phone number to make him go away. The whole thing left me feeling wrung out.

Everyone looked pretty wasted, except Karen who could apparently live on alcohol and loud music. Ex and Chogyi Jake had spent almost the whole night in occult work, preparing the house and shed. Aubrey had done the lion's share of the carpentry and appliance installation. He sat on the floor now, early afternoon light slanting in the window and catching the beginning of stubble on his cheek. I wondered what he'd look like with a beard. *Tired*, I thought, *but not because of the facial hair.*

"The wards on the house aren't elegant," Chogyi Jake was saying. I pulled my attention back to our little security briefing. "But they are effective. If we'd had another week, we could have done them in a less obtrusive way."

"Effective beats pretty every time," Karen said. "You did the right thing."

"What haven't we done?" I asked.

"The cargo van's still just a cargo van," Aubrey said. "And we don't know where the girl is."

"And we don't have a plan for what to do once we have Sabine safe," I said. "The part where we actually kill the rider is going to be important."

Karen smiled at me.

"I've been planning that for years," she said. "I've got it under control."

"More to the point," Chogyi Jake said. "We're exhausted. Ex and Aubrey especially, but all of us."

"All right," Karen said. "It's Friday. Why don't we take the night off. All of us?"

Ex shook his head. No. His skin looked thin as parchment, and the severe ponytail was off center. The stubborn expression was one I recognized. If I'd slept more I'd have been more patient with him.

"Ex," I said. "We aren't any good to anyone if we pass out. You spent all last night getting the house ready. The night before that was casting Marinette out of Aubrey. How long have you been awake?"

"I'm fine," he said, anger buzzing in his voice.

"Jayné," Chogyi Jake said. He shook his head gently. I was pushing Ex, and he wasn't in a mood to be pushed. Karen came to my rescue.

"Sorrow can be alleviated by good sleep, a bath, and a glass of wine," she said. To my surprise, Ex barked out a laugh. Karen grinned and held out her hand. "Come on, Preacher-man. I'll drive you home."

I mouthed *thank you* to her as Ex grunted and rose to his feet.

"I've got some cleanup still to do," Aubrey said. "Just nails and saws, but . . ."

"I can come back," Karen said.

"Don't," I said. "We'll take the rental. We're fine."

"You're staying?" Ex said.

"I want to spend a little time in the place," I said. "Get to know it."

It wasn't entirely true, and Ex seemed to know

that. There was a flash of something—disapproval, I thought—but it was gone as quickly as it came.

"Come on," Karen said, taking Ex by the arm and leading him to the door. I watched them through the picture window as they got into Karen's car and headed out along the long, winding driveway.

"Okay," Aubrey said. "What exactly is his fucking problem?"

"Guilt," I said. "He has once again failed to protect us. From ourselves, from the world. He feels responsible, and so he self-flagellates. And he lets us know he's doing it because . . . I don't know. Because it's more fun that way? He's pretty much always been like this, if you'll recall."

Aubrey made a low sound that might have been agreement or disgust or a little of both. Chogyi Jake yawned. He hadn't shaved in a couple of days either. Facial hair wasn't his strong suit, but his scalp had grown a downy black stubble and he ran a palm over it now.

"I want to go over the cargo van," he said. "I don't think it would be wise to do more than that without some rest."

"You need help with that?" I asked, hoping that the answer would be no.

"No," he said, smiled, and walked out the back door. Leaving me and Aubrey alone together, which was what I'd thought I wanted.

"I'm going to have to kill Ex if this goes on much

longer," he said. "I just thought you ought to know that."

"He's really getting under your skin, eh?" I said, sitting on the couch. It creaked under me.

"I guess so," he said. "You're probably right, though. He's just being Ex. I'll get some rest. Things will look better."

"If I hadn't been pushing us all so hard these last few months, we wouldn't have been so fried coming in," I said. "I think there's blame to go around."

Aubrey chuckled and sat back, his fingers laced together, his exhausted gaze on me. I felt myself starting to blush.

"So, we should probably talk," he said.

"I was thinking that."

"You want to start, or do you want me to?"

I took a deep breath. Outside, Chogyi Jake started the van's engine, then let it die. Through the picture window, I could see the soft grass, bright green with the first growth of spring. The back of our little Virgin Mary. Pray for us now and at the hour of our really awkward conversation.

"I'll go," I said. "I've been kind of avoiding . . . well, us. There's a lot tied up in it, you know? You're married, and I didn't find out until after we'd fallen into bed. You're separated and Kim's seen other men, so it's not like you're *married* married."

"You grew up in a particularly religious home," Aubrey said. "Having taken vows means a lot to you."

"And I hate that it means a lot to me," I said. "All of that. But . . ."

My heart was ramping up, a slow leak of adrenaline giving my blood a little electric push. It felt like looking over a precipice, even though it was only really confessing.

"There's something I haven't been telling you," I said.

"It's okay," Aubrey said, gently. "I already know. Eric told me about your mother. The affair. Everything. I absolutely understand why the idea of being with a married guy would be a deal breaker."

There have been a few times in my life that a few syllables—just words in sequence—felt like being hit in the head with a brick. When my supposed best friend in college confronted me and blew up my carefully constructed life. When my lawyer had explained that I had inherited the equivalent of a small nation. When I'd crawled out of his bed and discovered that Aubrey was still married.

And now.

"Wait," I said. *"What?"*

"Your mother's affair," Aubrey said. "Eric told me about it. How your folks almost got divorced."

"My mother had an affair?" I said, standing up. "When the fuck was this?"

Aubrey's eyes went wide.

"I don't know," he said. "It sounded like it was just after they were married, but I didn't—"

"My mother? Had an affair?" I said. "You don't understand. My mother doesn't have a sexuality. She's like a Stepford Wife."

Aubrey looked up at me from the floor, his arms crossed.

"So, I guess that wasn't the thing you weren't telling me about," he said.

"No," I said. "I wasn't telling you that I've got your divorce papers. Kim left them in Denver, and I never handed them over to you because I felt . . . conflicted or something. My mom had an affair? *My* mom? Who with?"

"Eric didn't know," Aubrey said. "He only knew about it because your dad went to live with him for a few months after it happened. Well, after it came out. Apparently your dad was pretty wrecked by the whole thing. Kim has divorce papers filled out?"

I couldn't imagine my father and Uncle Eric in the same room, much less living together. But the big break between them hadn't happened until I was in high school. Of course they'd had a history before that. They'd grown up together, gone to the same schools, known the same people. They were brothers.

If it was true, if something had happened, maybe my father would have turned to Eric. Maybe they'd had the kind of relationship back then that would allow it, even if it had all gone to hell later. But my mother?

All my life, I had seen her as a pale shadow of a woman. She'd made dinner, cleaned house, taken me and my two brothers to church. She had done as Dad, the full-on patriarch of the house, told her. The few times she had talked about a life before marriage, it had been when Dad wasn't around. Mousy, repressed, controlled, and oh-my-God asexual. I'd always been amazed that my folks had managed to have three kids. And my father—razor-cut hair, starched shirt, reading the Bible and scowling—had seemed like the perfect match for her.

And she had had an illicit affair that almost ended the marriage? The idea of her wrapped in some lover's embrace, risking her reputation—her *soul*—in order to have sex, was insane. She would never have done it. It wasn't possible.

Or maybe it was. A lifetime of interactions between my parents suddenly shifted focus. My father's gruffness and need for control suddenly looked like a constant need for reassurance. My mother's submission became a kind of years-long apology. Everything about my childhood—love, family, sex—came into focus.

"Jayné?" Aubrey said again. I was only vaguely aware he'd been repeating my name for a couple minutes.

"Sorry," I said. "What?"

"Where are the papers?"

"What papers?"

"The divorce?"

"Oh. In my pack."

Aubrey levered himself up with a grunt and passed into the kitchen, returning a minute later with the papers in hand. I watched him as he flipped through them, nodding to himself now and then, sometimes smiling wryly.

"And you've had these since Denver?" he said.

"Yeah."

"And you just didn't mention it because . . . ?"

"I was afraid you might still be in love with her and not sign them," I said. Apparently being in shock had a clarifying effect. I had barely admitted that fear to myself, and I sure as hell hadn't intended to bring it up here, with him.

Aubrey stood framed in the kitchen doorway, the light from behind him making him seem larger. Like a still frame from a movie, projected on a huge screen. Then he shrugged and took a pen from his pocket.

"Okay," he said as he signed them, "I can see that."

"Kim still loves you," I said.

"I know. And she's great, but . . ."

He folded the papers and tucked them into his shirt pocket. The urge to explain why she left him—that she'd been sleeping with Eric and her conscience couldn't take it anymore—rose in me, but I couldn't tell if it was because I wanted him to know everything or if it would only have been to cement his decision.

"My turn?" he said.

"Um. All right."

He squatted down in front of the couch and took my hand. His eyes were bloodshot and there were circles under them like bruises. The wounds on his collarbone and chest peeked out over his shirt, the scabs a black crust, the flesh around them puffy and red. He took my hand.

"What we did yesterday? I have to thank you for that. I needed . . . I needed something. Not sex, exactly. Or not just sex. But being with you matters to me."

My heart jumped up to my throat somewhere and got stuck. I fought to speak.

"Thank you," I said. It seemed profoundly inadequate.

"I'm a little messed up right now," he said, his face going a little colder, more focused within himself. "What happened with . . . Marinette . . ."

He'd been violated. His body hadn't been his own to control. I knew enough girls who'd had occasion to say the same things that I heard what he couldn't bring himself to speak.

"I understand," I said.

"If what we did was a onetime thing, I can accept that," he said. "If it's more than that, I'd love it. I love you, Jayné. You're funny and sexy and smart.

And vulnerable in ways you seem totally unaware of. And you make me laugh."

My chest felt hollow and full at the same time. *I love you.* The most common, used, trite words in the world, but my eyes were tearing up just the same. Aubrey wiped his thumb across them, and the world became a little less wavy.

"But seriously, I'm kind of messed up right now," he said. "And it may take me a while to get my head back on straight."

"Oh, I will so totally wait," I said.

"You don't have to," he said. "But it would be great if you did."

I leaned forward, slipped down to the floor, and wrapped my arms around him. We were both crying again. It felt wonderful and heartbreaking and a lot like relief. My uncle Eric broke it up.

"Hey. You've got a call."

I wiped my eyes with the back of my hand, kissed Aubrey quickly on the cheek, and went to the kitchen. My pack was open where he'd left it. The cell phone was in the side pocket. The caller ID said it was my lawyer.

"Jayné, dear, we've had something of a lead. Amelie Glapion? The grandmother?"

"Yes?" I said, looking for a seat. There was no table in the kitchen. We'd have to take care of that.

"A title search shows she owns several properties around New Orleans. Rentals, it appears. Her financial position is tenuous these days. Not enough diversity in the portfolio. She married her fortunes too much to the city, and between the hurricane and the housing market . . . well, I'm sure you understand."

"Then you have a good address for her?"

"Sadly, I have a half dozen," my lawyer said. "Who precisely lives where is somewhat obscure. If one were the suspicious type, one might call it a shell game. I can have each one checked, but since you specifically asked that no contact be made . . ."

"No, don't. Just send me the addresses and I can take it from there."

"I thought you might say that. Did you know, by any chance, that Glapion was Marie Laveau's married name?"

"Marie Laveau, like *the* Marie Laveau? Voodoo queen of New Orleans?"

"The very one. Amelie Glapion appears to be in direct apostolic line," she said. "She's the silent partner of something called the Voodoo Heart Temple. Despite the name, it's a retail shop. I thought you might want it looked into?"

"Yes," I said. "That would be great."

"I'll proceed on that as well, then," she said. "And, dear? There is reason to suspect that Amelie may have powerful friends. Be careful."

My lawyer had never said anything like that in the time I'd known her. Her tone of voice was flat and considered. It carried more weight than shouting would have.

"I will," I said.

"Excellent. I'll be in touch."

I leaned against the kitchen wall, looking at the cell phone. Something was shifting uneasily in the back of my mind. Aubrey appeared in the doorway.

"Are you all right?"

"Just fine," I said.

"You sure?"

"Not a hundred percent, no," I said. "Middle eighties, maybe."

"I kind of dropped a bomb," he said. "I really thought you knew about your mother. The way Eric talked about it, I assumed it was common knowledge. I mean, not *common*. Family business."

"Family business," I said. The phrase tugged at me. Glapion was related to Marie Laveau, the most famous voodoo priestess of all time. Sabine was Amelie's granddaughter. The thought fluttered in the back of my mind, soft and elusive as a moth. If I hadn't been tired and jet-lagged, if I hadn't had three kinds of emotional whiplash in the last half hour, if I'd gone to bed instead of dancing and drinking, maybe it would have come clear.

As it was, I didn't figure it out until it was way too late.

ELEVEN

"They act like it will all come back," Karen said as we walked across Jackson Square. "It won't. Nothing comes back, it just moves on. The natural state of the world is recovering from the last disaster."

She looked over at me, surprised by my laughter.

"Sorry," I said. "It's just that I have about five different things going on right now, and that describes all of them."

It was the awkward hour of the morning, too late for breakfast, too early for lunch. Jackson Square was full anyway. Fortune tellers sat at folding card tables all around the square, each offering up some small divinatory specialty. Crystal tarot. Energy reading. Palm reading. Aubrey and Ex planned to go to the safe house with Chogyi Jake and perform the rites that would make our cargo van difficult for the *loa* to find. Karen and I had taken the job of checking the six addresses of Amelie Glapion; playing the shell game.

Only first, we were on our way to the Café du Monde for beignets and coffee. Gawking tourist girl, me.

The air was heavy with moisture, the wide sweep of the Mississippi just up a flight of stairs, echoing the cathedral directly across the square. On one side, the eternal hope and faith of religion, and across from it, the uncaring, amoral water that had drowned the city. Only not this part. Not here. So maybe the cathedral meant something more after all.

"It's a mess," Karen said. "There are still people paying property tax on houses that haven't existed since the hurricane. They can't get the assessors out fast enough. Gentilly. St. Bernard Parish. There are parts of this city that are dead. And it's better now. Oh God, it's better than it was right after the storm."

"You sound like you love the city," I said, then pointed at the tightly packed chairs under the awning. "Is that the place?"

"The very one," she said with a confirming nod. "I wasn't here before. I mean, I passed through once or twice when I was working with the bureau. But not since. Not until the rider decided to come back here. And no, I don't love New Orleans. I respect it. I respect anything that can take a bad hit and not go down."

Like my parent's marriage, I thought. Like Karen herself. Or even the serial-killing rider we were hunting, for that matter.

I had meant to spend the evening after we got back from the safe house reading up about Legba and Marie Laveau, the Voodoo Heart Temple, and demonically possessed serial killers in general. Instead, I'd sent e-mail to my brother Curt. I didn't say much, just hi, and I was doing fine and traveling a little. How were things at the homestead? In all the time I'd been hopping across the globe, I hadn't talked to my family. I hadn't even told them what Eric had left me. Writing to Curt was a step so small as to almost not exist, and still it was a big deal for me.

Somewhere along the line, I felt like I'd taken a big hit too, and that I was still standing back up. I promised myself again that tonight I'd do my homework. No more putting it off. Time to be professional. Maybe even after we were done with coffee.

We got a table, and an older Asian waitress took our order. Five minutes later, I was eating deep-fried dough in a thick coat of powdered sugar and drinking chicory coffee.

"I was thinking," I said. "The whole thing with Marinette?"

"How is Aubrey doing?" Karen asked.

"He's fine. Well . . . no, he's really not," I said. "But he's going to be. You know?"

Aubrey. Another one for the list of hard knocks.

"I understand," she said, sipping her own coffee. She took it with cream. I drank it black. "I'm sorry that happened. It's . . . scarring. If there's anything I can do to help. Even if he just needs someone to talk to."

"I'll let him know," I said. "Thanks."

"I feel responsible," she said. "I was the one who led you in there. Even when you expressed concerns, I just pushed on ahead. I'm not used to working with people. Not anymore. I think I forgot what it's like, risking someone besides myself."

"We're grown-ups," I said. "We could have said no."

Karen smirked into her coffee cup. Her eyes stayed sad.

"Fair enough," she said.

"What I wanted to talk about, though," I said. "That thing where the locals are still looking to kick Legba's ass for whatever got it exiled in the first place?"

Karen sat forward, her brow furrowed, and nodded to me to go on.

"I don't know if you knew this," I said. "Eric . . .

sometimes he worked with riders. Pitted the little ones against the big ones."

"No," she said.

"It was hard for me to get my head around too," I said. "But there is a certain 'the enemy of my enemy' thing going on. And if we could find a way to use them. Something that would weaken Glapion, or even just distract her—"

"I said no. That's the end of it. There aren't any of them that will side with us. If Marinette proved anything, it was that."

I sipped my coffee, frowning. That actually hadn't been the message I'd taken from Aubrey's possession, but Karen seemed sure of herself, and she'd been doing this longer than I had. We sat quietly eating our heart attack of a breakfast. My fingers played idly in the fallen powdered sugar, drawing a snake in the shape of a question mark and dotting it with a drop of coffee.

"I'm sorry," Karen said after two or three minutes. "I didn't mean to snap."

"Didn't notice that you had," I lied.

"You're kind," she said. It wasn't the first time someone had called me that, and I still didn't know what they were talking about. "I don't trust riders. Not any of them. I know Eric used to play with fire. I was more conservative."

Who wants to live forever, right? Karen said in my memory. If that was more safety-conscious and conservative, then Uncle Eric must have juggled running chainsaws. But maybe he had taken terrible risks on a regular basis. Maybe that was why he was dead now, and Karen was still alive. If my mother had indulged in a marriage-threatening affair, then literally anything was possible.

"He will heal, you know," Karen said. It took me a second to figure out she meant Aubrey. "It will take time, and he won't be the same. It's even possible that he'll be better than he was before. Right now, he's . . . damaged. Badly. But he's not out of the game."

"Like the city," I said.

"I talked with Ex yesterday after we left the safe house," she said.

"Did he tell you that it was all his fault that Aubrey and I got hurt?"

"Yes," she said, laughing. "Among other things."

"Ex is a good guy," I said. "But he can be kind of a dick sometimes."

"He's a good man," Karen said. "Confused, maybe. But at heart, I think he's a very good person."

"You're probably right," I said. "It's just that we work together, you know? He's been around since the beginning. He looks at me, and I think he sees the girl I was when he met me. That wasn't a good night."

Karen washed down the last bite of beignet with the last swallow of coffee. She'd timed it better than

I had. I still had half a lump of sugared dough and nothing to drink with it.

"Back to work?" I asked.

"Let's," she said. We walked back across the square, Karen taking my arm like we were old friends. Or possibly lesbian lovers, but I was going for the old friends vibe. Even the few minutes we'd been gone had changed the face of the square. More musicians were gathered. A face-painting table had set up, a thick-faced woman with stars and rainbows running down her cheeks acting as her own advertisement. Tourists wandered through the square, gawking and dancing a little and having their fortunes told. I'd spent my whole life hearing about New Orleans and Mardi Gras. Now that I was here, walking through it all, it seemed both more real and oddly smaller than I'd imagined. I wondered if it had always been this way, or if the glory days had passed. Or if maybe they were still coming.

"Hey, pretty lady!" a man called out from one of the fortune teller's tables. "Come! Come, sit! I answer all your questions. Tell your future."

"Qué será, será," I said gravely and kept walking.

Back at the hotel, Aubrey, Ex, and Chogyi Jake were waiting for the valet to bring out the cargo van. I waved, walking forward with Karen. Aubrey looked a little better. There was more pink in his skin and less in his sclera. Chogyi Jake bowed toward me, smiling. Only Ex seemed awkward and diffident. I thought it was about me until Karen detached from my arm, went to him, and kissed him hello. It involved some unsubtle groping and went on long enough that I got my jaw closed again. I saw one of the bellhops watching us with bare envy on his face.

My mind felt like its clutch had slipped out of fourth gear, and I replayed everything Karen had said about talking with Ex. I couldn't quite believe what was suddenly perfectly obvious. A stray breeze would have knocked me over.

"Well now," Karen said, pulling back an inch from Ex's lips. "Don't tell me you're ashamed of me?"

"Of course not," Ex said, putting his arm around her waist. Karen smiled and leaned into him. Ex looked at me as if challenging me to say something disapproving. Aubrey blinked. Chogyi Jake kept his constant smile, but it didn't reach his eyes.

So, okay. Ex and Karen had done more than talk. All right. It wasn't quite as weird as my mother having a fling, but it was right up there. Not that Ex wasn't a grown man. And Karen was wildly attractive. I just hadn't thought . . .

It wasn't my business, I thought, angrily. Ex wasn't my lover, and he could do whatever he wanted with whoever he wanted to. There was absolutely no reason that I should feel betrayed. Or jealous. Or replaced.

The tableau held for two seconds, then three. I

turned, waved down a parking valet, and gave her the ticket for the rental minivan. My momentary absence was all it took for the conversation to start again.

"We're going to start with the one farthest out," Karen said, "then work our way back in toward downtown."

"Check in before and after," Ex said sternly. "If something does happen, we need to know where to find you."

Karen smiled. A taxi pulled up and let out an older man in a Tulane University sweater.

"If something happens that Jayné and I can't handle," Karen said, "you three need to run like hell."

Ex's expression went stony, and then to my continuing surprise, he laughed. I looked at Aubrey, who shifted his shoulders in a near-subliminal shrug. Chogyi Jake didn't meet my eyes. The cargo van—white, anonymous, and belching smoke—arrived. The three men piled in, and we watched them drive away.

"You don't mind, do you?" Karen asked.

"Mind what?" I said, a little too sharply.

"That I fell into bed with your priest."

"No," I said, forcing myself to mean it. "No, of course not."

Karen sighed. It sounded like relief.

"Good. I told him you wouldn't care," she said, and the minivan hove into sight.

For months it had been me and Aubrey and

Chogyi Jake and Ex; just the four of us. Karen, as cool as she was, belonged outside the circle. Only now maybe she didn't. If Ex had a lover, and a lover who was really better equipped to fight riders than any of us, it was going to change things. I just didn't know how. It wasn't Ex I was jealous of, it was all of us. The little family that I'd made was changing, and nobody had asked me if I was okay with that. Maybe it was just because I had so little that protecting what was left seemed so important.

I let Karen drive, and half an hour later, we were in a decent-looking middle-class neighborhood, parked in the mouth of an alley, and peering down the street with binoculars. I had pretty much talked myself back to sane. As we drove through, I'd thought the houses looked pretty normal, apart from a bathtub ring four feet above the ground and the ubiquitous, eerie X mark that I'd seen out in Lakeview on the doors. Now that we had stopped, I began to notice other details. The yards with thick weeds and vines. Broken windows. The smell of mold and earth, like we were in the ruins of a place half reclaimed by nature.

But there were also kids navigating their bikes around the potholes, jumping off the crumbling curbs. Dogs barked behind fences. Someone was practicing piano, the slow, awkward march of scales fighting against a distant radio on a hip-hop station. More houses showed signs of life than of death. The house we were spying on—a red and brown two-story with bars on the windows—had a planter by the front door that was already thick with violets. And, as with all the others, the X. I remembered vaguely having seen pictures of it on the news right after the hurricane, but I'd never really known what it was. So I asked.

"It's the searcher's mark," Karen said. "After the hurricane, they would come through and check houses. When they were done, they'd put that on the front. It tells you who looked there, what date, and how many bodies they found. It's one of the new symbols. You can find it on T-shirts."

"Grim," I said.

"There are always two sides. At least two," Karen said. "The searcher's X is the symbol of the death. The fleur-de-lis is the symbol of the rebirth."

"It is?"

"Oh yes," Karen said. "It's everywhere now. It never was before."

"I thought you weren't around before," I said.

"I wasn't. But I have been since. Okay. We have something."

I put the binoculars back to my eyes. A black man in his middle thirties was walking up to the door. He had a white plastic grocery bag in one hand, and it tugged at his wrist as he unlocked the door. I watched as he went inside. None of the Glapions came out.

"They could still be in there," I said.

"Or they might not," Karen said. "Let's mark this one off and hit the others. If we don't have any luck, we can make another pass tomorrow."

We didn't have any luck at the next five houses either. Two, in the Ninth Ward, were ruins; the third showed signs of occupancy, but no one went in or out in the hour and a half we watched; the fourth was overrun by at least half a dozen children, all of them white; and the fifth—a duplex in an upscale neighborhood by the river—had mail waiting in the boxes for Adele Grant and Foster Middleton. Amelie, Sabine, and Daria Glapion were nowhere to be found.

"We can try again tomorrow," I said, trying to hide my disappointment.

"This was a good day's work. We've narrowed the field," Karen said. "We can scratch off the two in the lower Ninth. And I think the duplex isn't likely. It's a white neighborhood. They'd stand out. The same with the kids."

"So the one with the guy, or the empty one," I said.

"I like the empty one. But if the boys are done with the van, we could also split the work. One car watches one house."

I nodded. It made sense. Still, I felt restless. Karen slalomed through traffic, the rental blowing conditioned air against me in a losing battle against the day's heat, and my hand tapping my knee in a slow double beat.

I was used to the idea of riders being a secret, part of a hidden world that I'd stumbled into. Driving through New Orleans, I started to wonder if that was true. I saw a Voodoo BBQ and Grill. A local football team, the VooDoo. A Voodoo dry cleaner's. Did they know?, I wondered. Was it all supposed to be a joke and kitsch? Local color? Or did the people who named their businesses know that there were predators on the streets?

Generations had lived and died here, but the riders, the *loa*, had been there the whole time. Individuals or lineages. I had the sense that they were a part of the city, woven in with it, and that their presence had changed the nature of the city itself. New Orleans was only partly human. It was also something else; a great, broken, sprawling artifact. A church. A gate.

A temple . . .

My thumb made its double tap against my knee, paused, tapped again. I realized I'd been playing along with my heartbeat, and I knew what I'd been trying to tell myself.

"You know," I said. "There's someplace else we could try."

THE VOODOO Heart Temple was at the edge of the French Quarter. If we hadn't known to look for it, it would have been easy to miss. The street was filled with the small, desperate shops that live off the scraps of real attractions. The three-story buildings shadowed the street without cooling it. Together with the awnings over the sidewalk, the faded sign would have been easy to miss. It was in the shape of a real heart—fist-shaped and muscular with yellow deposits of fat—pierced by two long spikes. The windows were dim, but not dark. The door stood open.

"Well, there's certainly enough room for an apartment above it," Karen said, idling on the street. "At a guess, there's probably an entrance in the alley behind it too."

"All right," I said. "How about if you take the car around to see what the back looks like. I'll hang here and window shop until you get back. If anyone comes in or out, I can play all clueless white tourist."

"Don't go in," she said.

I gave her my best *Hello. Not stupid.* look and slid out of the car. Karen and the minivan rolled on, turned a corner, and were gone. I walked slowly, peering in windows and trying not to look obvious. The shops were small, dim, and tacky. A lingerie shop with yellowed lace teddies in the front. A souvenir store with a display of dusty Mardi Gras beads and T-shirts. I noticed two shirts with the fleur-de-lis and one with the searcher's X. Maybe a third of the storefronts were empty, small signs or just business cards on the doors announcing what property management company to contact if you were looking for a lease.

"Tell your fortune?"

I'd noticed the black girl sitting on the sidewalk. Her skin was the color of dark chocolate, her hair in beautiful braids, her clothes grubby and worn. She couldn't have been more than ten or eleven. When she smiled, she looked like raw mischief.

"Five dollars for a question," she said. "Fifteen for a whole reading."

I glanced up. Given where the girl was sitting, I could easily be at her side with a good view of the Voodoo Heart Temple. It would save me pretending to look through windows of closed stores, or loitering obtrusively. Besides which, the idea of a kid making up fortunes like it was a lemonade stand tickled me. I sat beside her, fished through my backpack, and came up with a ten.

"What'll this get me?" I asked.

The girl narrowed her eyes, considering the bill like a doctor with an interesting patient at a clinic.

"Short reading," she said.

"Done."

She plucked the ten from my hand, pushed it deep in her pocket, and visibly composed herself. Her expression was so serious, and so clearly an imitation of the buskers and tarot readers of Jackson Square, that I couldn't keep from smiling. The girl opened her eyes, took my right hand, and considered it. Her grip was soft as moleskin.

"You a very powerful person," she said. "But you don't know it. You think you do, but you don't. You worried about your heart—will you find a man, and all like that—but you don't need to worry. He'll be along when the time's right."

"Good to know," I said. She looked up at me, annoyed at the interruption. Something shifted behind the window of the Voodoo Heart Temple. Someone passing by the curtains, I thought.

"You don't trust yourself," the girl said, "but you ought to. You know more than you think. You have hard times ahead, but if you pay attention and find your real power, you'll make it through better than when you started."

The door of the temple shifted. I looked down at my palm, but trained my attention on my peripheral vision. I didn't want to stare, but also I had to know when to glance up.

"And this is important, so you listen," the girl said.

"Okay," I said.

"It wasn't your mama's fault. She loves you, and she loves your daddy. She had a worm inside her when it happened, so you be gentle with her."

Adrenaline flooded me, cold and fast and electric. The girl was looking up at me through her eyelashes.

"What?" I said, at the same moment that the teen-ager who'd emerged from the temple called out.

"Daria! You get back here right now!"

The girl and I looked across the street. Sabine Glapion stood on the far sidewalk, her hands on her hips, her face bent with impatience.

"I've got to go," the girl said, dropping my hand. "You remember what I said, now."

"I will," I managed as she skipped across to her sister.

TWELVE

I checked Ex, Aubrey, and Chogyi Jake out of the hotel as soon as we could get there. Karen and I took their stuff and piled it in the back of the rental, then drove like hell to the safe house. No cultist-driven deathmobiles pursued us. Mystical beasts failed to rise from the lake to swallow us. The only change was a strong wind that kicked up, stippling the water with small, angry waves and pushing the minivan to the left. I didn't even start to calm down until we reached the safe house.

I'd sat there, on the street corner, with Daria Glapion. The girl with the Sight had held my hand, told my fortune, and Legba hadn't come out to kill me. I felt like a bullet had buzzed past my ear, and it left me a little nauseated. Karen, on the other hand, was equal parts glee and banked violence. She paced through the living room like a tiger in a cage, her blue eyes bright. Chogyi Jake, Ex, Aubrey, and I all sat on the couch or the floor. Behind her, the picture window blazed with the red and gray of sunset. The wind complained and threatened, and the trees bent and shifted like they were nervous.

"Okay," she said. "This is perfect. We know where the girl's hiding. Daria didn't identify Jayné, so we still have the element of surprise. We have the safe house ready. We can have Sabine in hand by the end of the week. Aubrey? Chogyi Jake? I'm going to need you two watching the temple and the streets around it. We need to know Sabine's routine. Where she goes, who she talks to. Everything. If she's holed up in the apartment over the shop, we'll need to know that. Amelie might be going in and out too. She has responsibilities to her congregation."

She was rubbing her hands together in delight. I'd always thought that was a figure of speech. Ex looked serious, but an echo of Karen's smile haunted the corners of his mouth, her pleasure reflecting off him like sunlight off the moon in a reminder of their relationship. It bothered me that it bothered me.

"We should still try to draw the girl out," Ex said. "Legba is going to have wards on the apartment just the way we do. Only since it's a rider, they're likely to be . . . unpleasant."

"Good point," Karen said. "We need a way to get her out of the building. Something that she can't ignore. Fire, maybe."

Chogyi Jake squinted and frowned. A particularly loud gust of wind rattled the back door. I didn't know I intended to speak until I did it.

"I think we should warn her."

Karen frowned.

"Who?" she said.

"Sabine. If she's in danger, she should know. If she understands what's going on, she can help us. Work with us."

"Why would she do that?" Ex said. "Some stranger off the street comes in and tells her not to trust her own grandmother?"

I hesitated, trying to focus my thoughts.

"Sabine must have seen the changes in her. I mean that's the point, isn't it? Legba was exiled, and now, after the hurricane, it's back. Amelie must have changed. The way she acts. The things she can do. Legba can't have been in her for more than two and a half years, I mean at the outside. And probably not as long as that, or Sabine would be dead by now, right?"

"I don't think we can assume that Sabine will have noticed a difference," Karen said.

"And Daria," I said, momentum carrying me

over Karen's objection. "I mean she's got this weird precognitive thing going on. She can't be on Legba's side either. Doesn't it make sense to try to get both of them, Sabine and Daria, on our side?"

"That isn't how this works," Karen said. "We don't tip our hand. We don't warn them. Once Sabine is locked up safe, we can—"

"And what about Daria?" I said. "If Legba kills off the people closest to the horse, you know, isolates it? Then why wouldn't Daria be in just as much trouble as Sabine?"

"Jayné," Ex said. Two familiar syllables, but they hit like a slap. "Karen has been tracking this rider for years. She's the expert. If she says this is how the thing behaves, we can safely assume that it's how the thing behaves."

"I was just asking," I said.

"You're right to ask," Karen said. "It's just that we can't reinvent the wheel here. We don't have time."

"I don't know," Aubrey began.

"Trust me," Karen said. "I know what I'm doing. If we can get Sabine away and safe, Legba will go crazy looking for her. It will overextend. That's when we can take it."

Karen laid out the plan, rough though it was. Aubrey and Chogyi Jake would watch the Voodoo Heart Temple, take notes, and build a profile of Sabine's actions. Ex and Karen and I would finish the work on the cargo van. We had magical wards on it, but we still needed to black out the windows and install handcuffs in the back to keep Sabine under control until we could get her to the prison shed out back. All through the conversation, Karen found opportunity and reason to touch Ex—leaning over a diagram of traffic in the French Quarter, her hand on his shoulder; sitting beside him on the couch, their thighs pressed together.

I got up and quietly walked out the back door. Night had fallen, but the wind hadn't died down. It drove last autumn's leaves across the grass and pushed my hair into my mouth. It played the trees like some huge, organic reed instrument; a saxophone playing free jazz until my ears wanted to bleed. I walked around the shed, pretending to look for places that Sabine might escape.

I wanted Aubrey to come out, to find me. To tell me I wasn't being stupid, that there was something worth thinking about in my questions. I told myself that my hurt feelings were just jet lag paranoia.

A year before, I hadn't even known that riders existed. Karen was seasoned and experienced; an expert. *The* expert. If she didn't think my objections were worth considering, maybe I was being stupid, and was just too stupid to know it.

I'd gotten just about to the point of leaving Ex, Aubrey, and Chogyi Jake to work with Karen while I went off to some kind of home for the mentally deficient when I heard the footsteps on the path. For a half second, I thought it was Aubrey. Another footfall, like a word in a familiar voice, told me otherwise.

"You walked out," Chogyi Jake said over the sound of the wind. "You're angry."

"Yeah, well . . ." I said.

Chogyi Jake nodded, squinting up into the darkness. Clouds scudded across the sky, glowing a dull orange from the city lights. He didn't speak, and I didn't either. His presence by my side felt like an affront at first. Who was he to come out and disturb my solitude? I didn't come breathe down his neck while he was meditating. Was it so much to ask for a little time for myself? And then, slowly, painfully, chagrin. He was just standing there. It wasn't like he was the one telling me I didn't know what I was doing. And then gratitude. I took a deep breath, letting it seep slowly out my nose. It was a relaxation technique Chogyi Jake had taught me. I should probably have been doing it more often.

I was about to suggest we head back in and get this abduction on the road when he spoke.

"I don't like her," he said.

"What?"

"Karen," he said. "I don't like her."

"Ex does," I said.

"Ex has had different experiences than I have," Chogyi Jake said. "I think there's weather coming. We should check the forecast."

"Why don't you like Karen?"

Chogyi Jake crossed his arms. He was wearing sand-colored slacks and a buff shirt lighter than his skin. The stubble on his scalp was in real danger of becoming hair, and I noticed a sprinkling of white at his temples that surprised me. I'd never thought about his age.

"When I was first learning to embrace and accept my own anxiety and suffering," he said, speaking very slowly, as if thinking each word twice before he said it, "I didn't do a very good job."

"The drugs," I said. This was only the second time he'd ever mentioned his career as heroin user, but the first time had made an impression on me. He nodded. A gust of wind brought the smell of the lake and diesel smoke.

"Something happens when you're a junkie," he said. "You never really come back from it. You . . . try to pass for a normal person. If you're good, you can fool people. Some people. But not another junkie."

"You aren't a junkie," I said, meaning it as comfort or reassurance. As a way to say he was my friend and I didn't care what he'd done.

Chogyi Jake grinned like I'd given him a puppy.

"Yes, I am," he said. "That's the point. And so is Karen. I don't think it was drugs in her case, but there was something. All the things she does to try to seem normal? All the games she plays? I've seen them before. I've done them."

"Like?"

"She is always slightly more approachable and friendly than anyone else in the room. She acts like you're intimates when you're in private, and disrespects you in public," Chogyi Jake said. "She found the man in the group most open to being seduced, and she seduced him. She's trying too hard."

"I don't see it," I said. "I don't see her acting all that different from me."

Chogyi Jake lifted a single finger. In the dim light, he looked like a woodcut of a Zen teacher.

"Like you turned to eleven," he said. "She's trying to pass for you, but it doesn't come quite naturally. I watch her, and I see the version of herself she wants me to see, but I also see *that* she wants me to see it. So I don't trust her."

"I think . . ." I said, then trailed off. *I think you're being paranoid. I think you're wrong. I think you're mistaking my desperate little sister crush on her for something weirder.*

I think maybe I don't like her either.

"Seduce is a strong word for it," I said after a while.

"She started quoting Thomas Aquinas at him as soon as she knew he was a priest," Chogyi Jake said.

"She did?"

He nodded. "I don't believe any woman with necklines that low quotes Aquinas without a motive."

Aubrey's head appeared at the kitchen window, looking out into the darkness. I took a step toward him, then paused. Chogyi Jake stood beside me, still peering up into the sky, as if the coming weather might have written a message there.

"What do we do?" I asked. The wind rippled across the grass, the small waves like lake water seen from above. Chogyi Jake scratched his arm.

"That Karen is . . . damaged isn't an argument that she is wrong," he said at last. "I don't have reason to doubt that the rider she is hunting is evil and merits destruction. There is no doubt that Joseph Mfume was a murderer and a sadist. And two *loa* have tried to kill you since we came to New Orleans. All of those suggest that Karen is telling the truth."

"Fair point," I said.

"If you restrict who you work with to the mentally well, you may find yourself short of allies. There are strong arguments against me. Or Ex. Aubrey. But don't put your trust in her."

"So I shouldn't be seduced by her," I said.

"Or cowed."

I ran through the last few days in my mind. The way Karen put her arm around me whenever we were alone. The irresponsible near-manic glee in the way she'd led us into danger at Charity Hospital. Her dismissal of my concerns tonight. I'd accepted all of it.

"You're saying I've been relying on the authority because she's the authority. FBI badass, years of experience, actually has a clue what she's doing, yadda yadda yadda," I said.

"Yes."

"And you think that's a mistake."

"Yes."

The wind paused as if it was catching its breath. In the moment's calm, I heard Ex laughing inside the house. A cricket chirped tentatively from the shed.

"This plan," I said. "It doesn't make sense to me."

"All right," Chogyi Jake said.

"I don't think Karen's going to answer my questions. She hasn't yet."

Chogyi Jake smiled and nodded like I'd said something nice about his shirt. He was giving me the space to think my own way through this.

"So I have to figure it out for myself, right?"

He didn't say anything. He didn't have to. I walked back into the house. Karen, Ex, and Aubrey were in the living room, talking intensely about how much free will a normal person had compared to someone with a rider. Or an animal with a parasite. I found my leather backpack, but my laptop case was beside the futon mattress I'd claimed as my own. I couldn't get it and get out without passing through the living room, so instead of slipping away quietly, I brazened it out.

"What are you doing?" Karen asked as I headed for the door.

"I need to check e-mail," I said. "The dead zone here is going to make me really nuts. You guys hang. I'm just going to hit a Starbucks or something. Back before you know it."

Aubrey half-rose, then hesitated. I could see that he wanted to come with me, but I walked to the door without him. I'd learned the lesson of Charity Hospital. I might be going into danger, and I wasn't going to have Aubrey be the shield for my risks, even if the risks were small. I was surprised when Ex objected.

"We should go with you," he said. "We can't be sure that Daria didn't recognize you. Legba could be setting a trap."

"I'll be fine," I said, then headed out the door before anyone could follow me. Heading down the driveway in the minivan, I saw Aubrey and Ex looking out the picture window after me, and Chogyi Jake sitting in lotus position in the backyard, his eyes closed. I got to the main road, navigated my way south again, and turned up the radio. The DJ was talking about a night of wind and rain, but there was no particular fear in her voice. Mere storms weren't going to faze a city that had survived a hurricane. The drowned have nothing to fear. I got onto the I-10, driving alone across the water.

The hum of tires against the temporary metal

grating that the southbound bridge had instead of
pavement was calming. The lake I passed over was
almost invisible in the night. I turned off the air conditioner and rolled down the windows, inviting the
thick, humid air of the real world into my hermetic
little box on wheels. It smelled like rain. A police car
sped past me, and the DJ played an old Pearl Jam
song I hadn't heard in years and I sang along at the
top of my lungs. Twin rows of brake lights strung
themselves out before me in the darkness. New Orleans rose up glowing beyond them.

All through my childhood, there had been rules
that bordered on commandments. In my father's
house, we were supplicants and sinners whose only
hope of redemption was in the obedience we offered
to the Lord, and the rules and strictures and demands of God were spoken in the voice of Andrew
Heller. I'd spent my childhood loving God because
He demanded it and fearing Him because He was
frightening, until one day the two finally came together in my mind and broke; God could not love
me and still permit hell to exist. There was either
eternal punishment or a loving and compassionate
Creator, but I didn't see how there could be both,
and that one thin crack of doubt—barely visible in
the eggshell perfection of my faith—broke everything. The rules of my father's house stopped being
the rules of the universe; the eye of God wasn't always watching me. I could sneak out.

I still remembered those first, tiny, unremark-able acts of rebellion: sneaking out of my bedroom window and sitting on the back lawn at midnight, wearing only my second-best socks to church on Sunday, silently reciting the lyrics to "Walk Like an Egyptian" instead of the Lord's Prayer at night. No punishment had come, and there had been a deli-cious, dangerous feeling. The hint that maybe I was actually free after all.

Now, driving away from Karen and Ex and Au-brey and even Chogyi Jake, I had a similar lifting and opening feeling in my heart. Of course I was afraid, and of course I was guilty. That was very nearly the point.

I drove to the French Quarter, put the minivan in valet parking in the hotel at which I no longer had a room, and pulled out my laptop. Two Google searches and thirty seconds on MapQuest got me what I wanted. My cell phone said it was 9:24. I re-checked the web page, got the number, and dialed, crossing my fingers. A man answered.

"Hello, this is Dr. Inondé."

"Hi," I said. "My name's Jayné? I saw on your Web site that you do private consultations?"

There was a quiet hiss. I imagined him rolling his eyes at another idiot tourist. I really didn't care what he thought.

"I do," he said, "but I am just closing the museum for the night. If you can come in the morning—"

"I'll pay you a thousand dollars for half an hour of your time if I can talk to you right now."

There was a heartbeat's span of silence, then the man laughed.

"I am at your service, Miss Jayné," he said.

"I'll be right there," I said.

The Authentic New Orleans Voodoo Museum—as opposed to the New Orleans Historic Voodoo Museum or the Voodoo Museum of New Orleans—was in a space no larger than a T-shirt store a block and a half off Jackson Square. The stores around it were closed, and the sign in the window also announced that the museum's hours had passed and to come back in the morning. A low red light still burned inside, and when I knocked, the door opened.

Dr. Inondé was, to my surprise, a white man in his early fifties wearing a Hawaiian shirt, loose linen slacks, and a ten-foot-long red-on-tan serpent as thick as my arm looped around his right thigh, up his side, and across his shoulders.

I stepped in, the acrid smell of burning twigs greeting me. The place had all the charm of a roadside attraction. Cheap red curtains draped around awkward oil paintings of famous practitioners of voodoo. One labeled "Marie Laveau" stared out from the far wall. I tried to see Amelie Glapion in the proud, dark face, but it looked more like Frida Kahlo.

"Miss Jayné," he said with a theatrical flourish of

his wrist, sitting at a low black table. "What can the world of the voudoun do for you tonight?"

As if he'd rehearsed it, a low roll of thunder murmured in the background and a pelting, angry rain began. I sat in the offered chair.

"Okay, look," I said. "I pretty much assume you're a fake, and I don't really care. The French Quarter's a small place, and I have to figure you know the competition, right?"

Dr. Inondé smiled and spread his hands, ceding me the point. His snake lifted its head, shifted its weight on his shoulders, and lay back down.

"Okay," I said. "For a thousand dollars. What do you know about Amelie Glapion?"

THIRTEEN

Dr. Inondé shook his head slowly, a small pink tip of tongue darting out to wet his lips. What was sensual and dangerous on his snake only made him look nervous.

"Amelie?" he said. "Why do you want to know about her?"

"When you're paying the money, you can ask the questions," I said.

He coughed out a single laugh, squared his shoulders, and leaned back.

"You think that I'm a fake," he said. The theatrical richness of his voice had faded, but hadn't entirely gone. "A show for the tourists. Well, most things around here are. That's where the money comes from, isn't it? People come here for the music and the mystery and the hope that some pretty coed will take her top off. It's what we have to offer. So sure, I ham it up sometimes. We all do. Amelie, though? She was the real deal."

"Was?"

"She hasn't been doing well these last years," Dr. Inondé said. "She and her family didn't evacuate for Katrina. They could have, God knows, but the Glapion clan doesn't leave this city."

My cell phone went off, Aubrey's number on the display. I turned off the ringtone, letting him drop to voice mail. I'd call him back when we were done.

"Sorry," I said. "Go on. She didn't leave?"

"She was like the captain of the ship. If her city was sinking, she'd go down with it. She lost her daughter."

"Sabine's mother?"

"You know Sabine, then? Yes. Sabine's mother, Annette. And there was a boy, Sabine's brother. Jean-Claude was his name, but everyone called him Jaycee. I don't know exactly how they died, but really there were so many dead. People forget that. There were bodies in the streets. Bodies in the houses. September eleventh was a terrible, terrible thing, but we lost more here. They say it's only two thousand dead or missing, but that's crap. They don't know."

The bitterness in his voice stirred something in the snake. Its huge, broad head shifted, its black tongue flickered against the man's cheek like a kiss. Dr. Inondé smiled, took the snake's head, and kissed it between the eyes.

"I'm fine, Doris," he said to the serpent. "I just get angry. Yes, Amelie lost her daughter and her grandson. And she had a stroke there at the Superdome. The stress was too much for her. If there had been a hospital to take her to, maybe they could have helped, I don't know. After the storm, she was walking with a cane, and her whole left side was just . . . dead-looking. Like a zombie. She's still a force to be reckoned with, but . . . it isn't the same."

"You sound like you know her pretty well," I said, leaning forward. The roar of water on the street surged while he shrugged. Doris the snake's head rose and fell.

"Everyone knows her, one way or another. That's who she is. The story is she's a direct maternal line to the divine Marie there. And the temple? Well, that's been part of the family forever. Amelie inherited it from her mother, and Annette was supposed to take it from Amelie. That's the way the Laveaus did it too. Mother to daughter. Only with Annette gone, Amelie had to step back in. I hear she's grooming Sabine, but the girl's sixteen."

"Grooming her for what?"

"To take over," he said. "Run the temple, do the

tourist trade. And Amelie holds rites. Invokes the spirits. I've never been, but from what I've heard it's a hell of a show. It's medicine too, you know. I remember it used to be Amelie would have eight or ten people a week show up at the temple instead of going to an urgent care center. Even had one boy who'd been shot, and when the paramedics were taking him to the hospital, he told them to go to the temple instead. That is how important Amelie Glapion was to this community. How do you put a sixteen-year-old girl in a position like that?"

The same way you put a twenty-three-year-old one in charge of a world-spanning empire fighting against riders, I thought. You do it because you have to. Because something went wrong.

"Maybe she thinks Sabine can handle it," I said.

"Well, I hope she's right," Dr. Inondé said. "We are competing for the same money, and God knows there's not as much as there used to be, but I would hate to think I helped them lose the family business."

Family business. There the phrase was again, tugging at me. The dark secret of my mother's affair, Amelie Glapion's rider cult and temple. The two ideas had wrapped themselves around each other like snakes on a caduceus. Dr. Inondé didn't notice my frown; he carried right on, waving a despairing hand as he did.

"And the young one? Daria? That poor thing. Sharp as a tack, but odd. You seem like the skeptical type, and I want you to know I respect that. There are any number of frauds in this business. I'm more than half a fraud myself, so I can say that. Daria Glapion gives me the heebie-jeebies."

She had a worm inside her when it happened, so you be gentle with her.

"Me too," I said.

"You've met her, then?"

"Once," I said. "And Amelie once, but we didn't really hit it off."

A flash of lightning turned the windows white, and a breath later, the thunder boomed. Dr. Inondé folded thick fingers together. With his brows knit, he looked more like a shop teacher than a houngan.

"Is this what you wanted to know?" he asked.

"I can't tell yet," I said. "I've heard stories."

"But you don't believe them," he said, as if offering sympathy. He thought I meant stories about voodoo, the supernatural, riders, and *loa*. I meant every word Karen had said.

"I believe something's going on," I said. "I just don't know what it is yet."

"But you're going to find out," he said.

"That's my job."

Dr. Inondé untangled Doris and put her on the table, then rose with a gesture that told me to remain where I was. He stepped past one of the cheap red curtains into an alcove I hadn't noticed. The snake looked at me with shining, empty eyes, then turned and slid down toward the chair where the man had been sitting like a cat curling up in a warm spot.

"For that thousand dollars, you can have this too," he said, passing me a red cloth pouch on a leather thong. It smelled like dust and old chicken, and I had an immediate, intense dislike of it. "It's gris-gris. Salt for the sea, ashes for fire, graveyard dirt for earth, and a baby's first breath for air. It's good medicine."

I didn't want to touch it, but I didn't see how to refuse. I took the thong in my fingers and lowered the thing into my backpack. When it was safely away, I took out my wallet and counted out ten hundreds onto the table. Dr. Inondé looked at the bills and then up at me.

"I don't want to know what's going on with this, do I?" he said.

"Probably not," I said.

He nodded, gathered up the money, and shoved it into his pocket.

"If I have more questions later?" I said.

"This sad fake is always at your service, Miss Jayné," he said in the theatrical voice. I smiled. He smiled back. As I opened the door to leave, a thought struck me.

"Inondé?" I said. "Doesn't that mean . . . ?"

"Flooded," he said with an apologetic rise of his brows. "You can pretend it didn't happen or you can make it part of the magic of the place. What other option have you got? And Dr. David Mackelwhite doesn't pull them in."

The rain hadn't slackened. Tiny streaks of silver and gray darted out of the sky and crashed onto the pavement like suicides. I walked under the awnings, as far from the street as I could manage, and my jeans were still getting wet. I thought about what I'd learned, if I had learned anything.

I knew that Amelie Glapion was possessed by a rider. That was firsthand knowledge, and I didn't have to trust anybody about anything. So that was the center to work from. Amelie was running a rider cult, and her granddaughter Sabine was attending rituals. I knew her other granddaughter Daria had the ability to see things that were true, but that she didn't necessarily understand herself. Again, that was direct evidence.

At one remove, I knew that the rider had been cast into exile, killed a bunch of people including Karen's old partner, and was now making its way back home. I knew Amelie Glapion had suffered a stroke at the same time New Orleans was wrecked by the hurricane. She had been a woman of serious importance in the community, but she was weaker now, and the community scattered.

I reached an intersection, ducked out from beneath the awning, and ran. The rain was hard, but warmer than I'd expected. My shirt and hair were soaked by even that short time. I double-checked my laptop carrier, but it was closed tight. Still, probably best to keep as dry as I could.

I turned down the street. A neon sign announced LARRY FLYNT'S BARELY LEGAL, white lightbulbs dancing above it. The pictures in the window showed airbrushed girls younger, I assumed, than I was. A woman in a bright yellow raincoat came out, lit a cigarette, and looked at me. She was wearing half a display counter worth of makeup, but underneath it, she looked tired. I smiled, and she nodded back. I had heard somewhere that the sex shows were the first businesses on Bourbon Street to reopen. At the time, it had been said in an approving voice, but I couldn't remember whose. I kept walking.

Nothing I'd heard conflicted with Karen's story. But if I were Legba, would I really choose Amelie Glapion for my victim? Someone that high in the community would be a coup, certainly, but I couldn't see why the rider would try to surround itself with people who were aware of riders and how they worked. If Karen was to be trusted, the local *loa* didn't think much of old Legba. Diving into an existing rider cult . . .

Maybe there was a reason. Maybe it made sense, if you looked at it from the right perspective. Eric would have known, could have put all the points in a line and seen what it all meant and what would happen next. But he was gone, and I was here.

And, much as I hated it, I did have someone I could ask. Karen had evaded my questions and played weird power games and all that, it was true. But if I wasn't seduced or cowed, I could insist that we talk about it. I'd present my questions in simple, clear words, and I'd just keep leaning until I had an answer. Then afterward, I could find a way to fact-check it.

I had just about resolved to head back to the safe house when I realized where, only half aware, I'd been heading all this time. I'd been walking and thinking, aiming for the dry spots and holding tight to awnings, and some part of me had known where it was headed. The Voodoo Heart Temple was right in front of me, its windows dark, its grisly sign swinging in the storm wind. I didn't see anyone inside, but I stepped out into the street, rain sluicing down me, and looked up. There, on the third floor, lights were burning. An apartment above the temple.

I needed to go. I needed to walk away right then and go to the hotel and get in my car and leave New Orleans. I tried to turn, but my body didn't move. I felt the cold distance come over me, the sense of being an observer in my own body. Something was wrong, and I knew it.

A voice, nothing more than a change in the tone of the raindrops. Three girls were coming along the street toward me, laughing and prodding each other. The one nearest the wall might have been Chinese or Vietnamese, I couldn't tell at that distance. The tall girl in the middle was black, gangly and awkward; a girl who hadn't quite grown into her body yet. The third—the one walking closest to the storm—was as graceful and beautiful now as she had been when I'd seen her in the flickering hell of Charity. Sabine Glapion.

And there, in the shadows of the doorway just before them, something moved. The raindrops paused, hanging in the air like crystal. The roar of the storm became silence. The two girls at Sabine's side froze in mid-stride, and Sabine alone went on for half a step.

I dropped my pack and my laptop in the street.

"Sabine!" I screamed. *"Run!"*

The thing that boiled out of the shadows shrieked; a wet, angry sound full of rage and hatred. Sabine turned and sprinted away, the dark thing surging after her, and me after it. The beast knocked the frozen girls aside with long, knifelike claws. Sabine ran into the suspended rain, her passage carving a tunnel through the falling water. I drew the psychic energy of my qi up from my belly through my chest, pressing the living force out my throat as I shouted.

"Face me!"

The thing hesitated, its great, inhuman head craning back to look at me. It had been human

once, I thought. I could see the places where the
rider hadn't transformed the flesh past all recog-
nition. The blunt, black incisors, the dagger-long
fangs were set in a jaw that belonged to a human
being. The weirdly expressionless eyes had been
a human's once. A man's, a woman's, or a baby's;
there was no way to tell. I leaped, my right foot
sawing through the unnaturally still air. The impact
jarred me like I'd hit a concrete wall, but the thing
fell back a step.

Before I caught my balance, it attacked. I tried
to block, and its claws bit into my arm. A closed fist
swung up into my ribs like a car wreck. Something
painful snapped. My own hand shot out, the heel of
my palm against the thing's face.

It took a step back, hissing. Stilled for a moment,
it seemed broad as a truck, thick shoulders of pale
skin mottled with deep veins of dark flesh. There
were too many joints in its legs. For a moment, the
only sound was the slow drip of blood from my
arm, then its chest expanded and it let out a sound
more like a storm than a shout. I felt the will and
power and rage in its voice. It was chaos and war
made flesh, and its hatred of me was as deep as a
mine shaft. The pain in my ribs was bright and ex-
quisite. I bent my knees, leaned toward it. When it
lunged for me again, I moved into the blow, under
it, and past the beast, driving an elbow into the
place where a kidney might have been in a human.

Its shriek had more to do with pain now. It wheeled to face me again.

I surprised myself by grinning. Its eyes flickered past me, down into the quiet of the suspended street. I could hear its breath, the low growl haunting the back of its throat. Sabine was getting away, and I could see the frustration in its face. A sense of profound peace came through my body, lifting and consoling me. My broken chest and mutilated arm hurt, but the pain didn't mean the same thing anymore. Even before I moved, I felt the violence spinning up within me like the singing of a choir. This, I thought, was what it must feel like to die.

I dove to the side, hands grasping the pole that held the sidewalk awning, and wrenched from my gut. The wood splintered in my hand, coming away like plucking a blade of grass. I landed in the street, club in hand, one leg back one forward. I felt angelic. I felt beautiful.

The thing turned, and this time the wood caught its claws. I darted in, hammering its shoulder with my fist, then danced back as it howled. The still rain hung around me like a veil. I battered the thing with a flurry of strikes, knee, chest, shoulder, belly. For a moment, I thought I might actually win.

It swung, and I fell for the feint, bringing my club to stop a blow that wasn't there. Its leg shot out, catching me just above the knee, and I stumbled with the sudden agony.

I saw the killing blow as it came. Knife-sharp claws carving the air, arcing toward my exposed throat. I wasn't going to be able to block it. I had no leverage to twist aside. I hardly had time to gasp.

But the blow didn't land. Something bright appeared at the thing's wrist, and the claws pulled wide, shredding my sleeve as I fell, but not breaking skin. From the black, shining pavement, I looked up.

A man stood in the middle of the sidewalk, a great black coat hanging from his shoulders like the robe of some exotic priest. His black skin shone like he was lit from within, and the close-cut gray of his hair was like a scrim of silver cloud in the night sky. A chain hung from his hand with a vicious hook at one end. The hook that had pulled the creature's attack aside.

"Not tonight, my friend," the man said in a Caribbean accent as I struggled back to my feet. His voice was velvet and stone.

The thing turned to him, then to me, then roared in defiance and frustration. I steeled myself for a fresh attack, but my leg wasn't quite where I thought it was. It didn't matter. The beast raised its arms, vanished, and the raindrops hammered onto the street. After the unreal silence, the storm was deafening.

I didn't realize I was collapsing until I was down, the asphalt rough and comfortable against my cheek. I coughed, almost certain that the warmth in my throat wasn't blood. I rolled to my back, watching the rain fall from the distant clouds down onto my face like a manga cliché.

Sabine Glapion appeared, looming over me. She was soaked, her blouse clinging to her skin, her eyes wide and horror-struck.

You're in danger, I tried to say. *Maybe you noticed.* Nothing intelligible came out. Then the black man was kneeling beside me. He had a long, careworn face, and a dark scar ran across one cheek.

"Don't move," he said, all concern and soft vowels. "You're hurt. You need a doctor."

"Y'think?" I managed, and he smiled a wide, warm, goofy grin. I lay back, darkness crowding the edges of my vision. The last coherent thought I had before I passed out was, *Oh shit. That's Joseph Mfume.*

FOURTEEN

In the years before I left home, I went to the emergency room exactly once. Christmas Day, when I was twelve, I had a stomach flu so bad I was getting dehydrated. My father put me in the car, gave me a towel to puke into, and drove me to the ER where they drugged my guts into submission and kept me alive with an IV drip. By the time I got home, my brothers had opened all my presents for me.

Since inheriting Uncle Eric's money, I'd spent a lot more time in the hospital recovering from wounds of my own and caring for the people who'd been hurt working with me. Swimming back to

consciousness, I recognized the dim fluorescent twilight, the smell of antiseptic, the squeak of nurses'
shoes against linoleum. I tried to remember what
had happened. A car wreck? No. Someone had
stabbed me. Or something.

I tried to sit up and my left side from collarbone to hip lit on fire. I fell back to the bed, gasping. The ceiling above me was all-white acoustical
tile. I came a little more awake. My right arm was
bandaged. My left knee was swollen to about twice
its normal size. I probed my ribs gently through
the thin blue hospital gown. My right side felt
merely sore and angry. I only tried touching the
left side once.

Joseph Mfume. I'd been fighting with something—a rider in its full, unhidden form—and I'd
been saved by the serial killer and rapist who'd
started the whole messy thing. I remembered Sabine Glapion standing in the unfalling rain of the
crossroads between the real world and Next Door.
Well, she'd still been alive last time I saw her, so that
had to be a good thing. I craned my neck, but there
were no clocks. I needed to find out how long I'd
been there. I needed to find out where exactly I was,
for that matter.

I needed to find Aubrey and Ex and Chogyi Jake.
The best I could manage was a nurse call button.
After what felt like an hour, I hit it again. A couple
hours after that, a nurse came, explained to me that

I had hairline fractures in two of my ribs, soft tissue damage to the connective tissue in my knee, and they'd stapled my arm closed where it had been cut. When I asked him who'd brought me in, he didn't know. When I asked for my stuff, he said he'd try to find it. He pronounced my name "Jane" and I didn't correct him.

A couple junior cups of fruit juice later, I was feeling almost human. The so-called hairline fractures hurt like hell anytime I moved or laughed or breathed in too deep, but I took comfort in the intellectual knowledge that they only felt shattered. I forced myself to sit up, then slowly, carefully, figured out how I could walk without mind-altering pain. By the time a different nurse appeared with my things, I could see the first, faint light of dawn in the windows.

My clothes were gone, cut off me by the paramedics. My laptop case was rain-soaked, but the interior looked dry enough that it might have escaped harm. The leather backpack I used as a purse was probably trashed. The scraps of paper inside were all waterlogged, and Dr. Inondé's unpleasant little gris-gris had leaked something gray and filmy over the interior pouch. I checked my cell phone's side pocket with a sense of dread. What I took for dead was actually just turned off, and when I powered it back up, it seemed fine. I had five messages waiting for me. I sat on the threadbare chair by the window, the hospital gown wrapped tightly around me in an attempt to preserve what was left of my modesty, and called voice mail.

"Jayné," Aubrey said at about the time I'd been talking with Dr. Inondé. "You hopped out of the house for a few minutes over an hour ago. What's going on? Call me as soon as you get this."

Then, more faintly, Ex said, *She's not answering?* and before Aubrey could reply, the message ended.

Oops, I thought, my belly tightening with guilt. In addition to getting my ass handed to me, I had probably just put my friends through a night of pure hell.

The next message was a few minutes later.

"Jayné," Aubrey said. "I've just called every Starbucks I can find in the phone book, and you don't seem to be at any of them. We're sending out a search team in the van. Call as soon as you get this message."

Two hours after that:

"Still nothing," Ex said to someone besides me, and hung up.

Fifty minutes after that, Aubrey again:

"*Fuck.* Jayné, if you get this, call in. We're covering as much territory as we can, but no one's found a trace of you. You need to call home. You need to come back."

Then an hour and a half after that, Ex's number again, but only the sound of two or three long, slow breaths together, and then nothing.

I pushed my hair back. The rain and the humidity were making it curl more than I was used to. My knee throbbed. My stitches itched. I'd screwed up.

I called Aubrey's cell number. He picked up on the first ring.

"Jayné?"

"Hey," I said. "Really, really sorry. Totally, deeply, profoundly sorry. Didn't mean to scare you. Didn't mean to scare anyone."

"I don't give a shit," Aubrey said, his tone speaking volumes of relief. "If you're okay, I'll kick the crap out of you later. We were all afraid you were in trouble."

I looked up through my eyelashes. The man in the room across the hallway was writhing in half-sedated pain, a wide, bloodless wound gaping in his belly. From farther away, someone screamed.

"Yeah, well," I said.

"You are okay?"

"I'm fine," I said. "But if you could bring a fresh change of clothes to Tulane University Hospital, I'd really appreciate it."

"Are you . . . Jayné? What happened?"

I replayed the night in my mind. Dr. Inondé and Doris the snake, the girl with the cigarette at the Barely Legal club, Sabine Glapion, the thing in the suspended rain. Mfume's concerned voice and goofy grin. The rider with its pale flesh and knifelike claws.

"I don't know," I said. "I don't know what that was."

I waited for what seemed like days, but wasn't more than an hour and a half. Aubrey and Chogyi Jake showed up with a fresh white button-down shirt, blue jeans, underwear, shoes, socks, and probably my least comfortable bra. In the thousand times I'd almost thrown it out, I had never thought putting on that particular example of underwire madness would feel good. Today, it did.

The nursing staff was very reluctant to let me go without talking to the doctor or possibly the police, but since it wasn't actually legal to restrain me, I was out of there fifteen minutes after Aubrey and Chogyi Jake showed up.

The morning was bright, clear, and warmer than I'd expected. Last night's storm was just puddles on the asphalt, thick humid air, and a few high clouds now. I could tell I was walking slowly because Aubrey kept getting a little way ahead and then dropping back. Chogyi Jake kept by my side, but I had the sense it was only that he was better at restraining himself.

When we got to the minivan, I crawled up into the passenger's seat and pulled the seat belt across, gritting my teeth the whole time. When Aubrey turned on the engine, the air conditioner blasted us. I leaned back in my seat.

"So," I said. "How bad did I fuck things up?"

Neither man spoke.

"Great," I said, closing my eyes.

"Perhaps," Chogyi Jake said, "you could tell us what happened?"

So I did. They both listened as I went through the whole thing. My decision to investigate on my own, my interview with Dr. Inondé, walking to the Voodoo Heart Temple, the foiled attack on Sabine, and being saved by Mfume. It only took fifteen minutes to do a rough recap; we hadn't even reached the lake when I was done.

Even with the hundred questions that I had—was the thing I'd fought in the street another aspect of Legba or a different rider altogether, what was Mfume doing there, why had he taken me to the hospital—I'd overlooked at least one.

"I wonder why you could fight at all," Chogyi Jake said. I turned to look at him over my shoulder. His expression was sour and puckered.

"What?" I said.

"When the rider attacked Sabine," he said, "time stopped. Just as it did when you were attacked at the hotel. The rain stopped falling. Sabine's companions couldn't move."

"Right," I said.

"You could," Chogyi Jake said. "Why?"

"I don't know," I said. "Maybe it's got something to do with the wards that Eric put on me."

"Yes," Chogyi Jake said, as if he'd tasted

something unexpectedly bitter. "The longer we go on, the more convenient those become."

"Mfume could move too," Aubrey said. "And Sabine."

"I figured Sabine could move because she was the one under attack," I said. "Just like with me back at the hotel. And Karen was able to interfere with that one, so there is a way for normal people to break into that spell. Maybe Mfume knows how to do it too. I just don't understand why he would. But I figure we'll ask Karen."

"I'm not sure how well that will go," Aubrey said.

I shifted to look at him. A dull ache bloomed in my knee. He was looking ahead at the road, and very much not at me.

"She's a little pissed off?"

"THEY'RE FUCKING gone," Karen said.

The safe house looked different in the light of middle morning. The tiny cracks in the wall where the structure had settled over the course of years looked like crow's-feet at the corner of an old woman's eye. The picture window seemed to include the wide swath of unmowed, semi-tended lawn. The Virgin Mary gravestone had turned its back on me.

"Jayné!" Karen barked.

I looked back at her. The mixture of guilt and resentment and wordless outrage in my heart was old, familiar territory for me. She stood in the doorway between the living room and the kitchen, her arms folded. She didn't seem shorter than me now. Her anger filled the space.

"The Voodoo Heart Temple is empty," she said. "Locked up, closed, and everyone inside gone to ground. Can you explain to me exactly what the fuck you were thinking?"

Aubrey, just behind me, took a step forward like he was going to protect me. Chogyi Jake was sitting on the counter by the kitchen sink, and I was pretty sure he would have jumped in if I'd given him an opening. Of my three guys, only Ex seemed as pissed off as Karen.

"I didn't go there to get involved," I said. "I was just walking, and I guess it was on my mind. I wound up there, and when I did—"

"You thought, *I know what would be fun. I'll tell the enemy we're here*," Karen said. "And now, I'm back at square motherfucking one. That's *great*."

The words stung. I felt my jaw sliding forward, my lips pressing tight. I felt the crushing weight of having been a disappointment.

"Hey," I said. "There was a lot of weird going around last night. What about Mfume? Why would he take me to the hospital after I got hurt? And the rider that was after Sabine? It didn't look or act anything like the thing that jumped me when I got to town. That one was a snake, and this one—"

Karen growled and ran her hands through her hair. Her eyes seemed to spark with anger. Ex, leaning against the wall behind her, might have smiled, or it might only have been my paranoid imagination.

"I don't know. I don't have answers for any of that, and I can't get them, because I don't know where the bad guys are," Karen said. "I didn't bring you here for your cool Nancy Drew imitation. I wanted help getting Sabine to safety and then killing Legba. That was it. I had an advantage as long as I knew where they were, and you have pissed that away."

How many times had my parents given me a lecture like this? How could I have failed my test? Where had I been, and who had I been with? Why had I lied about whatever tiny thing it was? It all came back to the same thing, however they phrased it: how could I have been so stupid?

I could see my old room, my books, the cross over the bed, my CDs with all the Christian bands on top, and all the secular ones tucked at the bottom of the pile. I could smell the fake floral stink of my mother's favorite laundry detergent. The knot of guilt and shame and anger and outrage in my stomach brought all the details back with it.

I was twenty-three and on my own. I'd thought I'd grown up. I'd thought I was through with this. Stupid me.

"I saved Sabine Glapion's life last night," I said, my voice shaking. "That thing was going to kill her."

"You *didn't* save her," Karen said, "because it is *still* going to kill her. Only now, we don't have any way to stop it."

"How would things have been better had Sabine died in the street last night?" Chogyi Jake asked softly. Karen turned to him like a fighting dog that just noticed a new opponent, like my father shifting attention to my little brother.

"Don't, Chogyi," I said. "I'm okay. I understand you're upset, Karen, and I'm sorry that I tipped your hand. But I found Amelie Glapion once, and I can do it again."

"Your lawyer can, you mean," Karen said. "All you've done so far is fail and have someone save your ass at the last second. I'm not sure that's the kind of help I need."

The lump in my throat was an enemy. I couldn't speak around the humiliation. Karen gathered herself, shook her head, and forced out a slow, hissing sigh.

"Look," she said, "this isn't your fault, okay? It's mine. This is a big deal. It's hard, and I didn't understand how inexperienced you are. I was thinking about Eric and all of the things that he could do, all of the tricks that he knew, and I put you in his place. That was unfair of me, all right? I expected too much."

"I think we can regroup," I said. "There are still a lot of things that I can—"

"No," Karen said. "Jayné, just . . . just no."

"I can fix this," I said.

But the silence in the room told me I was wrong. I couldn't. Aubrey's arms were crossed, his face set in stone. I could see the pain in the way he held himself. Ex's raised eyebrows told me that he agreed with Karen. Only Chogyi Jake was unreadable.

"I appreciate everything you've tried to do," Karen said. The softness in her voice was worse than the anger had been. "But I think I'd better run this operation solo from here on in."

I looked for words, didn't find any, nodded, and walked out. My knee didn't bend the way I was used to, and the staples in my arm itched. A gentle breeze stirred the branches. I felt like the trees were talking about me. I stood by the small statue of the Virgin, looking away from the house with her. The door opened and closed behind me. Aubrey's footsteps came close.

"Are you okay?" he asked.

"I'm fine," I said, and he put a hand on my shoulder. I leaned into him, then flinched as my ribs reminded me that I'd been injured. He had been too. Probably worse than I had.

Somewhere there had to have been a place where I could have done it right. A decision that would have kept Aubrey out of Charity Hospital when

Amelie Glapion's cult opened the way for Marinette, a question I could have asked Karen that would have put everything in context. I felt like my head was filled with cotton ticking; my throat was thick and heavy with the aftermath of shame.

Karen was right. I was flailing in the dark, and if I did anything right, it was only happy coincidence. I had let them all down, not just Karen. I'd put Aubrey in harm's way. Chogyi Jake had put his faith in me, and when I'd gone out to investigate for myself, I'd blown it. Ex . . . well, he'd been spending his nights with Karen, so maybe he at least was having some fun.

"I think they're on the same side now," he said.

I pulled myself back to the present. "What?"

"I was thinking about it back there. Mfume and Karen must be on the same side, since they're both trying to protect Sabine. I just wonder why he would be."

"Well, maybe they can hook up and work it out," I said. And then a moment later, "It doesn't matter."

Aubrey stepped in behind me, his arm draped gently around my collar to keep from pissing off my ribs. When I leaned back into him this time it hurt less. The door opened behind us, then closed again, but no one came to disturb us.

"Whatever you want to have happen," he said. "You know I'm going to back your play, right?"

"It's what I love about you," I said. I felt him

react to the word love. A bird called, shrill and trilling, from the trees behind the house. Near our little prison. Its voice was high, complex, and beautiful as jazz. Months of nosebleed-busy work, days of trauma and danger and injury and failure, and years of the day-to-day struggle of just being me all folded together. I let a couple of exhausted tears escape the corners of my eyes.

"I just want to go home," I said.

FIFTEEN

We left New Orleans that night, packing everything into the rental minivan and driving to the airport even before I'd bothered to make a reservation. Chogyi Jake checked our database and found a four-bedroom house I owned in Savannah. I called the lawyer, arranged for someone to drop keys off at the house, got four first-class tickets online, and walked up to the Delta counter to let them divest us of our luggage.

Going through the ritual humiliation of security, I felt like a piece of candy someone had put in a tin can and shaken. I was all chips and rattle. We got to the gate just in time for boarding. The flight crew were all professionally thoughtful, getting us bedded down in our flying Barcaloungers before letting the hoi polloi in coach shuffle past.

Once we were in the air, Aubrey curled up against the window and slept. When Ex headed up to the bathroom, Chogyi Jake leaned forward.

"You seem tired," he said. "You should sleep."

"I should," I said. "I will. It's just . . . I really screwed that one up, didn't I?"

"I don't know," he said, but he wasn't smiling. It was odd to see him looking somber, and it did exactly nothing to improve my mood. "If you consider that we came here less than a week ago, and in that time you've been assaulted by riders three times, Aubrey has been possessed and exorcised, we've bought a house and a car and fitted both with wards, added to which—"

"Hey, could we talk about this a little later?" I said. "I'm just . . . I'm not up to it right now."

Now he smiled. I could see my own exhaustion mirrored in him. Added to which Aubrey and I had fallen back into bed together, I thought. And my childhood had been reframed by my mother's sexual indiscretions. And, added to *that*, I'd screwed everything up. I didn't know how much of that he saw in my eyes, but some, I thought. Enough.

"Later, then," he said, and sat back. I didn't know how he managed to so clearly retreat into himself without actually moving more than an inch. I sat back in my soft plastic chair and waited for the unpredictable gods of the airline industry to get me the hell out of Louisiana.

This wasn't the first time I'd failed. In fact, it seemed just then like everything I touched was a failure. I'd have expected to be more used to it. And I knew what Chogyi Jake was going to tell me: we had all gone into the job exhausted; we'd been running since we touched ground; it was a complex situation, we didn't know all the facts, and our ally was perhaps not the least fucked-up person I'd ever known.

I could give myself all the excuses. The truth was, I was disappointed because I'd wanted Karen to like me. Or if not that, respect me. I'd wanted her to see that I was capable of handling myself, of taking over the job Eric had left me, of being the person I was pretending to be. If she had looked at me—preferably over the steaming corpse of the rider—and said that I reminded her of herself when she'd just been starting out, I would have done just about anything for her.

But.

I actually managed to doze for a few minutes before the captain came on the loudspeaker and announced our descent into Atlanta. An hour layover in an airport, then the flight to Savannah, then . . . what? I couldn't bear to think about it.

The Atlanta airport was alive with a wide, varied stream of people. Harried business types in gray suits and power ties, college-age men and women traveling in sweats and sneakers, a tour group at least two dozen strong speaking something that sounded like German but might have been anything. It took me a few minutes to realize we were traveling on a Friday. After the first few months of bopping around the world, setting my own schedule, I'd started to lose track of things like days of the week. We navigated through the concourse to a Houlihan's bar, the four of us crowding around a small table made of something equal parts wood and plastic. A television overhead blared about a particularly god-awful earthquake someplace in China, bright images of dust and violence fighting with the bar's dark, fake comfort. When the drinks came, my beer was warm and tasted weirdly like cut grass. I put it down after two sips.

"Okay," Ex said sharply. "Postmortem."

"Ex," Aubrey said, shaking his head, "I think maybe we'd better—"

"Postmortem," Ex said again. "We just had something go off the rails, right? So before we start forgetting things or romanticizing or justifying ourselves or whatever, why don't we get this out of the way."

Ex's pale eyes were hard. From his breath, I had the suspicion that he'd started on the drinks while we were still in the air. A man at the next table started talking into his cell phone loud enough to compete with the dying Chinese above us. It hadn't occurred to me until just then that by getting us fired, I'd also screwed up Ex's love life. He must have spent the whole flight to Atlanta stewing. I didn't want to talk about it, but I owed it to Ex to at least let him vent a little.

I reached for my lousy beer, thought better, and grabbed Aubrey's rum-and-coke instead. Chogyi Jake put his hands flat on the small table.

"Ex. I think this would be a mistake," Chogyi Jake said, his voice low and penetrating.

"No," I said. "It's okay. He's right. We screwed up, and we ought to face that straight on."

"It seems to me that we had a real failure of leadership," Ex said, "and that seems to underlie a lot of the trouble we've been having up to now too."

A failure of leadership. The phrase was like a gut-punch.

"We've been having trouble?" I said, trying to make it a joke.

"We have," Ex said. "For instance, let's look at the division of labor. Jake and I are setting up a secret hideout to hold off the bad guys, and you're . . . what? Clubbing? Maybe it's just me, but that doesn't seem like a very good use of time."

"Hey!" Aubrey said, frowning.

"That wasn't my idea," I said. My voice was higher and tighter than I'd expected it to be. "Karen suggested it."

"And there's another example," Ex said. "Karen. Was she the boss back there? Or were you? Or was Aubrey?"

"I think we should—" Chogyi Jake said, but Ex barreled over him.

"Everything fell apart *because* no one was in charge. Myself, I thought that since Karen was the one that called us in, she would at least be consulted before we went in and screwed everything up."

"What is your problem, Ex?" Aubrey said. "You're talking like everything that's gone wrong here is Jayné's fault."

"Well, there's a hypothesis," Ex said, his lip rising in a sneer. "Why don't we explore that."

Something in my brain hit overload, and the pain and shame and sorrow all shifted into rage. Ex was attacking me, kicking me when I was down. I was betrayed.

"Why don't we not," I said. "This was a bad idea. The postmortem can wait."

"And now, just like that," Ex said and snapped his fingers, "you're the boss again."

At the bar behind Chogyi Jake, an older man turned to look at us. The volume of our conversation was starting to rival the television. My hands were on my knees, fingers digging into my legs.

"Why are you doing this?" I said, keeping my voice down.

"I understand that you wanted to be like Karen," Ex said. "Karen's a very accomplished, experienced, wise woman. She's in control of her own sexuality in a way that nobody who's barely out of high school could be."

"My sexuality? How the fuck did my *sexuality* get into this?" I said, my voice buzzing with anger. "Jesus! Who's feeding you these lines? Is this Karen, because I'm pretty sure she already chewed me out."

"Just let me finish," Ex said. "I think you owe me that much. Karen is powerful, and she's sure of herself. It's perfectly understandable that someone who wasn't would overcompensate."

My rage topped out. It felt like calm. The exhaustion of travel, the humiliation of failure, the hurt of Ex's ambush—all of it fell away like shrugging off a jacket. The sound of the bar and television faded. I think I laughed.

"Walk away from this table," I said.

"No. You owe me at least—"

"Ex, you're fired. Now walk away," I said. All of us were silent for a heartbeat. "That *powerful* enough for you?"

Ex went pale, then flushed red, then pushed back from the table and stalked out into the terminal, his black shirt and pale ponytail vanishing into the river of humanity. None of us spoke. I finished Aubrey's rum-and-coke, walked to the nearest restroom, and sat in the stall with my head in my hands until it was time to board the plane.

Ex didn't make the flight.

I WOKE up in an unfamiliar room. The bed smelled like dust. The ceiling was canted oddly, like the dormer of an old house. Cream-colored paint took on the orange of the soft, translucent curtains. I didn't know who or where I was, and I had the sense that I didn't want to. I lay on my pillow, savoring the moment of sleep-induced amnesia. Something on my arm itched—a wide, ugly cut. And then like a lead weight pressed on my sternum, it all came back.

We'd reached the Savannah house after midnight. An envelope with the keys had been waiting for us under the front mat. We hadn't spoken on the flight. We barely talked on the way in. I'd walked through the house once to quell my only semi-rational fear that something or someone might be hiding in it, then found a bedroom, stripped down to T-shirt and underwear, curled up, and collapsed. My clothes were still in the pile by the door, and I pulled on my jeans before venturing out.

The bathroom was just down the hall, and someone had laid out my travel pack and robe. I showered, brushed my hair, brushed my teeth. All the little rituals that reminded me I was human.

Wrapped in the soft terry cloth of my bathrobe, I made my way down a flight of white-painted stairs and into the scent of bacon and coffee and the sound of ecstatic voices raised in song and filtered through a cheap radio.

The kitchen was all done in yellow tile and oiled hardwood. A slight haze of smoke hung in the air, a remnant of the pan-fried bacon still draining grease onto folded paper towels. The radio on the sideboard shone silver and sang gospel. My stomach woke with a physical lurch.

"Hello?" I said. "Anyone here?"

"Jayné!" Aubrey's voice called from the back hall. Two sets of footsteps came toward me; Aubrey and Chogyi Jake. Reflexively, I wondered where Ex was, then remembered. I plucked a strip of bacon off the pile just as they came in.

"She wakes," Aubrey said, moving in for a brief hug that was only made awkward by the bacon in my fingers and the brief but intense pain of my broken ribs. Chogyi Jake opened the refrigerator and took out a couple of eggs. In the moment before the door closed, I caught a glimpse of orange juice and bread.

"Someone's been shopping," I said. "What time is it?"

Aubrey shut off the radio and sat up on the counter.

"Seven thirty," he said.

"Wow," I said. "I didn't sleep much."

Chogyi Jake and Aubrey exchanged a look.

"What?" I said.

"It's Sunday," Chogyi Jake said. "You've been asleep for over thirty hours."

"Oh," I said, then, "Wow. I slept a lot. What did I miss?"

"Very little," Chogyi Jake said. "We did a rough inventory of the house. I bought some groceries. There's cable television and broadband access."

"We watched a couple movies last night," Aubrey said. "We needed to wind down a little."

"Good," I said. Chogyi Jake cracked the eggs onto a skillet where they sizzled and popped. "And you're both all right?"

"A few nightmares," Aubrey said. "More Marinette fallout. Nothing I can't handle."

"Fine," Chogyi Jake said. "Thank you for asking."

"No word from Ex, then?" I said, already knowing the answer. Aubrey shook his head, then looked down. I could see the banked anger in the way he held his shoulders and the set of his jaw. Chogyi Jake flipped the eggs.

"I'm going to go put the tools up," Aubrey said.

"Tools?" I said.

"There's a sealed closet we're trying to take a look at," he said. "May be nothing. Or it may be where Eric stored something. More data for the wiki."

"No rest for the wiki-ed," I agreed. "Or, y'know, maybe a little."

Aubrey moved toward me, hesitated, then kissed the crown of my head, and walked back along the hallway. I watched him go with a sense of regret I couldn't quite explain.

"How's he doing really?" I asked softly enough that my voice didn't carry over the eggs.

"He's wounded. We all are," Chogyi Jake said. "He tries to protect you from the worst of it. The rider shook his confidence in himself."

"My fault again," I said.

"If you say so."

"Ex would say it for me," I said.

"He might have," Chogyi Jake said, then killed the fire and lifted the eggs onto a plate for me. "I am going to betray a confidence. I don't like to, but it's the choice I've made."

"Um. All right," I said, reaching for a fork.

"Ex has certain feelings for you that he has tried to deny," he said.

My fork stopped on its way toward the eggs. I stared at Chogyi Jake.

"Certain feelings?" I said.

"He's a complicated man," Chogyi Jake said. "His previous experiences with women have been scarring."

"Wait a minute. Ex has a thing for me?"

"He does. And when he attacked you at the airport, it wasn't what it seemed."

"So what was it?"

"He needed your permission to leave," Chogyi Jake said. He paused for a moment, and I had the impression that he was gathering himself for some particularly unpleasant chore. "He and I spoke about Karen when we first went to New Orleans. We both knew the pressure that she would put on you, just by being who she is. He played on that. He needed you to push him away because it was the only way he could leave."

You don't have to apologize to anyone, Ex said from my memory. Meaning you're good enough, Jayné. You're fine just the way you are. Of course he'd been saying *I love you.* I closed my eyes.

"Well fuck," I said.

"When Aubrey was taken by Marinette . . ."

"I asked Ex to save the guy he most wanted to see out of the picture," I said. "He sucked it up, did the right thing, and then I fell into bed with Aubrey."

"You did," Chogyi Jake said. "What Ex said wasn't a reflection of your capabilities, or even of his real opinion of you."

"But he and Karen were lovers . . . they probably still *are* . . ."

"He took up with Karen after he'd just found you and Aubrey in bed together," Chogyi Jake said. "Karen was there, she was . . . available. I don't believe he loves her, and I don't believe she loves anyone."

"You really don't like her much, do you?" I said,

putting down my fork and rubbing my eyes with the palms of my hand.

"No," he said, thoughtfully. "I really don't."

"Does Aubrey know?"

"That I don't like Karen?"

"About Ex."

"Ah. No, I didn't see a reason to tell him. Ex would be humiliated and hurt if he knew I'd told you. But it didn't seem to serve you or Ex to keep the secret."

"And so you broke your promise not to tell," I said.

"I made that choice, yes."

From the back of the house, I heard something banging. A hammer against wood. In the distance, a car alarm blared and went silent.

"Thanks," I said. "Thanks for that. Aubrey and Ex. Hell. Just tell me that you don't have a thing for me too."

Chogyi's silence dropped a charge of adrenaline into my blood. He looked away, his customary smile replaced by a grimace of embarrassment.

"Chogyi?" I said.

"I have . . ." he began, faltered, then tried again. "I am not perfectly comfortable with this. It isn't you personally, but . . . I don't find Caucasian women attractive."

For the space of three heartbeats, we were silent.

"I don't think of myself as a racist," he said

defensively, "it's just that with white women, that little frisson is never *there*."

My laughter brought Aubrey back into the kitchen. His confusion, looking back and forth between me and Chogyi Jake, also struck me as comic, and set me off again. Chogyi Jake was blushing, but maintained a dignified countenance until I could get myself under control.

It felt good to laugh. It felt good to relax and to have slept and to be with friends instead of pushing and pushing and pushing to run some race I didn't even know how long it was. It felt safe.

I didn't realize until that moment how long it had been since I'd felt *safe*.

"Is everything okay?" Aubrey asked as my hilarity faded into mere giggles.

"Just fine," I said. "Perfect."

That night, we ordered pizza and found a movie rental joint with a good selection of old science fiction. The microwave in the kitchen didn't work, so we got a new one and some popcorn. Chogyi Jake was right. We were all wounded, and we were tired—worn so thin, I felt like you could see through us. I dedicated the evening to just hanging out, being relaxed, recovering. Chogyi Jake and Aubrey sat on a living room couch of old lady floral-and-lace. I lounged on the floor, my back against Aubrey's shins. I had never seen *Close Encounters of the Third Kind,* so we'd gotten that and *Young Frankenstein* as a Teri Garr double feature. A light rain was falling against the windows, Gene Wilder and Peter Boyle were singing "Puttin' on the Ritz," and my mind had a pleasant, unfocused hum.

It would have been perfect, except that I kept feeling that we were missing someone. Part of my mind expected Ex to come in or call out from the other room. The guilt at having lost my temper with him was growing, and I caught myself wondering where he was and whether he'd come back if I asked him. I wondered if I wanted him to.

He was probably fine. I figured that he'd gone back to New Orleans and Karen Black. I didn't know if it was more comforting or sad to imagine the two of them together. On the one hand, I believed Chogyi Jake when he said they didn't really love each other. But even without that romantic spark, there was something to be said for companionship. Just being with your friends. I didn't want to think of Ex without that. Nor, despite the sore spot that her dressing-down had left, did I wish a life of solitude on Karen.

It was hard just then—with my popcorn and my movies and Aubrey and Chogyi Jake—to imagine that I'd ever wanted to be like her. Yes, she was competent and powerful and certain, but she'd lost so much along the way. Her career. Her parents, killed in that fire. Her partner, murdered by the rider. All her friends from the FBI thinking she was nuts.

When I thought about it, she was one of the most isolated people I'd ever known.

The most *isolated*.

Fuck.

I sat up sharply, a dozen small things that had haunted the back of my mind falling into place. Amelie Glapion's voice asking me what I was doing in her city. Marie Laveau passing the mantle of voodoo queen down to her daughter. Marinette's buzzsaw-in-meat voice saying, *You have no place here*. Aubrey calling my own mother's scandal *family business*. Mfume and the rider that attacked Sabine. Parasitic wasps. Different riders with the same powers, the same ecological niches.

"Jayné?" Aubrey said.

"The movie," I said. "Turn it off."

SIXTEEN

The screen was empty gray. Night had turned the windows of the house into dark mirrors. Some brave, early spring cricket sang defiance at the world, as likely to attract a predator as a mate. Aubrey and Chogyi Jake sat on the couch together, the bowl of popcorn forgotten between them.

"Okay," I said, pacing the floor, my mind bouncing around like a monkey behind my eyes. "So here's the thing. I think we've been wrong the whole time."

"About what, exactly," Chogyi Jake asked. From anyone else, it would have felt like an attack. In his voice, it was just an opportunity to be a little more exact. I took a deep breath and tried to put the whirling cloud in my mind into a straight line.

"It doesn't all fit together, does it?" I said. "We're looking for this rider that got voted off the island, but we're seeing this old lady who's been leading a voodoo cult in the same place for years."

"But we know she's a rider," Aubrey said. "She tried to kill you."

"Legba tried to kill me," I half-agreed. "But Legba doesn't make sense as the exiled rider. Amelie Glapion's been doing the whole voodoo queen thing for years, and her family's been at it for generations, right? I mean Amelie was grooming her daughter to take over, and now Sabine."

"I thought that was what makes her a good target for Legba," Aubrey said. "That she's . . ."

"What? Powerful? Prepared? Surrounded by people who know how to deal with riders?" I said. "That's my point. If I'm the exiled rider, she's the last person I'd want to possess."

"Maybe her cult wasn't really dealing with riders. Maybe they were just a religious thing. Fakes," Aubrey said. I could hear in his voice that he was struggling to follow me.

"They knew enough to open the way for Marinette. Dr. Inondé said they were the real deal," I said. "I think Legba's been in Amelie Glapion the whole time, and probably her mother before her.

Legba isn't the exile. Legba's been in New Orleans the whole time, going from mother to daughter down through the generations, just like with Marie Laveau. Like a family business."

"Then what's Karen been chasing?" Aubrey said.

"You remember what Karen said about riders being mistaken for each other?" I said, finding the words as I went. "About there being another rider that can do that stop-time thing that Legba did?"

"The one that had the same ecological niche," Aubrey said, nodding. "Like the wolves and hunting cats."

"Carrefour," Chogyi Jake said. "Its name was Carrefour."

"And the Freddy Krueger on steroids thing that went after Sabine didn't look anything like the snake monster that came out of Amelie," I said.

"Different riders," Aubrey said. "You think there's two different riders."

"So Carrefour—*not Legba*—gets kicked out of Haiti," I said, waving my hands to illustrate each point, "and it rides Mfume up to Oregon. Only Mfume gets caught. He's stuck in prison, so it . . . I don't know. Shifts. It moves into someone powerful enough to be useful. And then it starts isolating the new horse, right? It kills her partner. It kills her parents."

"*Her* parents?" Aubrey said. "You mean you think *Karen* . . ."

Chogyi Jake made a small, satisfied sound in the back of his throat and smiled thinly. There was no particular pleasure in the expression.

"The hurricane injured Legba badly," Chogyi Jake said. "Amelie Glapion suffered a stroke. The intended heir died, leaving Sabine to be promoted whether she was prepared for it or not."

"Vulnerable," I said. "It left them vulnerable. Carrefour found out, and it figured this was its chance to come back."

"The wolves start dying out, and the hunting cats come in," Aubrey said, starting to follow my logic.

"And so Karen comes to New Orleans," I said. "Maybe it takes her a while. Maybe she doesn't know it's happened or exactly who Legba's riding. There's a bunch of people who say they're voodoo queens or houngans or whatever. Maybe Carrefour needs to figure out who the right target is."

"Or who would get the new daughter organism," Aubrey said. "With Amelie's daughter dead in the storm, Karen—Carrefour—would have to find out who was going to be the next host."

"Exactly," I said. "But it turns out even the riders who used to be part of Carrefour's team—the Petro *loa* like Marinette—have closed ranks against it."

"Marinette," Aubrey said, then paused. He seemed lost in himself, but only for a moment. "She hated Karen. She hated Karen more than she hated Legba."

"And right after the exorcism, I asked Karen about trying to recruit the local riders. She shot me down because she knew everyone was against us," I said, still pacing. "Carrefour didn't have any local allies. And Carrefour had kept Karen isolated, so there wasn't anyone *she* could bring in."

"Except the hired guns. Meaning Eric. Meaning us," Aubrey said.

She'd kept me off balance. She'd taken me out to the club instead of leaving me to my research. She'd dismissed me every time I'd questioned her. She'd seduced Ex. And when I started doing things on my own and asking too many questions, she'd told me to leave.

I'd been a chump.

"It answers everything," Aubrey said.

"Well. Not everything," Chogyi Jake said, "but it—"

I held up my hands, palms out. My fingers were trembling. My blood felt slightly electric.

"Okay, hold on. Before we get too freaked out, let's just . . . look at it. I mean, maybe I'm wrong," I said. "When I went missing, who was with Karen?"

Chogyi Jake and Aubrey glanced at each other. I couldn't stop talking.

"I'd just said how we ought to warn Sabine, Karen said no we shouldn't, and then I went AWOL, right?" I said. "If Carrefour is riding Karen, it might think I was running off to spill the beans. It freaks out and decides to go after Sabine right then. But that can't be true if one of you guys was with Karen the whole time. If she has an alibi for the time when I was getting my ass kicked, then I'm wrong.

"So was she with someone when it happened?"

The silence wasn't any longer than two or three breaths together. It seemed like hours. Aubrey cleared his throat.

"No, she wasn't," he said. "I think we have a problem."

THE FIRST flight back to New Orleans left at five in the morning, but had a huge layover and didn't get us on the ground until early evening. A later flight would actually get us there earlier. Waiting in the terminal with the Monday morning business commuters, I kept reminding myself that by not going immediately and as fast as I could, I'd actually get there sooner. Intellectually, it made perfect sense, but my guts wanted the rush of speed, the appearance of heroic action. Something.

Because I had missed the cues, because I had been pushing myself too hard and letting myself get distracted, Ex was sleeping with a serial killer that slaughtered its lovers. I wanted to take it all back, to fix it, and I wanted to do it now, dammit.

"Joseph Mfume was part of a jailbreak from the Oregon State Penitentiary two years ago," the lawyer said from my cell phone. "The reports were that they recovered a body from a river that was identified as him, but apparently that wasn't quite true."

"Right. And the others?"

"Only preliminaries," she said. "Kent and Catherine Black died in a fire eight months after Mfume was incarcerated. The insurance paid off, so the adjusters didn't think it was particularly suspicious. But . . ."

"But Karen worked arson cases," I said, remembering the detail from the original background report.

"Exactly," the lawyer said. "Michael Davis died in a rock-climbing accident."

"Were there any witnesses?"

"None so far, but I only got your message this morning. There's still a great deal of work we can do."

"And Glapion?"

My lawyer sighed. It was a tight, percussive sound.

"We're looking, but the records in New Orleans weren't anything to be proud of even before Katrina. We have the addresses I've already given you. None of the business records have other addresses. I've put alerts on all their accounts, so if there are any transfers of funds big enough to require reporting, I can find that for you."

"But she's got to be in New Orleans," I said, trying not to whine.

"And if you want to live in an under-the-table economy, there's probably no better place," she said. "There are any number of people there who are living entirely off the books. There always have been. It's New Orleans."

"Okay," I said. "All right, can you just . . . let me know if you find anything?"

"Absolutely. And I have some inquiries that I'm waiting to hear back on. If I get anything substantive, I'll be with you immediately."

"Thank you."

"Be careful, dear."

"I will."

I hung up. Chogyi Jake closed his cell phone as Aubrey returned with two paper cups of coffee and one of green tea. A four-pack of identically tied businessmen looked over at us with an air of disapproval. It was petty of me, but I hoped they were on our flight. And in coach.

"Still nothing?" I said.

"He isn't answering," Chogyi Jake said. "Either he doesn't have the phone with him, or he's chosen to ignore us, or . . ."

"Or Karen has done something to keep him out of contact," Aubrey said. "Anyone care to bet? What about the lawyers?"

I lifted my cell phone.

"No joy," I said.

"Shit," Aubrey said conversationally.

"Yeah."

"They may still be using the safe house," Chogyi Jake said. "The wards are still in place. It would give Karen the protection she wanted."

"That would be nice," I said. "In that sort of what-are-we-going-to-do-now way."

"It's one rider," Aubrey said. "We can take it."

"It's not just a rider," I said. "It's a rider and Karen Black. She may be demon-ridden, but she's still smart and trained and better at this than any of us. And part of what she's trained at is shooting people. This wasp picked itself a really good caterpillar."

"Caterpillar?" Chogyi Jake asked.

While Aubrey explained about the parasitic wasps and the caterpillars who love them, I pulled up my laptop and checked e-mail. I was hoping for something from Ex, but instead I got a raft of spam. And one other message.

It was from my little brother, Curt, replying to the note I'd almost forgotten sending. I opened it.

Hey, good to hear from you. What are you up to these days, anyway? ParentalForce is acting like they never had a daughter. Creeptastic. I'm good, except school bites. I got busted cutting class. It was like they'd caught me with a crack pipe up my nose.

There's a new pastor. Mom thinks he's great, Dad's not

so sure. I figure he'll be busted for kiddie porn in three . . .
two . . . one . . . As long as he keeps his queer-ass hands
off me, I don't care.

Anyway. It's good to know there's life out there. With
you and Jay gone, I've got to Praise the Lord for all of us.
Ugh! Whatchaupto anyway?

I read the e-mail twice with a growing sense of
vertigo. There wasn't anything new in it, except that
somewhere between the time that I'd left home and
now, my baby brother had turned into a teenager.
The little kid with the black hair and dark eyes, the
serious expression, would never have written that
e-mail. When I'd left, he was the only one of the
three of us who would pray without being told, the
only one who didn't push back at getting up early
for church, the only one who'd seemed like maybe
all that God and angels stuff really meant something
to him. And now he was joking about pornography
and cocaine.

Now he was sounding like me, and I was surprised how much it bothered me.

My fingers hovered over the keyboard, waiting for
some idea what I could say that wouldn't seem moralistic or simplistic or like the sort of thing a grown-
up would say to a kid. I was lost. *Hey, little brother.
Got more money than God, busy fighting demons and
unhealthy love triangles. And no one says "queer-ass"
anymore. Hey! OMFG! Mom screwed around!*

What had I expected? That everything back at home would stay just the way it had been when I left, a picture of the paternalistic, creepy American family trapped in amber? That my little brother would always be little? I'd made my break, gone to a secular university on my own money, and failed. I wondered whether Curt thought that was cool of me. I wondered whether I did.

Maybe I should have . . . not *stayed* there, no. But kept in touch. *Something*.

"Jayné?" Aubrey said. "Are you all right?"

"My brother," I said, and shook my head. "It's just some family business."

I looked at the screen again. Somewhere down the concourse, a baby started crying and then stopped. I typed without thinking, my hands moving of their own accord.

> Hey, little brother. I'm okay. Made some friends I actually like this time. Got some kind of big stuff going on, but it'll be cool.
>
> Take care of yourself, okay? I love you.

My fingers stopped. There had to be more to say, something wise or solemn or even just useful, but I couldn't think of anything. It struck me that just the way the Curt I'd known when I left home would never have written the e-mail he'd sent, the Jayné I'd been would never have told him she loved him. So maybe we were both different people now. Maybe that was the point.

I hit send and closed the laptop.

"Are they boarding yet?" I said.

"Another twenty minutes," Chogyi Jake said.

I muttered something obscene and scooped up my coffee cup. I wondered how much money it would have taken to charter a jet of my own, and whether it would have taken more time or less. I closed my eyes.

Of course, I was doing it again. We were rushing off into the teeth of God-knew-what without a plan, without preparation, without actually knowing what we were up against. It was the same mistake I'd made the last time I'd flown into New Orleans. It struck me for the first time that I wasn't just risking myself and Aubrey and Chogyi Jake. I was also putting Curt's big sister on the line, and oddly that had some weight to it. I made myself relax, and once relaxed, think.

The sounds of the concourse seemed to fade, my breath slowing in the centering meditation Chogyi Jake had taught me lo these many months ago. My muscles released a little. My mind didn't stop jumping around, but it slowed. Like mud settling to the bottom of a pool, my thinking started to clear.

I really couldn't see taking on Karen directly. I was still feeling the pain from the last fight. Aubrey wasn't healed from his exorcism, for that matter. If

we were going to take on Carrefour and Karen both
and have a hope of getting Ex out alive, we had to
have more than the address of the safe house and
some good intentions. There had to be a plan.

I had to know Carrefour's weaknesses. I needed
someone who'd taken the rider on and beaten it.

Put that way, it was obvious.

"I hate this job," I said out loud.

"Sorry?" Aubrey said. I opened my eyes.

"This job," I said. "It looks like crime. It smells
like crime. It makes me associate with criminals."

"What did we do?" Aubrey said.

"Apart from help hide a great big pile of bodies
like the day after I met you?" I said with a grin.

"Yeah, besides that." Aubrey smiled back.

"Well, not much," I said. "But you're not who I
was thinking about."

"No?"

"Nope."

"I was thinking the same thing," Chogyi Jake
said. "The enemy of my enemy."

"Exactly," I said.

"Am I being dim here?" Aubrey said. "What are
we talking about?"

"We need your friendly neighborhood serial
killer," I said. "We need Mfume."

SEVENTEEN

We landed in New Orleans a little over five hours later. The flight had been wildly uncomfortable, the cramped seats made infinitely worse by the almost random stabbing pain in my cracked ribs. I hadn't rested at all, but I felt more annoyed than exhausted. The rental joint was out of our usual minivans, so we wound up in a luxury sedan that got maybe six miles to the gallon, but had every conceivable bell and whistle, including self-heating seats and programmable memory that shifted all the mirrors to the right height for any given driver. Anyone who saw us and didn't at least consider carjacking just wasn't paying attention.

The air smelled of the Gulf, the lakes, the river. The sun, already low in the west, was wide and red and angry, and the highway hummed beneath our tires.

"Okay," Aubrey said as he drove. "What's the plan? I mean, it's not like we can just put up signs and find Mfume. The lawyers don't know where he is. We don't know where he is. The police think he's dead."

"Just head for the French Quarter. I'll navigate you in when we get close."

"You have something?"

"It's a desperation move, but yeah," I said. "Something."

The Authentic New Orleans Voodoo Museum looked cheaper and smaller in the gray shadows of twilight. The doors were open, and a low chanting spilled from tinny speakers out into the street. The air was thick with incense. I could see Aubrey's uncertainty, and looking at the tawdry signs and tourist-trap flyers, I felt a little unsure myself. But the worst I could do was fail. I led the way in.

"Miss Jayné! How can the world of voudoun be of service to you this night?"

"Dr. Inondé," I said. "Hey, Doris."

The snake shifted to look at me with its other eye, black tongue flicking the air. We four human beings and the giant snake effectively filled the room. The place seemed smaller than the first time I'd been there, the red curtains more dusty and threadbare, the portrait of Marie Laveau even less flattering. I sat down, rooted through my backpack, and pulled out the ugly little charm he'd given me. Even with a little rain damage, it still felt like holding a spider on my bare palm.

"So," I said. "You aren't actually as much of a fake as we said. Are you?"

Dr. Inondé looked at Aubrey and Chogyi Jake as if sizing up my bodyguards, then shrugged.

"I know a few things," he said. "Not much. Some. You need some juju done?"

"I do," I said. "I need to find someone named Joseph Mfume."

Dr. Inondé sat with a grunt. His eyes seemed to lose their warmth for a moment.

"You have anything this Mfume fellow owned? Shirt. Book. Anything?"

"No," I said. "But I think he's been hanging around with Amelie Glapion."

"So you want to find this Mfume fella, or do you want Amelie Glapion?" he said.

"Either one would do," I said. "I don't want any trouble. I just need to talk to them."

Dr. Inondé shook his head, smiling apologetically.

"You seem like a nice person, but there isn't enough money in the world to make me cross Amelie. If she doesn't want to be found, there's no finding her. You know what happened to her after the last time you came in here? Something tried to kill her granddaughter."

"Yeah," I said. "I was there. I was one of the people who helped save Sabine."

"Were you now?" He didn't sound convinced.

"Jayné could have been killed," Aubrey said with an anger I hadn't expected. "The least you can do is try to help."

"It turns out Amelie and I have an enemy in common," I said. "The thing that's after Sabine is also threatening a friend of mine."

The wind shifted the door. Somewhere nearby, a band burst into full-throated jazz. Someone yelled in what might have been celebration or distress.

"Come back in an hour," Dr. Inondé said. "We'll talk."

I nodded my thanks, and together the three of us walked back into the deepening darkness. Aubrey made an impatient sound. Behind us, the museum door shut, and I heard the deadbolt slide closed.

"Do you trust him?" Chogyi Jake said. He managed to make the question sound like idle curiosity.

"Not particularly," I said.

"So what do you think he's doing in there?" Aubrey asked.

"I think he's asking permission," I said. "We may not need magic after all."

Jackson Square at twilight was still populated. Tarot card readers, T-shirts, face-painters; they were

all there, sitting at folding card tables, sitting on
cheap plastic chairs, but it had the feel of day's end.
The sky above us was sliding from blue to gray to
black. A slow, heavy breeze was wafting in from the
south. The men and women at the stalls seemed
tired. Not listless, but worn down. They'd spent another day feeding off the story and mystique of New
Orleans, or else propping them up. Maybe the two
were the same.

Restaurants were coming sluggishly to life, the
early dinner crowd rolling in without filling the
tables. It wasn't Mardis Gras, there wasn't a festival
going on. It was just a Monday night in the jazz
capital of the world, the home of American voodoo,
the Crescent City, the Big Easy. The fallen city doing
its best again, because that's all there was to do. I
looked through the clean glass at the starched linen
tablecloths, the classic black lacquered wood. The
smell of pepper and seafood wafted out across the
sidewalk as we passed the corner of Decatur and
St. Ann, but it didn't make me hungry. My belly was
knotted tight, my gaze flickering between the faces,
hoping and dreading to see someone familiar.

"I don't think we should go back," Aubrey said. "I
think we're making a mistake."

I paused, looking at him closely for the first time
since we'd come back to the Quarter. His shoulders
were pulled forward, his head hung low, almost like
he was cradling something to his chest. Chogyi Jake

tilted his head, inviting Aubrey to go on. A kid on a bicycle swerved around us and pedaled out into the gloomy narrow streets.

"Let's . . ." Aubrey said, gesturing to the south. We started walking again, Chogyi and I flanking Aubrey, who seemed to be struggling to find the right words. We got halfway down the square before I broke the silence for him.

"Mfume could have killed me," I said. "Sabine could have. Seriously, when that thing in the rain was done with me, any third-grader with a nail file could seriously have kicked my ass. They took me to the hospital."

"Is that the issue?" Chogyi Jake asked. "Safety?"

"Yes," Aubrey said, and then, "No. Not exactly. I mean . . . Okay, I understand that they didn't take advantage of it when Jayné was vulnerable. And maybe they can team up with us. Maybe all of us want something that we can work with, the way we did with Midian in Denver. But . . ."

Frustration buzzed in his voice. And fear. He was looking for the words that would say what he needed, but he was my scientist. His vocabulary was all about predation and genetic frequencies, host behavior and parasite load. Even after feeling Marinette take his body from him, he couldn't say what he felt.

I could. I took his hand.

"But these things are demons," I said.

"Yes," he said, the word rushing out of him. "Yes, they're evil. These things are evil and they're smart and they're dangerous. Even if we have a common enemy, how can we leave ourselves open to things that can do what they do? What do we do if something happens?"

We reached the steps at the southern end of the square and started up them. High overhead, an airplane's contrail caught the last rays of sunlight, glowing gold and fading quickly to the gray of spent cigarette smoke.

"You mean now that Ex is gone," Chogyi Jake said, clarifying the thought. "Now that being possessed isn't something we can easily undo."

"What are we here for?" Aubrey said. "Are we trying to stop Carrefour? Or Legba? Or both? Ex is a grown-up. And after all the crap he pulled on Jayné, I don't really see that he'd welcome our help anyway."

Aubrey stared out at the dark water, frowning, not meeting my eyes or Chogyi Jake's. I didn't know what to say. Without betraying Chogyi Jake's confidence, I couldn't explain that Ex was in trouble partly because he had a thing for me and I hadn't picked up on the signs. I couldn't say that I was pissed off at Karen for fooling me and at myself for letting her without approaching industrial-grade pettiness.

And it didn't matter, because Aubrey knew why we'd come: Ex was in trouble, and we could help. I didn't really understand what he was saying.

Chogyi Jake did.

"Was it that bad?" he asked.

Aubrey snapped his head back like the gentle words had been a slap. His grip on my hand went so hard it almost hurt. I didn't let go.

"I can't explain it," Aubrey said softly. "I don't know how to say . . ."

"I'll presume," Chogyi Jake said, stepping in. "You knew intellectually how it all worked. In your time studying with Eric, you'd seen riders and what they can do. But, irrationally, you thought you were different. You wouldn't have said it, not even to yourself, but you suspected that the people who were ridden—who were *taken* by riders—had some defect, some weakness in them that let it happen. Not that they deserved it, not in a moral way, but that somehow they were at a greater risk. You knew more, you controlled yourself more effectively, you were safe, if only by comparison. And then it happened, and you found out you were wrong. Now all those protective lies are gone. The dangers you used to ignore, you can't ignore any longer. You're left naked all the time. Vulnerable all the time. Constantly in danger."

Aubrey was weeping a little, but otherwise his face was stone.

"It happened to you too?" Aubrey said.

"No," Chogyi Jake said. "Not possession. Or not by riders. Something else. But I lost that sense that the rules didn't apply to me. I still miss it sometimes."

"I don't think I can do this," Aubrey said so softly I almost didn't hear it, even standing right beside him. "I don't think I can face them anymore. I thought . . . I thought I could."

It was an apology, and it was meant for me.

I didn't know what to say. I'd known that Aubrey was in trouble since the second I'd seen him turn toward me, there in the ruins of Charity. He'd told me that he was messed up by it; he'd said the words and I'd agreed. It wasn't the same as seeing him fold. When I'd fallen into Uncle Eric's strange, occult world, Aubrey had been the one I called for help. He needed help now, and I didn't know what to say.

So I faked it.

"Tough shit," I said. "I know you think you're weak, but *I* don't. I think you're strong. You're scared? Yeah, welcome to the club. I've been doing everything at three times the sane pace for months because I'm scared. I hid your divorce papers since Denver because I was scared."

"You hid his divorce papers?" Chogyi Jake said, but I barreled on.

"Ex freaking out and ditching us wasn't exactly a statement of his confidence and heroism. *He's* scared. Chogyi just told you he's been scared so long he's gotten used to it. I'll bet you everything I've got that Eric spent half his life working through adrenaline rushes.

We're all freaked out. We're all scared. You don't get to bail on me just because of that."

Aubrey took a step back, trying to pull his hand out of mine, but I held tighter. I was screwing it up. I was saying the wrong things. All I could hope for was to make his shame at being frightened worse than the fear itself.

"If you walk away on this one, I swear to God, you'll walk away on the next one too," I said. "And the one after that. And then you're done, right? Then Marinette wins."

"Jesus Christ, Jayné," Aubrey said. His voice was shaking. "You don't know how hard this is."

"I don't care how hard it is. You can do it," I said.

Aubrey opened his mouth, but no words came out. Instead, he took a long, shuddering breath. In the dim light, his eyes glimmered with tears, but he set his shoulders. Chogyi smiled, watching us both. I didn't know if he was judging Aubrey or me or both. Or neither.

"Damn," Aubrey said. "Just . . . damn. Don't treat me with kid gloves or anything."

I moved close and put my arms around him. It was easy to forget how big he was—wide through the shoulders and ribs, solid, reassuringly male. I hoped I hadn't just screwed him up worse.

"I'm sorry," I said. "I should have been gentle. That was shitty of me, wasn't it?"

He took a breath before speaking. I figured that meant yes, but he'd let me slide.

"Eric told me that if I kept at it, there'd be something like this," he said. "A crisis point. There's nothing you said that he wouldn't have."

"The divorce papers thing?"

Aubrey laughed. It sounded pained.

"Okay, maybe not that part," he said. "But he'd have kicked my ass. You even sounded like him there at the end. I just . . . I didn't mean to . . ."

I put my head against his shoulders, and he wrapped his arms around me, squeezing until my cracked ribs screamed with pain. I gritted my teeth and took it. I had it coming. People walked past us. The river murmured to itself, water hushing against the pilings. The soft sound of a city—traffic and birdsong, barking dogs and pounding radios, sirens and voices and the bells of the cathedral—washed past us.

"Um," Chogyi Jake said. "Jayné?"

I looked up.

Bracketing us on the promenade, a dozen people stood, staring at us. Most of them were black, but a couple were white or Asian. Their expressions were the blank of soldiers ready for a fight. I pushed Aubrey back and stepped toward them. In the glow of the street lamps, the faces looked cold. I knew them. That man had been one of the drummers at Charity Hospital. The woman across from him had danced naked, calling the riders down into her body. And staring at us with deep, dark eyes, Sabine Glapion stood near the back of the crowd.

Struggling up the steps behind them, Dr. Inondé held Amelie Glapion's elbow. The old woman's head shifted from side to side like a serpent testing the air. And behind them, the deep black skin and graying hair of Joseph Mfume. The handful of tourists peering out over the darkening water took a look at the scene and scattered. My heart was thumping behind my ribs like it was trying to get out. All of the smartass shit I'd just said to Aubrey about fear drained out of my mind like it had never been there. I just wanted to get the hell out.

Amelie Glapion reached the back of the crowd, her cult parting before her. Dr. Inondé met my eyes and nodded with something like apology. I wondered what our chances would be if we all leaped into the river. It didn't look like it was going that fast, but I remembered something about still-looking waters sucking people down.

"Okay," I said softly enough that only Aubrey and Chogyi Jake could hear me, "this might have been an oops."

Amelie came forward, leaning on her cane. Her drooping face was ashen and sour. The air around her seemed to crackle with power that her body alone couldn't begin to justify. Her eyes shifted from me to Aubrey, from Aubrey to Chogyi Jake, from Chogyi Jake back to me with the intensity of a predator sizing up prey.

I felt the subtle shift in my body that I'd come to associate with the onset of violence. When Amelie spoke, her voice was Legba's; deeper than a human throat could fashion, rich with threat and power.

"What the *hell* you think you doing in my city?"

I wanted to swing forward, to fight my way free, pulling Aubrey and Chogyi Jake along with me. My body almost vibrated with the need to strike, to scream. I forced myself to speak like I was using someone else's mouth to do it.

"Carrefour tricked me," I said. "I've come to you. I need help."

These were demons. They were predators: tigers, wolves, sharks. I looked into Amelie Glapion's eyes, and something else looked back at me. Something inhuman. Someone made a sound that was neither word nor whimper. I risked a glance. Daria Glapion, her face frozen with anxiety, held her sister's hand.

"Well now," Amelie said, "that's more like it."

The woman turned away, and the moment broke. The air itself seemed to slump back. Aubrey touched my shoulder, and I startled. Around us, the cultists were starting to move. At the head of the stone steps that led down to Jackson Square, Amelie Glapion stopped and turned, looking over her shoulder at us.

"You waiting for something?" she asked. "Come on."

EIGHTEEN

Someone walking down the street might not have seen anything. An old woman walking pretty well with her cane. A few people accompanying her. A teenager leading a younger girl by the hand. Three touristy-looking types looking unaccountably nervous. A deeply black man with a long face and goofy smile walking by himself. Another group walking in the same direction. A white man in a Hawaiian shirt strolling behind the rest. Apart from everyone moving in the same direction, there was nothing about it that looked different than any other night in the French Quarter.

It felt like being marched to prison.

The Glapions and half their followers before us, Mfume and the other guards behind. I wondered if this was the kind of negotiation Eric had done, and if it was what had gotten him killed. Ahead of us, two of the cultists stepped close and put supporting arms around Amelie Glapion's waist. Wherever we were going, it had to be close.

We turned down one street, and then another into a side street so narrow, I couldn't imagine two cars actually passing each other. Thin trees pushed up, bare as sticks and struggling toward the sky. The brick buildings were painted over, pale colors turning to shades of gray in the darkness. The wrought-iron rails of narrow balconies looked thin enough to break between two hands, and the air stank of a backed-up sewer. All the doors we passed were closed, all the windows dark. I had the sense of walking into a tendril of dead city, as if the destruction of the Lower Ninth had cut a blood vessel, and even here where the city hadn't suffered the flood, its tissue was dying.

Amelie and her entourage stopped at what had once been a storefront, its windows smeared now with gray paint. I was close enough to see Amelie's eyes close for a moment. When she opened them again, there was a stiff determination in her expression, but no strength. One of the cultists—a woman—fumbled with a key chain, unlocked the door, and stepped aside. Amelie Glapion led the way like the general of a failing army, and the rest of us fell in behind her. Aubrey, beside me, shuddered as we passed the threshold, but that was all.

Inside, we passed through a wide space with dark wooden flooring worn in a pattern that outlined where shelves and pathways had once been, through an ornate archway that numberless coats of paint had muddied, and into something that might once have been an office. A particleboard folding table stood in the center of the room, a tablecloth of yellowed lace stretching across it. Fifteen or twenty lit candles burned at either end, black candles on my right, white on my left; the air was hot from the flame and stank of hot wax and honey. An ancient carved-wood chair sat on the other side of the table like a throne.

Three canvas army cots were against one wall, pillows and sleeping bags on each. The one farthest from me had a stuffed bear, worn from use and affection. As I watched, Daria walked to that last cot, threw herself onto it, and turned to look at us.

It reminded me of the gang warfare scenes from *The Godfather* and of the safe house I'd bought in Pearl River. Amelie Glapion and her granddaughters had gone to the mattresses, and so had we. Amelie Glapion made her way to the throne, sat carefully in it, and turned her gaze to us like a queen considering the ambassadors of some particularly ill-favored

nation. It was theater. It was the appearance of no-
bility and power, confidence and influence built out
of baling wire and bubble gum; the trash and debris
of the world transforming itself into something holy.
The Church of Something from Nothing, and for a
moment, I felt genuinely moved by it.

The rider in her—Legba—spoke again.

"You have come to my city uninvited and unwel-
come," it said with the old woman's tongue. "You
come with the tools of a thief and an assassin, and
you conspire with the outcast. For any of these, I
would break your flesh and cast you into darkness.
But the hollow one tells me you fought in my child's
defense."

Sabine, behind me, spoke. Her voice was strong
and musical.

"She did, Maman Legba. Everything he said was
truth."

Amelie Glapion cast a sour, inhuman glance over
my shoulder at her granddaughter, then shrugged.

"For this I grant you indulgence. Now you say
you've come for my help against the outcast," the
rider said. When it spoke again, the depth and
power were less, the voice more human as if the
thin, ill woman were grabbing the microphone from
a fallen angel. "Why the hell should I believe that
shit?"

I stepped forward. Legba's eyes, snake-black,
stared out at me from Amelie's face. I remembered

its shining skin, its teeth, the presentiment I'd had that first time we'd met that it would die or I would.

"Karen Black lied to me," I said. "She told me that there was a killer loose and that she needed my help to stop it. I didn't know she was Carrefour's horse. And she is, right?"

"She is."

The voice came from the shadows to my left. Mfume was leaning against the wall, his arms crossed. His smile was strangely encouraging.

"Okay, then," I said. "She called me here under false pretenses. And then she . . . sent me away again. But a friend of mine's still with her. He's sleeping with her. He doesn't know what she is either."

"He's an idiot," Amelie said. Or Legba. Or maybe they agreed with each other.

"He is sometimes, yeah," I said. "But he's my friend. And I want him back."

"And you need my help to do that," Amelie said. It was strange hearing the two separate beings in the single voice, but I felt I was getting the feel of it.

"Yours, yes," I said, then nodded toward Mfume. "And his."

"What price are you offering?" Legba asked.

The room was silent. It was what Karen had asked me. It was how, I had to think, Eric had gained his wealth, his power. I didn't know what to say. I hated how much I sucked at this part.

"I'm offering to help you break Carrefour's

power," I said. "I'm your enemy's enemy. As long as that's true, we can work together."

"Well ain't that convenient," Amelie said, though I had the sense that Legba within her was considering the offer. "You work with her, you dance to her tune, you screw up my home, and then you come here all ready to get behind me. How do I know you're not still working for her, just getting in here so you can stab me in the back? Hmm?"

It was a fair question, and I didn't have an answer.

"What price are you asking?" I said.

"A pact," Legba said, and I knew from its voice the word meant something deep. I had heard a little about agreements with riders and wizards and other nasties. *Binding of intention* was the phrase that came to mind. I felt something in my belly squirm and flutter, and then settle.

"I will accept a pact with you," I said and immediately thought, *Holy shit, I will?*

Amelie Glapion rose and held out her right hand. I stepped forward to meet her. When I put my hand in hers, her fingers closed on mine like a trap. Her will, her qi, the caduceus-like spirits of woman and rider pressed into me, and reflexively, I pressed back, the heat in my belly rising to my shoulder, down to my hand out through my fingers. When Legba spoke, I saw Amelie's teeth had changed to the rider's forest of knives.

"Until Carrefour is destroyed, you will not act against me or mine. You will respect my will and shall act in no way against me," Legba said. "Nor shall we slaughter you, though it be our right to do so."

"I accept this," I said, and Glapion dropped my hand. We both stepped back. I felt like something electric and profound had happened. I was energized and a little nauseated. Amelie Glapion sat in her throne and chuckled. Her eyes were human again, her voice her own.

"Well now," she said. "Ain't you the subtle one?"

"Um," I said. Then, "Thanks?"

"I'm going to rest up now," she said. "I'm a tired old lady, and this shit's too much to keep up all day long. Then we can talk about how to kill that sonofabitch wants to hurt my girls."

Amelie started to rise and faltered. The two drummers hurried to her side, lifting and supporting her. Even by the warm light of the candles, I could see her face had taken on an ashy color and the drooping along her left side had become more pronounced. From one moment to the next, she had gone from being the mask worn by something huge and powerful that lived just outside the world to a fragile old woman, exhausted by walking and needing care. The two things seemed like they should cancel out, that the rider's power and the woman's vulnerability should somehow average to a middle value. They didn't.

There was a rush of sound that I didn't recognize at first as voices. The cultists were speaking for the first time since they'd surrounded us. Men and women, old and young, they were all talking now in low voices. Some were smiling, others shaking their heads.

"Thank you," Sabine said.

"For what?" I said, though *You're welcome* would probably have been more polite.

"For helping Maman," she said. I followed her gaze. Amelie was reclining awkwardly on one of the cots, helped down by one of her group. "It was hard for her, losing the Temple. I was afraid . . ."

Sabine shook her head. Sixteen. Curt's age. She looked older, but it was probably only that she carried a heavier weight. I had the urge to put my hand on her shoulder, but I stopped myself. I had just bound myself to a spiritual parasite from Next Door who intended to possess this girl, continuing a line of devoured women that reached back over a century. I made myself complicit to her sacrifice.

Only until Ex is back, I thought. Until Carrefour is destroyed. That was the deal, and after that we would see where we stood. Maybe there would still be a way to get Sabine out safely.

I hoped so.

"Thank you," she said again.

"It's early days," I said. "Thank me when it's over."

She smiled, and a small dashing movement careened into her side. Daria Glapion hung on her sister's arm, grinning.

"I told you she'd come back," Daria said to her sister, and then to me, "I knew you would."

"You did?" I said.

"Not *knew* knew," Daria said. "Just normal knew. I was right though, wasn't I."

"You were," I said, and the little girl grinned in triumph.

The crowd began to thin, Amelie's congregation going about the business of setting watch, getting food, or whatever the business of the rider required. There were only three cots. They couldn't all be sleeping here. One of the drummers caught my eye and looked away nervously. I wondered what I seemed like to them. Early twenties college dropout with too much money in the company of a couple slightly older men. Put that way, it didn't sound like an uncommon sight.

On the other hand, when Marinette had taken Aubrey, I'd beaten one of their gods in single combat, so maybe that would be a little intimidating.

"Let me get you something," Sabine said. "Do you need something to eat? Drinks?"

"I'd take a Coke," I said. I needed to eat—we hadn't had anything but airplane food since breakfast—but my gut was still unsettled from the pact. Aubrey shook his head, and Chogyi Jake asked for green tea, if there was any to be had. Sabine, her little sister in tow, went off, playing the hostess because her mother was dead, her grandmother was dying, and there was no one else to do it. Chogyi Jake watched her, smiling.

"Well," Aubrey said, his voice an almost-perfect imitation of not-panicked. "The place isn't too bad. As lion's dens go."

"Yeah," I said. "I think it worked, right?"

"I don't know," Aubrey said. "What exactly did we agree to?"

"Not kill each other until Carrefour's cooked," I said. "At least I think that's right."

"More precisely," Chogyi Jake said, "you agreed not to act against Legba or its coterie, and it agreed not to kill you. I believe it could still imprison you or inflict injuries that weren't actually mortal. That doesn't seem to be its immediate intention, though."

"Great," Aubrey said. "And we're covered in all that too, right?"

Chogyi Jake tilted his head.

"I think that depends on whether 'we will not slaughter you' was you-singular or you-plural," he said. "On the up side, if we aren't covered by the protection, we aren't bound by the restrictions either."

"Right. Good to know," Aubrey said, and I laughed. I couldn't help it. The tension and fear and strange energy of the rider made me giddy. Chogyi

Jake and Aubrey looked at me, which only made it worse. It wasn't funny, except it was.

"A little slack here," I said, wiping away small tears of hilarity. "It was my first pact with demons, okay?"

One of the cultists cleared her throat in a low, but distinct signal. Quietly, the groups of people started to file out. On her cot, Amelie Glapion lay with her eyes closed, hands folded, her breath regular and deep. At rest, she looked ancient; her eyes sunken, her cheeks collapsed.

I'd never known my mother's mother, but Grandma Heller had died when I was twelve. We had all gone to the funeral, even Curt who'd still been in kindergarten. My memories of the trip were vague, half-recalled and half-imagined, but the image of the old woman in her coffin—hair pulled gently back, lips in a secretive smile—remained. In her death, she'd looked more alive than Amelie Glapion did now.

Sabine returned, an actual glass bottle of soda in one hand and a paper cup steaming and smelling like tea in the other.

"I couldn't find green, but I got some normal kind," she said softly as she handed the cup to Chogyi and the soda to me. "I'm sorry about Maman. She needs a lot of rest these days. She usually only naps like this for a few minutes. She doesn't mean any disrespect."

"No," I said. "No, it's fine. But maybe we should . . . you know, go someplace?"

Sabine nodded sharply, her gaze jumping to her grandmother and back to us. Her brow furrowed, and a soft, familiar accent came from behind us to rescue her.

"Let me take them," Joseph Mfume said. "There is a conversation that we should have anyway, and now is as good a time as any."

"Thank you," Sabine said. "I should find Daria. She's like to sneak out to the street and start telling people's signs if no one stops her."

"Off you go, then," Mfume said with a mock solemnity. "You need not care for these three. I will see to them."

He led us through a smaller archway to a thin staircase lit by a single bare bulb. Single file, we went up the steep wooden steps, down a short hallway, and out through warped French doors to the balcony overlooking the street. The night air was muggy but cool. The sky glowed with the city's reflected light, but not so much that the stars couldn't fight their way through. Mfume took a pack of cigarettes from his shirt pocket.

"Forgive me. It's a terrible habit, but it's my own," he said as he took one out. He lit it with a kitchen match drawn along the iron rail. In the sulfur flare, he looked older than I remembered him. Careworn. He had tattoos on the backs of his hands. I hadn't noticed that before. He breathed out a cloud of gray and smiled at me. "I'm pleased to see you again, and looking so well. I was worried about you."

"Some cracked ribs, a few staples to hold my arm together," I said. "Good as new. These are my friends. Chogyi Jake. Aubrey."

"Thank you," Aubrey said as he shook the killer's hand. "You didn't have to take Jayné to the hospital like that. I want to say how much I appreciate that you did."

"It was nothing," Mfume said, gesturing with his cigarette, the smoke leaving a faint contrail in the air. "It was the least I could do."

"She doesn't look good," I said. "Amelie. Or Legba. Whatever. She doesn't look good."

"She isn't," Mfume said. "And it's getting worse. She has less energy. She's confused more often. I'm no doctor, but I think she has had another stroke. At least one. Perhaps several."

"She is bound up with the city, isn't she?" Chogyi Jake said.

"I don't know," Mfume said. "She might be. The first stroke and the hurricane coming at the same moment seems too poetic to be simply chance, but . . . other people suffered as well. Suffered worse. And she isn't as young as she once was. There may be no reason to assign a spiritual significance to it."

"Did you know her daughter?" I asked. "Sabine's mother. The one that died."

"No," Mfume said. "No, I didn't come here until after all of that."

"You came for Carrefour," Aubrey said.

"In a sense," Mfume said and took a drag from his cigarette. The ember glowed in the darkness like a fire on the horizon. His hooded eyes and long face considered each of us in turn.

"I suppose," he said, "it would be simplest if I began at the start of things."

NINETEEN

"I grew up in Haiti, one of the fortunate few," he said. "I was well educated. I never wanted for food. It marked me as a child of great privilege. The poverty in Port-au-Prince is unlike even the worst desperation in the States, and the countryside makes the city look like the promised land. I knew nothing of riders or voudoun. It was superstition. Something for the servants and the beggars on the streets. My family was Catholic, and I grew up within the church and the protective light of Christ Jesus.

"That didn't go so well as I might have hoped.

"I was twenty-four when Carrefour took me. I

had been accepted to law school in the States. My family was very proud. There was a girl I had been seeing, beneath my station, but very beautiful. I went one night to say my good-byes to her, and she took the news of my good fortune poorly. We fought, and . . . she bit me. Hard enough to draw blood.

"I hid the injury, and thought nothing of it. Three days later, she came to my family's house, weeping and demanding that I return something to her, but she could not say what precisely I was supposed to have taken. I know now, but at the time I thought she'd gone mad. We sent her away, and I went on with my preparations.

"I left Haiti on my sister's eighteenth birthday, and I have never gone back.

"At first, all seemed well. I was taking classes, making new friends. Being in the States was more than living in another country. It was a different world. I thought that the dreams were only that. They came every few weeks, and they were not precisely the same, but there were some elements in common. A sense of having been betrayed, and of both rage and the power to act upon it. Asleep, I was the righteous vengeance of God against those who had wronged me. Once, early, I woke to find my bedsheets slit. I thought at the time they had been ripped in the laundry and I'd made it worse in my sleep.

"I began dating a classmate. Cassandra, her

name was. She was beautiful and intelligent. She'd been born poor in New York and fought her way through the public schools. She worked twice as hard as any of us. I think I began with her just to see if it was possible to distract her. I had been with women before, but Cassandra was a level above them all. I fell in love with her as I had never done, and so she was the first that Carrefour killed."

He seemed to sag against the iron railing. His gaze was lost in the air before him. We didn't say anything.

"I didn't know that the devil had come inside of me, you see. Not then. Not for years. To begin, it was only that the dreams got worse, and after I'd had one, the whole next day I would be in a foul mood. And then, I started becoming suspicious. Cassandra would study at the library very late, just as she always had, but I became convinced that she was meeting someone. Another man. There was no evidence, of course. It was the rider whispering in the back of my mind, but I believed the thoughts were my own. It persuaded me.

"I had a key to her apartment. I believed that I only intended to frighten her, to show her that betraying me was foolish. I can say that what I did seemed right at the time. It seemed innocent. I went to her apartment one night, parked several streets away so that she would not see my car. I waited with the lights off. And when she came in . . .

"I believed that I was doing it, you see. They were my hands. My arms. It was my voice. Even if it felt as though I were only watching it happen, how could that have been true? And as it was going on, I felt a terrible sense of peace. Because this is what Carrefour does, you see? It feeds you its rage and its pain, it ties you into a knot. Then when it takes control of you, there is the reward. Peace. Pleasure. Transcendence, almost.

"When Cassandra was gone, I sat with her body for hours. I was horrified. I was stunned with grief. And I was confused, because I had enjoyed what I had done to her. What Carrefour did to me was like training a dog. Punishment and reward. Classical conditioning. And it worked.

"I withdrew from the law program. I was afraid to be around people who had known Cassandra. I moved. Not out of the city but across town. I found work at a small accountancy doing simple data entry. And the beast within me grew stronger. The woman who came in twice a week to help with filing be-friended me, and four months later, I killed her too.

"Of course I hated myself, but the pleasure—the release—of my crime was the only peace Carrefour allowed me. It began speaking to me then, a voice within my head. And sometimes it changed me. My fingernails became knives. My skin grew pale. I wasn't a fool. I was hearing voices. Hallucinating. Clearly, I had suffered a schizophrenic break, but with what I had done, who could I ask for help? Three times, I tried to kill myself, but the rider would not let me. I slaughtered two more women.

"I was quite mad by then. I believed that I had been possessed by a demon, but I also believed that I was making that up. I thought I was innocent, and that I was a monster best shot on sight. My victims deserved it and they did not. I began stalking women who had made no overtures of friendship toward me. And beneath it all, there was the sense of betrayal and the rage and the hunger for vengeance that was the rider's. I learned the name Legba and of *loa* and the power of the crossroads between our world and theirs.

"Each time I committed my crimes, the sense of peace and relief that came with it would deepen. I don't know if it was Carrefour learning how better to control me, or only that I had been broken of my grief and guilt. Broken of it or accustomed to it. For a day, two days, three I would be myself again. The world would have some tiny ray of hope. I could eat. I could sleep. I told myself that it was over, that I could stop. But inevitably, Carrefour would shift in the back of my mind, and I knew it was happening again.

"And then an angel of God's grace by the name Karen Black saved me."

Mfume paused, considering his cigarette. Aubrey squatted down, his back against the rough stucco of the wall. In the dark, it was hard to make out details, but I thought he was sweating. Marinette hadn't ridden him for more than a few hours, and he was listening to a lifetime under the rider's whip. I couldn't have imagined a worse nightmare for him.

Mfume plucked a fresh cigarette from his pack, lit it from the butt of the last one, and flicked the still-burning ember down into the street. It glowed like a falling star, then went out.

"By this time, Carrefour was manifesting within my flesh whenever it saw fit. Angry, I would grow bigger. Wider. I split my pants and shredded my shirts. My hands would sprout knives. And it walked in the crossroads. I could stop the world. Go where I wanted. Take what I pleased. When I found that we could do that, Carrefour and I, I thought that we would never be stopped. But it was reluctant to use that power."

"Why?" I asked.

"I think it was afraid of being found by others like itself," Mfume said. "The crossroads is the natural habitat of riders, and Carrefour was always very aware of being in exile, away from its home. Unsafe. And it was that hesitance that saved me.

"I don't know precisely how they found me out, but I can't imagine it was that difficult. I was past concerning myself with hiding evidence or trying to behave unsuspiciously. One morning, I rose, showered, dressed, and stepped out of my door into a trap. Half a dozen people surrounded me, guns drawn, screaming that I should lay down on the ground. I could feel Carrefour's surprise, its anger. It was preparing to step into the crossroads, and to all of those good people it would have seemed that I had simply vanished. But Karen acted on instinct. She dove for me, wrestled me to the ground. And in the struggle, I bit her. I tasted her blood, and Carrefour took its opportunity. Between one breath and the next, it was gone."

"When Karen talked about the rider," Chogyi Jake said. "She said that even once it had moved to a new host, its former victim was loyal to it. That you loved it."

"Of course I did," Mfume said. "It had been the only thing that could bring me peace. For years, it had insulated me from the worst of my pain, my guilt, my horror. And then I was left not just alone, but empty. Hollow. Carrefour was a dark and terrible God, but it was mine. And God had abandoned me.

"At the trial, I saw it. She testified, and I saw it in her eyes, looking out at me as it once had from the mirror over my sink. I cried out. I begged," Mfume said, then chuckled. "The judge told me that if I wanted to get an insanity plea, I would need to become a much better actor. She had, I think, very little sympathy for my situation."

"And so jail," I said.

"Just so," he said. "I was sent to the state penitentiary. I was monitored throughout the day and night. I could not eat except when I was told. I could not walk for exercise except when I was told. I had no clothes of my own. No books of my own. My family would not speak to me. They were ashamed and frightened. Of course they were. What else could they have felt? Alone, abandoned, imprisoned, crushed by grief and guilt and horror, I also came to understand that I felt more free than I had in years. Even in the nights when I woke weeping and calling for Carrefour to return to me, I was slowly, painfully, becoming myself again.

"I had once aspired to become a lawyer, and so I knew how to study. I read widely on spirits and possession. Most of what I found was useless, but now and then, there would be something that spoke to my experience. You can't imagine how strange it felt to find references to Legba and the *loa* and to confirm all the things I had imagined at the time to be my own private ravings. I came to understand what I had been, and what had been done to me. I came to see that what had happened to those women had not been my doing. That I was not a monster."

"But Karen," Aubrey said. "She had it now."

"Yes," Mfume said. "The penal system has very few avenues for the prisoners to keep tabs on the police, but I did what I could. I heard about it when Karen left the FBI, and I sent her letters. I begged her to see me. When she did not, I wrote to her partner, Michael Davis. I thought it was a hopeless attempt, but he came. He spoke to me.

"He had seen the changes in her. The anger, the sense of having been betrayed. When he had first met her, she had been the consummate professional, her personal life kept at home. Since apprehending me, those boundaries had begun to break down. She had become sexually aggressive in ways that alienated her from her colleagues. He saw her manipulating the people around her to no clear end. Every time he reached out to her, he had been refused or redirected. When I told him what had happened, he didn't want to believe me. But two months later, he returned. I don't know what had happened, but he knew that Karen was no longer herself."

"And then she killed him," I said. "I'm pretty sure she burned her parents to death too."

"Yes, I heard of that," Mfume said. "There was very little I could do. I was a convict. A serial killer in jail without hope of parole. I was on record saying that I had been possessed by a demon. I was like the Groucho Marx joke. I wouldn't trust anyone idiotic enough to find me credible. And so . . . I escaped."

"Okay, you could expand on that a little," I said. "You just said, *Wait, this sucks,* and walked out?"

"At my prison, there was a meditation group. An outreach to help people within the system become well. I joined it at first because I wanted to find some purely psychological peace. But as I coordinated my reading on the *loa*, my practice with the group, and my experiences being ridden by Carrefour, I found a way to walk in the crossroads."

"You taught yourself magic?" Aubrey said.

"There is a certain amount of spare time in prison," Mfume said. "And I was better prepared than most. I used what I learned. And one day, yes. I walked out. Since then I have been hunting Carrefour, but it has Karen now, and she is a very clever, very resourceful woman. When I learned that the hurricane had injured Carrefour's enemies, I felt certain that the rider couldn't resist. I came here, made contact with Legba, and offered my services in exchange for its aid."

He spread his hands to show the world before us, the dark streets glittering with lights, the black sky glowing.

"Okay," I said. "But how come I was able to get involved when it tried to kill Sabine?"

"You have also lived in the crossroads," he said. "Learned how to step between the moments."

"Yeah, only no. I really haven't," I said. "Seriously, I didn't know about any of this a year ago."

"Her uncle put some protections on her," Aubrey said.

Mfume looked from one of us to the other and shook his head.

"I know of no protections that would do what

you describe, but my knowledge is . . . opportunistic. I am no master of this art."

"What does Carrefour want?" Chogyi Jake said.

"I didn't know its agenda until I came here," Mfume said. "Not precisely. I knew it hated Legba above all other *loa*, but not why. I knew it sought to return to its place. Having spoken to Amelie and her granddaughters, I believe I understand now, but you must take everything I say on this for what it is: my best guess."

"Consider the caveat emptored," I said. "What've you got?"

"Legba is also a master of the crossroads. It controls the path by which *loa* pass into human bodies, and it is the gatekeeper between the *loa* and all other riders. It has terrible power, but it is also weak in some ways. It is more involved with humanity than other *loa*. It is connected to the world in a way the others—even Carrefour—are not. Each person Legba enters into, it never leaves. It dies with them."

"That's a shitty design," I said.

"No, it's not," Aubrey said. His voice was stronger than I'd expected. Less shaken. "It's normal. Pretty much any terminal or chronic disease works the same way. When a tuberculosis patient dies, all the bacteria in their lungs go with them. The point is to get daughter organisms out before that happens. To spread."

"And so," Chogyi Jake said, "Sabine."

"Sabine," Mfume agreed.

"But Legba's still in Amelie," I said. "Sabine's not being ridden yet, right?"

"No, not right," Mfume said. "Legba is also in Sabine. *A* Legba. Growing to maturity. Finding its strength and hers."

"And she knows?" Aubrey asked. "She's okay with it?"

"She has always known," Mfume said. "It is what her family has always been. Only now Carrefour intends to pull it out, to sever the connection between the rider and the bloodline that has protected it."

"Why not just kill Sabine?" I asked. "I mean, since we're being bloodthirsty and all."

"Once the rider is vulnerable, it can be eaten. Its power can be taken on by Carrefour. Once it alone controls the crossroads, it believes it can take Legba's place, and force the *loa* to renounce its exile."

"Can it?" I asked. "Will they take it back?"

Mfume laughed. In the distance, as if in answer, a car alarm chirped.

"The political life of the *loa* is beyond me," he said. "It's possible that Carrefour is tilting at windmills. Or things might all go just as it intends. Unless someone stops it."

"Meaning us," I said.

Mfume stabbed out the last of his cigarette on the rail, tiny sparks raining down to the street below us.

"We are in the right place at the right time," he said. "And so yes. Us."

"Well," I said. "At least we're on the same side."

"Are we?" Chogyi Jake asked. "It seems we all have similar goals, but our agendas aren't all the same. Legba wants to protect itself and its offspring. We want to find Ex and get him out of harm's way. Those aren't really the same thing. And if I understand Joseph, neither one are what brings him here."

"Your friend's right," Mfume said. "We are on the same path for the moment, but this is a marriage of convenience for all sides."

"So what's your agenda?" Aubrey asked. He managed not to make it sound like an accusation.

"Isn't it obvious? I've come to redeem my redeemer," Mfume said. "I intend to save Karen Black."

TWENTY

The war council was held at the same table where Legba and I had made our pact. The candles and lace tablecloth were gone, and a cheap torchiere lamp had been plugged in, filling the room with rich halogen light and the smell of burning dust in more or less equal degrees. Amelie Glapion sat on her throne, surveying the room with a critical expression. Her nap had returned her to sharpness, but I was more aware of her as an old, fragile woman than I had been. To her right, Dr. Inondé looked like a mildly apologetic salesman. To her left, Sabine sat, her face still full with youth but managing to mimic her grandmother's severity. Chogyi Jake, Aubrey, and I took the other side of the cheap folding banquet table, and Mfume sat at the head, both with the group and also apart from it. Daria was curled on her cot, a sleeping bag pulled up to her ears, snoring quietly.

Some kind soul had run out for coffee. I had a paper cup with café au lait just slightly too hot to drink. The others had drinks of their own, except for Chogyi Jake and Amelie Glapion.

It was ten thirty at night, and dark as midnight.

"We don't know where she is," Amelie Glapion said, "and she can't find us neither. So that's where it stands. Either we keep her held off until Sabine can watch out for herself. Or else we take her on."

Sabine nodded. She knew what was happening. And what was more, I could see from the way she held herself that she accepted it. She was going to be the host of a rider for the rest of her life, and in this place, in this context, she thought it was a good thing. And God help me, I was starting to see her point of view.

"How long is it going to take for Sabine to pupate?" Aubrey asked.

The room went silent, all eyes turning to Aubrey as if he'd said something inappropriate.

"*Excuse* me?" Sabine said. I hopped in.

"How long before the *loa* in you is strong enough to fight off Carrefour?" I said. Then, "He's a biologist. He talks like that sometimes. Don't sweat it."

"The longer it goes, the stronger it grows," Amelie said. She was herself; I didn't hear any trace of the rider in her voice. "The child will come into her own, but it ain't all that different from real kids. It happens when it happens, you know?"

"Generally, the longer we can hold her off, the better it'll be," I said.

"Except," Mfume said, planting the word like a flag. Attention shifted to him. "You mustn't underestimate Karen Black. Once, I was able to keep a rough sort of track of her. Once, we were certain that we had time, that we could arrange this confrontation to fit our schedule. Instead, Carrefour has gathered new resources. It discovered us at the temple, and except for Miss Heller's intervention might already have taken Sabine. And it has vanished."

"Yeah, that was me," I said. "Well, us. The wards where it's hard to find with spells and cantrips and stuff? That was our fault."

"We cannot assume that stealth gives us power," Mfume continued. "Karen is very good at what she does. We may believe that we are safe only because she allows us to think it. The illusion serves her, and waiting gives her the tempo."

"But we *do* know where she is, don't we? We know where the safe house is," Aubrey said.

"And she doesn't know that we three are back in the game," I said. "So she won't know that's compromised. If nothing else, we could send someone out to take a look. And if she's not there, maybe Ex would be, and we could get him back too."

"Ex?" Amelie Glapion said.

"My friend who's sleeping with her," I said. "The one we came back for. He's another problem. He used to be a priest, and he knows how to pull a rider out of the host body."

"So Ex like in exorcist," Amelie Glapion said. "You're telling me this bitch got a warded house and a working exorcist out of you?"

"And a van," I said. "A warded van so she can move around without being seen."

"And you got what?"

I felt myself blushing a little.

"She told me some stories about my uncle. And there was a favor or two she was going to owe me."

"Owe you," Amelie said.

"Yeah."

"Owe you like not actually do for you, but maybe someplace down the line."

"Like that."

The old woman shook her head in disgust.

"Either this bitch really is that good or you've got to get a whole lot smarter," she said.

"Little of both," I admitted.

"But the safe house," Aubrey said. "I know going out there's a risk, but—"

Chogyi Jake leaned forward, his fingertips tapping the tabletop like raindrops. His expression was

focused inward, the way it did when he was thinking through a particularly knotty problem.

"It may not be a risk we have to take," he said.
"I put the wards on the house and the van both. Ex
and Aubrey here both helped, but I was central to
all of them. If I can be used as a focus, perhaps we
can break them through me."

"What exactly did you do with them?" Dr. Inondé
asked, and the conversation sailed over my head
like a kite. Medial foci, ekagratva, veve, and primal
aether bounced across the room with occasional
pauses for translation and clarification. It was like
Amelie Glapion, Chogyi Jake, Aubrey, and Dr. Inondé had turned into occult economists; I didn't
know what they were saying, and I was fairly certain anything I said was only going to make me look
dumb. Instead I finished my coffee and leaned back
in my chair.

There was a certain joy in disengaging from a
conversation. It let me see all the things going on
at the edges of the talk. The way Sabine leaned in
whenever her grandmother spoke, as if she was trying to drink in each word. The way Amelie Glapion's
eyes darkened when the rider within her stirred and
took interest. Mfume's poker face, built in prison to
give nothing away. The angle of Dr. Inondé's head
as he leaned forward, drawing something on a nap-
kin for Chogyi Jake to look at. Mfume and Aubrey
started up a side conversation about the geography

around the safe house. Sabine said something about Soleil Noir and got shushed. Daria, on her cot, stirred, sat up, stretched.

When I got up to throw away my coffee cup, Daria walked sleepily over to the table and crawled into her grandmother's lap like a child half her age. The old woman or possibly the rider ran long, thin fingers over the girl's back and shoulders, soothing her even as the debate raged on. I thought I saw tears in the young girl's eyes. They should have been a warning.

"We can try it," Dr. Inondé said. "The only danger is to you."

"I don't think it will be a problem," Chogyi Jake said.

"Um, sorry," I said. "I was just over there. I missed that part. What danger?"

"I have some connection to the wards we put up," Chogyi Jake said. "By using my mind as a focus point and Legba's power channeled through me, we believe I can inhabit the original work and undo them."

"Check," I said. "And the danger part would be?"

"It leaves me open for a time," Chogyi Jake said. "It is possible that in that period one of the *loa* or a different rider could take up residence in my body."

"And what would we do about that?" I asked.

Chogyi Jake's smile could have meant anything.

"It's very unlikely to happen," he said.

"Lock him in a refrigerator until we get Ex back," Aubrey said.

"That sounds bad," I said.

"It wouldn't be good," Chogyi Jake agreed. "I understand that the stakes are high. But the chances are good. It's a risk worth taking. Safer, for example, than going to the safe house."

The room quieted. I was the only one standing, and all the others were looking at me as if waiting for something. As if it was my call.

Which meant it was. If I said hell no, I wasn't putting Chogyi Jake in harm's way, it would have been off. If I gave the thumbs-up, then it would move forward, and the consequences would be at least partly mine to carry. It seemed unfair at first, but I'd been the one who paid Chogyi Jake's bills. I was the one who'd entered into a pact with a voodoo demon. There was a pretty good argument to be made that I was the boss, and it made me wish I'd understood the mechanics of the thing better.

"It's the right thing?" I asked.

Chogyi Jake shrugged.

"It is what it is," he said.

"Okay," I said. "Let's do it."

Amelie Glapion put Daria down and reached for the metal cane that she once nearly killed me with. Sabine said she'd gather the others, Mfume walked to the back with a clear purpose in mind,

and Chogyi Jake and Dr. Inondé started moving the table back against an empty wall. Aubrey
walked to my side, his arms crossed. We hadn't
had time to talk, just the two of us, since I'd deliv-
ered the verbal smackdown on the boardwalk by
the river. Four hours earlier. It seemed like four
days.

His brow was furrowed, his lips pressed thin. I
put my hand on his arm and he looked up at me like
he'd just noticed I was there.

"How are you doing?" I said.

"Like a mouse in a snake pit," he said. "Jumpy as
hell."

"Yeah," I said. "I can see that."

"I don't know how they do it. Mfume. Amelie
Glapion. They had those things in their bodies with
them for years. I had to go through it for, what? Six
hours?"

"I think it's different for everyone," I said. "How
they come to it. What the rider is, maybe."

"Yeah," he said. "That too. I mean . . . I look at
Sabine. Specifically Sabine. And . . . I don't know. It
messes with my definitions."

I looked over. The girl was back now, helping
the drummers set up on the floor next to the cots.
She was younger than any of them, but she acted
like their natural superior, telling each where to sit,
which way to face, which drum to hold.

"She's a black sixteen-year-old girl in a city with

no functioning infrastructure to speak of," Aubrey said. "She's got no parents. Her grandmother has had at least one stroke, and maybe several. She's got a little sister to take care of."

"And a demon growing inside her," I said.

"But that's the thing," Aubrey said. "That's what she has going *for* her. Without being heir apparent to the whole voodoo queen thing, she'd be totally screwed. You look at her situation on paper and you'd think here's a girl who's going to wind up as a prostitute or homeless or something really bad. But she won't. She'll wind up the voodoo queen of New Orleans. Her life is going to be better because of that thing in her."

"Yeah," I said. "I know."

Sabine turned, looking past us, and waved at another of the cultists, her hand fluttering like a bird. The man trotted to her, his head bent at a deferential angle.

"Mutualism," Aubrey said in a tone that meant *Who'd have guessed it?*

"Meaning?"

"Legba's not a parasite," he said. "Not technically. A parasite is either detrimental to its host or functionally neutral. Usually detrimental, if only because it's diverting energy resources. But if it's actually doing the host good, that's not parasitism anymore. That's part of a mutualistic relationship. There are bacteria that fix nitrogen for plants, and the plants provide energy to the bacteria. Either one would fail without the other."

The eldest drummer tapped a wide-mouthed pottery drum, a low, dry sound filling the room. He nodded to Sabine.

"I don't know whether that makes me happy or creeps me out," I said.

"How do you mean?"

"Well, either that means Sabine's got a really nice rider and more power to her, or else the world is so fucked up that the best she can hope for is demonic possession."

Aubrey took a deep breath, letting the exhalation filter slowly through his mouth and nose.

"Guess it's how you look at it," he said.

Amelie Glapion returned to the room. A young man at her side carried a bag of corn meal, and together they went to the cardinal directions, the man pouring out the bright yellow meal in shapes, figures, and ideograms of inhuman languages while Amelie and Legba within her intoned words and phrases that seemed to echo in a space larger than the room we were in.

As they progressed, the drummers took up the rhythm of the chant. Amelie Glapion moved from one veve to the next, taking small objects from her pockets—a crow's foot curled against itself in death, a sprig of rosemary, a cheap one-shot whiskey bottle, a handkerchief smudged with lipstick and something else. Her head began to bob and weave in its unpleasant serpentine pattern, and the air around us thickened with invisible things. I could feel the riders gathering, pressing at the film between the real, physical world and the abstract nation behind and beside us. Aubrey felt it too, and his hand sought mine out.

Chogyi Jake stepped in from the back, naked, his head bowed. Someone had drawn symbols on his skin in bright paints. I recognized the fleur-de-lis on his shoulder, the searcher's X on his breast, but there were at least a dozen others I didn't know. He showed no discomfort at his nudity, but walked to Amelie Glapion, knelt before her with his eyes closed, and raised his palms to her. One of the cultist women yelled and began to sway. Others joined her.

"Kisa sa a ye?" Legba shouted, Amelie's mouth widening more than the merely human would allow. *"Kisa sa a ye!"*

Mfume, across the room, sat cross-legged. A map was open on the floor before him, and he was passing his hands over it like he was feeling heat radiating from it. The dancing cultists shouted and whooped to the pulsing rhythm of the drums. Against my will almost, I found my body swaying too. My eyes closed almost without me, and I stepped out into the ceremony, drawing Aubrey along behind me.

I didn't know what I was doing. I didn't know what it meant, but the heat of the bodies before us, the pressure of Next Door, the danger and the lush, complex rhythm, the smell of fire and flesh, made it all feel right. One of the male cultists no older than I was had taken off his clothes, his dark skin shining with sweat. His erection seemed strangely comforting and familiar. It was a reminder that even among these spirits, we were first and foremost human; our animal nature made us part of this world, the physical, immediate, concrete. I heard myself shout, felt the rumble of the air in my throat.

The world became a dance, not bodies, not spirits, but the relationships between the two. Like an optical illusion, I was not my body or my mind, but the space defined by them. I tore free of my own shirt, delighting in the feel of air against my skin. Lust and hunger. Pain, sorrow, and joy. They were the tether of humanity that held me from spinning out into another world, and I honored them, fed them, and trusted them completely to hold me and to pull me back.

Like the report of a handgun, Amelie Glapion clapped her hands. The drums stopped, the dance stopped, and I stumbled, sitting on the floor. My head was spinning and I felt flushed and energized and a little nauseated. Chogyi Jake wasn't more than three feet in front of me, bracing himself with both hands like a man almost too drunk to crawl.

"Did it work?" I managed, and he nodded carefully.

Above us, Amelie Glapion sagged, leaning on her cane. Her face looked drawn. I felt almost unstuck from my body, like I'd just gone through a marathon of sex and liquor. I couldn't imagine how she felt. But a moment later, the half of her face that was still alive, smiled.

"I am *never* getting tired of that," she said low in her throat, and Mfume shouted.

"I have her," he said. His eyes were still closed. His fingers pressed onto the map like a blind man reading braille. I stood unsteadily, scrabbling at my cast-off shirt. Aubrey appeared at my side, and we navigated across the room.

The map was of New Orleans, but marked with ley lines in black and red and yellow. I saw the yawning darkness of Lake Pontchartrain, the snake-curve of the Mississippi. The gridwork of streets between the two like a crystal growing between the curves.

"Where is she?" I asked, pulling on my clothes. I was hoarse.

Mfume opened his eyes and knelt close to the paper. I could see his fingers trembling.

"She's . . . in the street," he said. "She's here. She's outside right now."

We were silent for a moment, and then with a roar like a lion, Amelie Glapion strode out toward the front room. I saw the glow of streetlight squeezing past the gray-painted glass as she opened the connecting door.

The explosion lit her in silhouette, a darkness standing against the sun.

TWENTY-ONE

I grew up in the '90s. All I knew about explosions came from the action films that my older brother Jay used to watch when my parents left him in charge. They were great big Jerry Bruckheimer things that billowed smoke and fire like a grand, implacable tide shot from three different angles. This explosion wasn't like that at all. It was sudden, sharp, louder than anything I'd ever heard, and over before I understood that something was happening.

I didn't black out or lose consciousness, but time seemed to skip. I found myself running forward, toward the empty doorway and the haze of smoke and the leaping light of flames without knowing what exactly I thought I was doing. I stumbled on something and fell forward. The floor was hot under my palms. The air smelled like acid. Someone behind me was screaming. With a sense of profound detachment, I noticed that my arm was bleeding where Carrefour had cut me. I forced myself to stop, to look at where I was and what I was doing despite my body's impulse to blindly react.

Amelie Glapion had been thrown backward into the room, which was a very good thing, because the street-facing storefront of the building appeared to be on fire. Six or eight of the cultists were skittering around the back. One woman had collapsed and was being carried; one of the drummers had her heels and Chogyi Jake—still naked and marked with voodoo symbols—her shoulders. Aubrey stood open-mouthed in the center of the room, balanced between the impulse to act and raw shock. I knew how he felt. The cornmeal veve were being scattered by running feet, blurring like chalk marks in a rainstorm.

"Jayné!" Aubrey shouted.

"I'm fine," I yelled back. "Find the girls! Get out!"

He hesitated.

"Go!" I shouted.

Something in the street cracked, and I saw a brief yellow-white light in the darkness at the far side of the deeper orange fire. Muzzle flash, I thought. She's shooting at us.

"Stay down!" I shouted. I could feel the vibration in my throat, but my voice seemed to come from half a block away. "Everyone take cover!"

I couldn't tell if they heard me. Amelie Glapion moved, her arm rising up slowly, like a strand of seaweed waving in a light current. I started toward her, and a strong hand grabbed my arm, turning me. Mfume's eyes were wide, his skin ashen. He had the crumpled map of the city in his other hand.

"Don't," he said. "It's too dangerous." His voice was only the bass notes. Like a stadium concert pressed into a fraction of a second, the blast had blown out my hearing.

"It's okay," I shouted. "I'll risk it."

A different thought struck me.

"You have to go," I shouted. "You have to get out of here. Now!"

"We can all go," he said. "I have to—"

"No! You have to get out. The cops are going to come. They're going to be here. If they find out you're alive, you're heading back to prison."

Mfume rocked back like I'd slapped him. He'd forgotten that he was an escaped serial killer. He looked around the carnage and panic, and his expression was anguished.

"I'll take care of it," I said. "Just go!"

"I will stay close," Mfume said. "I will find you."

"It's a date. Now run!"

He stepped back, hesitated, and then turned, running toward the back of the place. I wondered what escape routes he could find. I didn't think there was an alleyway behind the building, but there might have been a connecting passage or a way up to the roof.

I couldn't worry about it. Another volley of gunfire came from the street, then the screeching of tires probably about a hundred times louder than my abused eardrums could register. I crept forward. The fire in the front room was getting bigger. I couldn't see the darkness of the street on the other side, so I assumed that if Karen was still out there she couldn't see me. The doorway was bright, the flames dancing wildly. The heat came off it like an assault. I scuttled forward, grabbed Amelie's blouse at the shoulder, and hauled her back. Above us, the ceiling was almost lost in a roiling white smoke. A voice I didn't recognize shouted somewhere to my left. I heard glass breaking from up the stairs and hoped it had been intentional.

"It's going to be okay," I said, then looked down at the woman I was carrying and knew that it wasn't.

Flying glass had stripped the skin from her cheeks, revealing deep red tissue and white cheekbone. Her throat was bloody. Her hands hung in the air, laboring under their own weight. Her legs where they had lain nearest the fire were blistered. A sweet smell like cooking pork cut through the smoke, and I tried not to retch.

"I'll get you out," I said. "I'll get you out of here."

"There is no need," Legba said. Unlike every other sound, its voice was perfectly clear. "The woman is gone."

"But—" I began, then didn't know where to go. But she can't die. But she was just here a minute ago. But I still need her. I didn't know if I was weeping from the smoke or something else.

"Carrefour is a clever, deceitful beast," Legba said. "I had believed that we were safe. That there would be time. More time."

The woman's dead body, still animated by the power of its rider, shifted and rose unsteadily until it sat before me. The roar of the fire in the next room was like a waterfall. The dead lips smiled at me, exposing a hundred needle-sharp teeth.

"I have fallen," it said. "There is no longer any hope for this one. It is in my child's hands now, but she is weak. Young."

"Yeah," I said. "I absolutely get that."

"The pact you took with me is broken with my death," it said, "and I cannot bring myself to beg."

"Hey, don't. I mean, you don't need to beg or anything. I said I'd stand up, and I'll do it."

The eyes were black, the woman's flesh losing its own form, shaped more and more by the thing still alive within her. Alive, but fading. I glanced around, and we were the only two left. The others had gotten out. The three empty cots against the wall were barely above the lowering smoke. The heat of the fire was like a hand pressing against my cheek. The undead voodoo queen of New Orleans considered me.

"We have not been allies," it said.

"I'm not saying I'd marry you," I said. "It's just . . . I'll look out for the kids. I'll do what I can."

It looked out toward the street. I coughed. I was getting a little light-headed.

"First the flood and now the fire," Legba said, as if laughing at some private joke. "Go, then. Leave me. Save my city."

I should have run. I should have been running the whole time.

"I will," I said.

Legba took my hand, and I could feel its strength failing. Without knowing I intended to, I leaned forward, cupping the dead woman's skull in my palm, pressing her forehead to mine. Something seemed to pass between us—not magic, not spirit, but understanding. And grief.

"Go," the rider said. "I will clear your way."

And the world stopped.

Silence rushed in where the roar of flames had been. The roiling smoke stilled. Amelie Glapion's body nodded toward the front room, and I rose. The air seemed to tingle, but the heat wasn't unbearable.

I walked toward the front room and its ongoing conflagration. Bright flames hung in the air, still as stone but glowing. I brushed one with my hand like I was petting a cat, and it felt like velvet.

The street came more clearly into view with each step. The blackened shell of a car lay on its side in the middle of the pavement. Men and women were crowded on the sidewalk across the street, and down far enough that the heat of the flames was bearable. Two policemen stood like temple guards, keeping the crowd back.

I wondered how long it had taken—five minutes? ten?—to go from the sense of power and freedom and safety of Legba's ward-breaking dance to this. I caught a glimpse of Aubrey near one clump of people, his arm raised to shield his eyes. He didn't react as I came near, not even to breathe.

I turned back toward the fire.

"Okay," I said, my voice no louder than a conversation between friends. "Thanks. I'm clear now."

A breath later, the world turned back on. The roar of the fire, the distant sirens, the assaulting smell of burning wood and spent explosives. I felt a tug at the back of my mind, like a kid yanking on her mother's sleeve, and I knew that Legba— the Legba that had lived in Amelie Glapion—was gone. Aubrey shifted to the side, squinting into the fire.

"Hey," I said.

He yelped, whirled, and then scooped me up in a bear hug that made me yelp right back.

"Ribs! Watch the ribs!"

"Right," he said. "Sorry. But you're out. You got out. Daria, she collapsed. I mean, I think she's okay now, but I had to carry her out. I saw you going after Amelie, and then I didn't see you go past, so I thought you were still . . . I thought . . ."

"Guess that was kind of dangerous," I said. I felt disconnected. Like the world was still at one remove, and I was still moving through the crossroads. "I didn't really think about it."

"What about Amelie?"

"She didn't make it," I said. "She's gone."

Aubrey didn't answer. At the far end of the street, a fire truck arrived, its lights flashing and its siren clearing the path of onlookers. Another police cruiser was behind it, then two, then five and an ambulance. The city of New Orleans had arrived at the crisis. They were on it. I crossed my arms and watched, unable to offer anything but moral support. Slowly, like I was waking from a dream, human concerns started to occur to me.

"Chogyi Jake," I said. "He was . . ."

"He's down there with the others."

I looked where he pointed. Down the block, a small cluster of people had set up a kind of ad-hoc relief station. Two people lay on the sidewalk, three others standing or squatting beside them. Chogyi

Jake was sitting on the curb, someone's jacket wrapping his hips. Daria Glapion stood beside him looking back at us. Even from half a block down, the fire reflected in her eyes.

"Come on," I said.

The police, reinforced by the newly arrived squad cars, pushed the crowd further back and the firefighters rushed in. Chogyi Jake looked up at me and smiled wearily.

"Not the evening we had in mind," he said.

"No joke," I said and sat down beside the girl.

Daria didn't turn toward me. Her eyes were fixed on the pyre, tears flowing down her stark, impassive cheeks. I sat with her in silence for a minute. The firefighters pulled a long hose that looked like canvas up to the fire. With shouts and hand signals, the water started, spraying out into the flames. The smoke thickened.

"I'm sorry," I said.

The little girl nodded.

"I would have saved her if I could," I said. "But your grandmother was already gone when I got to her."

"I know," Daria said.

The matter-of-fact tone of voice together with the pain in her eyes, the bravery of her composure, was heartbreaking. I wanted to put my arm around the girl, to scoop her up and hold her and let her cry, but her dignity seemed to forbid it. Here was a child not even in high school. She had seen her city assaulted, had lost her mother, her brother, now her grandmother, and all she had left in the world was a sister who . . .

A sister.

"Where's Sabine?" I said, my voice sharper than I intended. "Who's got Sabine?"

"I couldn't find her," Aubrey said, shaking his head. "She was already gone."

Chogyi Jake and Daria turned to me in silence.

"Well, fuck," I said.

"SHE MAY be with Mfume. Or Inondé, wherever he is," Aubrey said. "We don't know for certain that Karen got her."

I'd rented us a room in the same hotel we'd stayed at when we had first come to New Orleans. Chogyi Jake was in the bathroom, showering off the last of the voodoo markings from his skin. Daria was sitting on the crisp, white linen sheets looking out the open French doors to the patio and the darkened courtyard beyond it. Aubrey couldn't stop moving, pacing, rapping his knuckles on the walls and tables as he passed them, and I was sitting in a deep, cream-colored oversized chair. My hair smelled like smoke.

"I don't think we can assume she got away," I said. "If she's not with us, we have to act like Karen got her. Hoping for the best isn't really an option here."

"Call him again," Aubrey said. "Maybe he'll be there."

I didn't fight him on it, but I didn't expect anything to come of it. I dug through my pack, pulled out the cell phone, and pulled Ex's entry out of the contacts list. As I listened to the phone ring, the shower water stopped. By the time Ex's recorded voice said he was away from his phone and to leave a message, Chogyi Jake stepped out of the bathroom wearing a fresh pair of blue jeans and a white T-shirt.

"Any word?" he asked, and I shook my head.

"Okay," Aubrey said. "Let's take stock here. We don't know where Sabine is—"

"So we have to assume Karen's taken her," I said.

"Right," Aubrey said. "So Karen's taken her. Mfume and Inondé are MIA. Ex isn't answering his phone."

"Does she know we broke the wards?" I asked. Chogyi Jake's brow furrowed for a moment.

"I don't know," he said. "If she didn't specifically check, she might not. And unless she's been listening to the message we left for Ex, she may not know we've come back at all."

"Oh, I never told him we were coming back," I said. "I never told him Karen was possessed. I just said he should call us."

"In that case," Chogyi Jake said, sitting on the

bed beside Daria, "I can't see how she'd know we're here."

"Okay, so we've got something in the plus column," I said. "What else?"

"We probably know where she is," Aubrey said. "And if we can find Mfume, we can be sure."

"If her intention is to pull the rider out of Sabine, that will take Ex some time," Chogyi Jake said. "Two hours. Perhaps three."

"Giving us maybe an hour to figure out whatever we're doing, and then do it," I said. "I don't think we're in the plus column anymore, guys."

The sense of despair was seeping in at the sides like ink soaking a sheet of paper. The last time I'd faced Carrefour, it had almost killed me and I still hadn't recovered. Aubrey had been on the edge of freaking at least twice already, not to mention his wounds from exorcising Marinette. Chogyi Jake had been the focus of a ceremony already. We were tired, and we were hurt, and we were going to go to the safe house and confront Karen Black and the thing inside her. I didn't like our chances.

Daria shifted. She looked empty. Shell-shocked.

"Hey," I said gently. She turned to me. "How're you holding up, kiddo?"

"You can't take it on," she said. "You should call for help."

"I would," I said with a sense of growing loneliness. "I don't have anyone to call."

Daria's expression became quizzical.

"I do. I've got lots of people," she said and started ticking off fingers with each name. "Aunt Corrie and Uncle Bo. Aunt Sherrie. BP and Omar."

"Wait, who?" I said.

"Legba's community," Chogyi Jake said, his voice chagrined. "The ones that aren't being treated for smoke inhalation."

"They're going to know what happened by now," Daria said. "Somebody would have called somebody as soon as they got out from the fire. They're probably just trying to figure out what's going on."

"How many people were in your grandma's . . . group?" I asked.

"A hundred," Daria said without pausing. "It's always a hundred. Ten tens give it power and strength. Grandma said we needed that."

"And you can get ahold of them?"

Daria held out her hand. She couldn't have been more than twelve, and I had the feeling she was more in control of the situation than I was. I gave her the phone. Her small fingers traced a number. I heard the distant ringing as she held the phone to her ear. Then a click, and a woman's voice.

"Auntie Sherrie? I'm with someone you need to talk to. She's going to help Sabine, so be gentle with her, okay?"

Without waiting for a reply, Daria held out the

telephone. Her expression was eerily mature and more than a little pitying.

"You *really* need to find out who you are," she said.

I put the phone to my ear.

"Hi," I said.

"Who is this?" a woman's voice asked. I could hear the fear and the anger, but something else too. Something protective and fierce.

"My name's Jayné," I said. "I'm a friend. Kind of. We don't have time to get into that part. What's important is Carrefour killed Amelie Glapion and abducted Sabine."

The woman on the other end said something obscene.

"I know where they are," I said. "Get as many people as you can and meet me at Jackson Square in half an hour."

"I'll be there," the woman said, equal parts promise and threat. She dropped the connection. I put the phone back in my pack with a sense of unreality.

"Well?" Aubrey asked.

"Daria's right. Put it in the plus column," I said. "We've got a cult."

TWENTY-TWO

Something happened when I was ten or eleven years old that, maybe because it didn't have to do with leaving home or supernatural beasties or who that cute guy in French was, I hadn't thought of in years. The Conroys were a family that went to our church. The father was a big, bluff man with thinning blond hair and a bright red face, his wife was short and about as wide as she was tall, and their three boys were named—I'm not making this up—Huey, Dewey, and Louis. Pronounced Lewis. We weren't close to them. We didn't go to the same schools, our dads didn't work together, our mothers didn't hang out. They were just some other people who went to the same place we did on Sunday, listened to the same sermons, milled around at the same picnics and ice cream socials and so on.

And then their house burned down, and they came to live with us for a month.

My clearest memories of that time involved waiting in the hallway for one of the boys to finish with the bathroom and the smell of the cabbage and sausage casserole that Mrs. Conroy made as a thank-you dinner. When my brothers and I talked about it, it was always in the context of, "Holy shit, do you remember when those people invaded our house?" After they left, we didn't stay in touch. The only thing we'd ever had in common was our church.

Until that night in the dark, bleak hours of the morning, a cold fog rising from the ground in Jackson Square like a thousand cheap Halloween ghosts, I hadn't thought about how amazing that really was. The Conroys had been nothing to us, and we'd let them come into our home, sleep in our living room, borrow our robes and slippers, and watch our TV with us just because we were all part of the same group and they were in trouble.

The thirty men and women standing in Jackson Square, waiting for me and Daria would have stood out in my church like blood on a wedding dress. Never mind that there were no blacks at my church; there also weren't men with decorative scars on their necks or women who looked like they could chew through two-by-fours on the strength of rage alone. But something was the same, a sense of belonging together, of unspoken loyalty, of real community that filled me with a nostalgic longing.

There was also the impression that they'd happily beat an outsider to death with a pipe and sink the body in a swamp. There was less nostalgia with that one.

The whole time she'd been with us, Daria had been quiet. As soon as we saw the cult waiting for us, Daria ran to a thick-shouldered woman, wrapped her thin arms around the woman's belly, and started crying. Her sobs were low and violent, and I felt inexplicably responsible for them.

"Hey," I said. "I'm Jayné."

"You're the one came and screwed up the ceremony at Charity," one man said. He looked familiar. Now that I was close, and they were all around me, there were several who looked like I'd seen them before dancing in the belly of the dead hospital. There were more, though, that were new to me. I didn't see anyone who'd been in the fire, who'd witnessed the pact I'd taken with Legba. That was kind of too bad.

"Yeah, sorry about that," I said. "I didn't really understand the situation. I screwed up a lot of things."

"It's not her fault," Daria said. "Carrefour lied to

her. Soon as she saw what was happening, she came to Gramma for help."

"Seems like that didn't work out too well either," the thick-shouldered woman said.

"Treat her with respect," a man's voice came ringing from the gloom. "Amelie accepted her."

Dr. Inondé loomed up out of the fog. He wasn't a particularly imposing sight. The damp had soaked his shirt and hair, sticking both to him in unflattering ways. He nodded to me and Aubrey and Chogyi Jake, then went and knelt beside Daria and murmured something that the girl nodded back to. When he stood, he looked tired but determined.

"Look," he said. "I was there. Carita Lohman was too, you can call her. Or Tommy Condoné. Or Harold Jackson's son. We were all there. If it wasn't for this girl and her friends, Carrefour would have been able to do a lot worse than it did."

"Did bad enough, seems like," a thin, angry-looking man said.

"Okay, look," I said. "I know where Carrefour took Sabine. I can take you there, but . . . I need a promise."

"Who the hell are you to make demands of us?" the thick-shouldered woman said.

"Sherrie!" Daria snapped, standing back a step from the woman and wagging a finger at her like a mother scolding a child. "I told you to be gentle with her. So be gentle."

It was a ridiculous sight. Daria was small and slight and young; a girl play-acting at being adult. Sherrie looked like she'd be at home in a street fight. But when Daria spoke, Sherrie looked abashed.

"I'm not trying to hold things up," I said. "It's just that we aren't all going into this with the same exact agenda, and I don't want things to get weird. The exorcist that Carrefour's using doesn't know he's working for a rider. He thinks he's saving Sabine. So when we get in there, don't hurt him. He's not the bad guy."

There was a silent motion in the group. I couldn't tell if it was a good thing or a bad one. I felt like I was standing on the high-dive board, looking down at an empty pool. But I had to keep going.

"And," I said, "the horse? The one Carrefour's riding? Her name's Karen. She didn't pick any of this either."

The voice of the crowd was easier to interpret this time, low and unhappy. Angry. I felt Aubrey and Chogyi Jake step in toward me, closing ranks. Dr. Inondé looked embarrassed on my behalf.

"You want to go into a fight but just don't hurt anybody," Sherrie said.

"I just want to try and do the right thing," I said. "We have to do what we have to do, but if there's a chance . . . if there's a way to keep Karen alive, we should. This isn't her fault."

"And if we don't promise, you're going to let

Legba be cast down and Sabine die," Sherrie said.

"No. If you won't, then we'll try to stop Carrefour without you," I said. "It's just not as likely that it'll go well."

"Then I guess we promise," Sherrie said, raising an eyebrow.

A police car driving past the square slowed but didn't turn on its flashing lights. It wasn't every night someone set off a car bomb in the French Quarter. Thirty angry-looking people standing around Jackson Square at two in the morning was only going make the authorities jumpier. I didn't think taking everyone back to my hotel was going to work either.

"Okay, look," I said. "I've got a car over at my hotel like five minutes from here. The place Carrefour took Sabine is out in Pearl River, but it's a little hard to find. Can you guys grab your cars and follow me out?"

"We'll be there," Sherrie said.

"I'm coming too," Daria said.

I said, "No, you aren't," at the same moment Sherrie said, "Like hell you are."

"She's my sister," Daria said to both of us. "You can't keep me from coming."

"Sweetheart," Sherrie said. "Your grandma would come back from the dead to kick my ass if I took her baby granddaughter into a fight. And if you believe I can't keep you from coming, you don't know me as well as you think."

"I'll take care of her," Dr. Inondé said. "We'll stay at the shop. Doris likes her."

"Doris doesn't like anything," Daria said, outraged. "She's a *snake*."

I nodded to Sherrie, then Aubrey, Chogyi Jake, and I all started back toward the hotel. I noticed I was breathing hard; adrenaline burning off through my lungs.

"How long have we got?" I asked.

"If the rider in Sabine is as intractable as Marinette," Chogyi Jake said. "An hour. Maybe less."

"If we're too late, I think those people may kill us," Aubrey said.

"I had that feeling too," I said.

The drive out to the safe house had never seemed longer. Fog pressed in at the car windows, the murmur of the tires against the pavement hissing like a constant, breathless voice just too low to comprehend, and behind us, a string of headlights. The rider cult, following close. With each mile we covered, my stomach knotted more tightly until I was skating along the edge of nausea.

I was pretty sure that somewhere along the line I'd intended to be careful, to plan, to think things through rather than rushing headlong into unknown danger. And here we were, Aubrey leaning over the steering wheel as he broke the speed limits, Chogyi Jake in the backseat in deep meditation that I recognized as a preparation for battle, and me sitting powerless in the passenger's seat squinting ahead at the darkness or backward into the light. I didn't know what we would find at the safe house. The new Legba might already be eaten, Sabine and Ex already dead. Or Carrefour might be waiting for us. Karen could be in the trees with a sniper rifle, prepared to pick us off as we drove up the street.

She might not even be there.

"Jayné?" Aubrey said. "You okay?

"Fine. Why?"

"You keep saying *shit shit shit shit* under your breath," he said. "I didn't figure it was a good sign."

"Copro-vocal meditation," Chogyi Jake said from the backseat, his voice calm and amused. "I'm doing the same thing, only on the inside."

I laughed a little, and in the mirrors, I saw Chogyi Jake, his eyes closed, smile too. I loved him just then. Not like a man, but just as himself. And Aubrey too. And even Ex, asshole that he sometimes was. It was the moment of clarity that put all the rest of it in perspective.

"I shouldn't have let him split up the family," I said. "I should never have put up with that."

Aubrey glanced a question at me, then looked back at the road.

"Ex," I said. "Fucking Ex. Well, and Carrefour. I should never have let them split us up. I mean this thing that we're doing? This is not the sign that I did things right."

"But we have to do it," Aubrey said.

"Yeah," I said. "Because of Ex."

"Would you turn away otherwise?" Chogyi Jake asked. He sounded deep and calm as a temple bell. "If Ex had been with us in Savannah, and you had the same epiphany, would you have turned away?"

"Yes," I said. "Oh hell yes. You wouldn't have gotten me back here for anything."

"Interesting," Chogyi Jake said.

"It's not that I don't like Sabine," I said. "She's nice. She's out of her league, and I totally respect that. But there are a lot of nice people in trouble out there, you know? I'm not even keeping this one from being possessed."

"And Legba?" Chogyi Jake said.

His tone of voice carried volumes. Legba, the shining serpent that made its way through the blood of Marie Laveau down through the generations. The rider that would keep Sabine and Daria from only being orphaned black girls in a dangerous, broken city. The demon that would not leave New Orleans even in the face of the city's inundation. Legba the mutualist, the builder of community.

And so, by implication, Carrefour who had raped and slaughtered Mfume's fiancée and Karen Black's partner and parents. Carrefour who had lied to me, seduced me as much as it had Ex. Carrefour who had bombed Amelie Glapion and whoever else had happened to be in the street at the time. Carrefour, the serial killer. The exile.

Did I really think there was no difference between the two? Or was it just that the difference wouldn't have been big enough to justify the risk of coming back?

I wondered what Eric would have done. I didn't know anything about his relationship with Karen Black except what she'd told me. There might not have been the consultations she'd told me about. The favors owed and paid. All I knew for certain was that he'd had her number in his cell phone, and that when she called, she'd assumed he would know what she was talking about.

"I think I preferred the muttering obscenities," Aubrey said.

"Sorry," I said. "I was just thinking."

"Yeah, I got that from the way I could hear the gears grinding in your head."

"Maybe I would have come back. For Sabine," I said, and we ran out of lake. We'd reached Pearl River.

The road to the safe house was empty, and we took it very slowly, turning our headlights off. The cars behind us—eight of them—followed our lead. We glided through the night in the glow of running lights, slow as a funeral. If we actually drove up to the house, they'd hear us for sure. I didn't know if it made more sense to try sneaking up on Karen

and Ex or going for the full frontal assault. Except
I really did want Ex to live through it, and Karen
too if I could manage it. All-out assaults tended, I
guessed, to have more of a body count. I weighed
my options and a shadow detached itself from the
trees and loped toward the car.

Aubrey yelped, but before he could gun the engine or turn the car to attack, Joseph Mfume's long
face was framed in the window, his finger turning a
fast circle that meant we should roll down the window. When Aubrey did it, the thick, unconditioned
air smelled like swamp and sweat.

"What are you doing?" I asked.

"Waiting for you," Mfume said and looked back
at the other cars. "And them as well, I take it."

"I got some reinforcements," I said. "She's really
here then?"

"Yes," Mfume said. "I followed it from the house.
Amelie? She's . . ."

"Gone," I said. "And Legba with her."

Behind us a car door opened and closed, and
then another. The cult preparing for battle. Mfume's
goofy smile looked strained and nervous.

"They have been in the shed for some time," he
said. "We have to hurry."

"I know," I said, then to Aubrey, "just park it here.
We'll walk in."

"You have a plan?" Mfume said.

"That would be generous," I said as I got out.

"I've got a bunch of general intentions and thirty or so people with cheap handguns and machetes."

"More effective than intention alone, I suppose," Mfume said.

The others were spilling out into the midnight-black street. The dome lights flickered on and off like a huge, understated Christmas tree. One car alarm chirped, and angry voices followed it. I felt some sympathy for whoever had made the mistake. We were all improvising here.

They gathered close, but I could see their eyes turning toward the gently curving drive that would lead to the safe house. I could feel them drawn toward it like moths toward flame; their queen was in danger, and they strained at the leash of my own tentative authority. I couldn't hold them back any longer.

"Okay," I said, my voice a stage whisper. "They're going to be in the shed out back . . ."

"We gonna need three groups," Aunt Sherrie said. "Omar, you take your crew and head around the left side through the trees, and don't go fast. You go too fast, you make noise like that goddamn car alarm."

"Sorry about that," a voice said from the gloom.

"Don't be sorry, just get your boys together," Sherrie said. "Elijah? You take Nick and Majora and any two others you like and secure the house. Anybody in there, you just keep right on going all the way around until you hook up with Omar, but if it's empty, you get in and hold it. Deny this bitch her fallback position, you understand?"

"Yes, Aunt Sherrie," a man with a voice like a landslide said.

"All right, then. The rest of y'all come with me. That means you too, Miss Thing," Sherrie said, looking at me. "We're the ones going to bell the cat, and I am *not* doing that job by myself. Omar, I'm going to give you five minutes to get in position. If we have to fall back, Carrefour's going to get drawn out, and you be ready to come in behind it. Now all you remember we're trying not to kill the preacher or the horse. Preacher, you just hold him down or shoot him in the knee. Whatever. The horse . . . well, do what you can."

"Um," I said, blinking.

"Two tours in Afghanistan, one in Iraq," Sherrie said. "I do *not* fuck around."

I had the almost genetic impulse to say *sir, yes sir,* but I sat on it. Mfume stepped forward.

"I will take the rider," he said. "Don't kill her unless I have fallen."

Sherrie cocked her head, then shrugged.

"You heard the man. Be careful with Carrefour until it kills this one. Then do what you have to do. Now let's go."

Half the cultists seemed to dissolve into the gray, moonlit mist, the others waiting to follow Sherrie's lead. She smiled at me with wide, white, tombstone teeth.

"This is your party," she said. "You go on ahead, we'll follow you."

Meaning, I understood, that if anyone was going to get shot from a distance, it was going to be me. I took a deep breath, then let it out slowly and nodded. Chogyi Jake and Aubrey came to my side, and then Mfume joined them. Five minutes, she'd said. They lasted forever and no time at all. Sherrie looked from her wristwatch to the drive, pointed at me, pointed at it. My throat was thick with fear and my blood felt like it was vibrating in its vessels.

I walked down the side of the path, the knee-high grass muffling my footsteps more than the gravel would have. The safe house slowly came into view, its windows glowing in the fog. No one confronted us but the Virgin Mary, looking more like a tombstone than ever. The shed was still hidden by the angle of our approach.

Aubrey trotted up to walk at my side, Chogyi Jake and Mfume followed close. Aubrey took my hand.

"I've got to stop getting us into situations like this," I said softly. "I'm seriously going to get someone killed."

"Yeah," he agreed. "You really are."

TWENTY-THREE

We made our way around the corner of the house. The white cargo van squatted at the back door, its windows black. I had the sense that it was watching us, though there was no one in it. The fog-wet grass soaked my shoes and the cuffs of my pants as I walked, cold and clammy and grasping. My shirt and hair were getting damp, and Aubrey's hand in mine was the only warmth I felt.

The thick air also muffled sound so that even the handful of crickets seemed to be singing from miles away. The prison that we'd made from our shed was a looming darkness punctuated by intense points of brilliant white light—the line around the doorway, the slats of the tin vent. I squeezed Aubrey's hand one last time and let it go. Hunching close to the ground, I moved forward until the dark, mist-soaked wood was almost close enough to touch. The voices got louder as I approached like someone turning up the volume knob. Ex, his voice hoarse, in a shouted litany. The higher, weeping voice of Sabine.

The world felt thin, changed, unstable as driving on ice. Whatever rituals Ex was doing to cast Legba out of Sabine's body had brought the Pleroma or Next Door or whatever we called it close enough to feel, and it made my skin crawl.

Someone came up on my left. Mfume, and then a moment later, Chogyi Jake and Aunt Sherrie. This was it. The big moment. We would gather all the cultists together, kick in the door and hope for the best. I steeled myself, but my hands were tapping busily at my knees, like my body was trying to get my attention. I had Chogyi Jake and Aubrey, Mfume and Aunt Sherrie, and at least a dozen of Legba's congregation. I was pretty sure, if it came to it, we could rush in and take them by force. A few cultists would probably die. Maybe Ex. Probably Karen.

So I had to try the other way first. I motioned Aubrey and Chogyi Jake to stop, then I waved Mfume and Aunt Sherrie closer.

"Get everyone around the shed," I whispered. "Not in line of sight, but close by, okay?"

"What the hell are you doing?" Sherrie said.

"I'm going in," I said. "I'll get the others out if I can. Just stay clear until I give the high sign."

Sherrie didn't seem to like the idea, but she nodded.

"Your funeral," she said, and I stepped up to the shed door and knocked.

"Ex! Karen! It's Jayné! We need to talk!"

I waited for a hail of gunfire, but all I got was a stream of invective from inside the shed. I heard men and women scattering in the thick, wet darkness and held myself steady. When the door swung open, the light was blinding.

"What the hell are you doing here?" Karen said, and for the first time I recognized the deepness and power in her voice as a rider. Carrefour was speaking through her, and the mask was beginning to slip.

"I need to talk to Ex," I said.

"Jayné?" he said from within. He'd stopped his chanting, but Sabine's keening cry didn't falter.

"Hey," I said. "Sorry for the shitty timing. But . . . I tried calling your cell phone."

"I lost it," he said.

Yeah, I just bet you did, I thought.

My eyes were adjusting. Karen was more than a movement within the brightness, and Ex had come to her side. The shed was lit by four halogen work lamps, hissing and hot as a furnace, and the gloom around us seemed deeper by contrast. Ex looked exhausted. His skin had a gray undertone, and his hair hung in his eyes, limp and greasy. His clothes looked like he'd slept in them. He held a crucifix in one hand and a book bound in black leather in the other.

Karen, on the other hand, almost glowed. Her eyes were bright as a fever, her hair pulled back into a ponytail, with only one stray lock to soften her face. She was wearing what looked like military surplus gear—thick canvas pants and jacket over a ribbed white T-shirt. There was something inhuman in the way she held herself. Carrefour was so close to winning that it could taste the victory, only here I was interrupting the party. Once the young Legba was plucked out of Sabine's body, Carrefour could turn on us all, but until then it had to keep the masquerade going.

I smiled as if I meant it and walked up like I assumed they'd let me pass. Karen almost held her ground, then with a growl like a dog ready to bite, she took a step back, and I went in.

The shed had seemed bigger when it was empty, but it was still a wide, high space. The halogen lamps burned in three corners, fed by bright-orange extension cords. A matte black shotgun lay against the wall like a presentiment of doom. The dirt floor was covered now with symbols in paint and earth like Amelie Glapion's cornmeal veves. The designs seemed to move in my peripheral vision, and they filled me with a deep unease. In the center of the floor, a black iron ring stuck out of the newly poured concrete. Sabine was chained to it, bright steel links going to manacles at her wrists and a tight leather collar at the throat.

Her clothes, ripped and bloody, were the ones she'd worn at the ceremony, the ones I had seen her in only hours before. They were almost unrecognizable. Her eyes were puffy and closed, and she rocked back and forth on the ground, whispering to herself. *Louvri le pót. Legba. Legba. Louvri. Please, please, Legba louvri le pót.* I wanted to sweep over to her, to wrap my arms around her and comfort her and tell her it was going to be all right, even though I thought it probably wasn't.

How had I ever believed this was a good idea?

"What's going on," Karen said. "Why are you here?"

"We got back this morning. I needed to see Ex," I said.

"He doesn't answer to you anymore," Karen said, moving to him in a fair imitation of protectiveness. She took his hand, and he let her. The confusion in his expression hurt to see.

"You fired me," he said, which wasn't exactly the same as Karen's statement.

"Yeah, I know. Look, could I just talk to you for a minute? Alone?" I gestured toward the door. If I could get him outside and out of the line of fire . . .

"No," Karen said. "We're in the middle of a ritual cleansing. Every minute we let it rest, the rider gets its control back over the girl. We have to get her free."

I nodded and smiled as ingratiatingly as I could. It was a doomed effort, but I tried.

"It'll only be—"

"What's going on here?" Karen said. Her eyes swept the door and walls like she could see through them. "Where have you been? What do you want?"

"It's okay," Ex said. "I can handle this."

She turned on him faster than a human could, a hand pressed to his sternum.

"Don't you fucking move," she said. "Something's wrong here. Are you alone? Did you bring someone here?"

"Aubrey and Chogyi Jake are outside," I said, nodding to the door. Karen lifted her head, sniffing the air like an animal. Ex stepped back from her, crossing his arms and frowning.

"I'd love to talk," he said, "but I can't."

Sabine's litany trailed away into a low keening. She looked up, her eyes no more than slits, as if she was seeing me for the first time.

"Jayné?" she said.

The silence that followed was like a thunderclap. The fear tasted like pennies and tinfoil.

"How," Karen said, her voice low and dangerous, "does it know your name?"

"You've got the wrong rider," I said. "Ex, get outside now."

Before he could move, Karen dove, scooped up the shotgun, and whirled. The barrel was pointing at my head, and it was big as a tunnel. And then Ex was between us, shielding me with his body.

"Karen!" Ex shouted. "Stop it! What are you—"

"She's with them," Karen said. "She's been taken over by them. Don't you get it?"

Ex looked at me, fear and pain in his eyes, and I knew he thought it was true. He had walked away from me, and I had gone and gotten myself possessed by a rider, and it was his fault for not protecting me. Months of living in close quarters made every nuance of his expression legible as a book, and I felt a surge of desperate impatience with him.

"Ex, you need to get out of here right now," I said. "Karen lied to us. She's possessed. She has been from the beginning. It's called Carrefour, and it's the exiled rider. The thing in Sabine never left New Orleans."

"But the girl's possessed," Ex said. "I know she is."

"Yeah, that's true. But it's not as bad as you think."

"Move aside, Ex," Karen said. "She used to be Jayné, but she's the enemy now."

"I can save her," Ex said. "I got the thing out of Aubrey, I can get it out of her too."

He believed her. He thought I had a rider. Karen

chambered a round, and Sabine screamed. I tried to step around Ex, but he shifted, staying between me and the gun. Some flying insect found its way into the furnace flame of the lamps and popped as it died.

"You can't kill her," Ex said.

"Oh," Mfume said from the doorway, "I think she can. The beast within her is quite capable of murder."

Karen turned, her face going pale as bone. Mfume didn't flinch when the shotgun pointed at him; he raised his chin in defiance. I had never been so glad to see someone ignore my instructions.

"You can fight it, Karen," he said. "I believe in you. I know that you can fight it."

The blast of the shotgun was deafening. One of the halogen lamps burst in long, streaming flames. The doorway where Mfume had been was empty, and I couldn't tell if he'd dodged the blast or been knocked back by it.

Karen screamed, a sound filled with rage and violence and joy. And like I had turned a switch, my body moved into action. I pushed Ex out of the way gently as lowering a baby into a crib, then hammered out one leg into the shotgun. Karen staggered back, trying to turn the gun toward me, and I kicked it again. I felt the mechanism buckle under my foot, and Karen slammed into the wall like a cannon shot, the wall actually cracking like something out of a cartoon.

Surprise widened her eyes, but only for a moment. Karen launched herself off the wall, swinging for me. I spun back as Ex tried again to put himself between us. Karen's open hand drove into my side, and I felt the snap of my weakened rib even before I felt the pain. I landed hard on my ass at Sabine's side. Ex was yelling something about being reasonable; Sabine was shouting desperately for Legba. Karen and I might almost have been alone in the room.

Her eyes were hard as marble, the little smile at the corner of her mouth ticked up a degree. Pale hair framed her face and made her beautiful. I knew that beside her, I must look like a drowned rat—fog-soaked shirt and jeans, black hair sticking to me like ivy on bricks. I had a hand pressed to my broken ribs. Every breath hurt like a bitch.

"You can't have them," I said, not knowing quite what I meant by it, but absolutely clear on my sincerity.

Karen snarled and brought her foot down hard. She was aiming for my knee, but only scraped along my shin as I rolled. Another blow landed on my shoulder, shaking my balance but not badly enough to keep me from regaining my feet. I was going to lose. I was hurt and comparatively weak, and Karen had years of training and a supernatural serial killer. I faced across the narrow space, and I knew that I had no chance standing against her alone.

I also knew there were thirty plus people just

outside the shed. I hadn't managed to talk Ex out to safety. I hadn't managed to get Sabine free.

But I had gotten Karen's undivided attention, and that was going to be enough. I bolted for the door.

The air outside was cool, the fog thicker than when I'd gone in. The house glowed, twenty feet away, and distant as a vision of elfland. I ducked by instinct and something whizzed past my head to thud against the wall. I skidded to a halt, the grass slick under my feet, and dropped to one knee. My side was on fire, my breath short. I was pretty sure nothing had punctured a lung but I wouldn't have put a lot of money on it.

After the brightness of the halogen lamps, the world was a tissue of shadows and mist. Karen roared out from the lit doorway, murder in her voice, and three dark forms tackled her. She went down, twisting like a cat. I heard a soft impact, and one of the bodies rolled free as two more piled on. Someone shouted, and a volley of answering calls came from the distant trees. My little army charged.

Ex appeared framed in the light, his crucifix held loosely in his hand, his mouth open in confusion. Chogyi Jake stepped out of the shadows, putting a hand on his shoulder.

"Don't kill her!" Mfume called out as the cultists of Legba descended on Karen. His voice was strained, but not weak. "Hold her down, but do not kill the horse!"

They piled on her like a football team, and Karen, screaming, went down under the sheer weight of bodies. I let myself sag a little. I'd gotten a cut on my neck, but I didn't remember when. A trickle of blood ran down my collarbone. Karen screamed. Someone cursed.

"Jayné?"

Aubrey was at my side. He looked worried.

"I'm okay," I said. "Don't hug me."

He knelt, his hand fluttering between my arm and shoulder, uncertain how to help and unable to keep from trying. I thought it was sweet.

"We have to get Sabine out and get Karen in there," I said. "Ex has to get Carrefour out."

"I know," Aubrey said. "I know. Don't move. You're hurt."

"Yeah. Clear on that. But I'll still be hurt later, and we need to fix Karen now."

"We've got it," Aubrey said. "We're taking care of it."

I let my eyes close. The sound of the tussle was like a television in the next room. Karen's voice was high, shrill, and animalistic. Other voices—Aunt Sherrie, Omar, other men, other women—competed with it yelling instructions or threats or shouting in triumph. Mfume exhorting them not to kill. I thought I heard Sabine wailing behind it all. I lay down, my head resting against cool grass. I felt like the ground itself was lifting me up.

"Mfume?" I said.

"His arm's pretty messed up," Aubrey said. "He won't stop, though. We tried to make him."

He's a big boy, I almost said, but it seemed like a lot of effort. I made do with a long, stuttering sigh. Running footsteps came toward me, familiar as a known voice clearing its throat. I opened my eyes to Ex.

"What the hell is going on?" he said. "They're killing Karen."

"They won't kill her. I don't think they'll even hurt her if they can help it," I said. "But we need to drive the rider out of her body."

"What rider?" he said. "She was fine yesterday. She's fine. When did she get possessed?"

There were tears in his eyes. Of course there were. In the rush and fear for him, I'd never taken a minute to think how this would look from his perspective. How it would feel. He'd been this woman's lover. He'd shared her bed and her body, he'd gone to her when I pushed him away, and it had all been a lie. Carrefour had used Karen, and Karen had used Ex. If he'd been prone to taking inappropriate responsibility for the safety of people around him before now, this one was going to send him through the roof.

"I can explain everything," I said. "But . . . Ex, I am so, *so* sorry."

I levered myself up. The blood from the cut on

my neck had soaked the parts of my shirt that the
fog and dew hadn't. Ex shook his head once, and
then stopped.

Everything stopped.

Aubrey went still, and the fighters in the dogpile.
The thickening mist froze where it was, and the
distant crickets fell silent. With a howl like meat
tearing, Carrefour rose up, scattering Amelie's congregation like leaves.

Karen was gone. The rider's body had broadened
and thickened, splitting the seams of canvas shirt
and pants. Its fish-pale skin was veined in black, and
claws like knives clicked at its fingertips. I scram-
bled to my feet. A flash of motion to my right was
Joseph Mfume pulling a length of silver chain from
his pocket with his good hand, his shotgunned arm
limp and blood-soaked at his side. Carrefour looked
from one of us to the other, and its broad, inhuman
face broke into a parody of a grin. I said something
obscene.

It had taken us to the crossroads, the natural
environment of riders, the place where the Venn
diagram of reality and hell overlapped. We weren't
thirty to one. It was just me and Mfume, neither of
us whole, against an engine of rage and death, and
suddenly I didn't like our odds.

Carrefour raised its bladed hands and bounded
toward me.

TWENTY-FOUR

I fell back, scampering toward the cargo van, thinking I could get it between me and the rider as cover. Carrefour loped forward, lashing at me as I ducked. The windshield shattered. Safety glass pattered down on me like hail. I spun around, my arms out like I was on a highwire and keeping my balance. One blow, and Carrefour had destroyed the windshield and peeled back a swath of metal from the van's hood. A second swing rocked the van with a low boom. Carrefour lurched around the corner of the van to face me.

Not every trace of Karen had vanished. I could

see the echo of her impish smile, something familiar
in the angle of the thing's shoulders and the way it
moved its arms. Traces of the woman still remained in
the beast, and if anything that made it worse. Carrefour blinked bloody eyes and shrieked. I saw the blow
coming, and I stepped under it. I sank my fist into the
mottled flesh where its solar plexus would have been
if it were human, and I heard its breath hiss out, felt
the heat of its body pressing against mine. The energy
of its qi, the raw will of its consciousness, writhed
against me and I felt a heat blooming in my own
belly, rising to press back. I shouted, and it growled,
set its feet into the soft ground, and pushed. I tried to
shift away, but it got a shoulder against my chest and
leaned in. Its weight pressed the air out of my lungs,
the door of the van behind me bent in an inch and
then another. My broken ribs flared with a pain that
put stars in my peripheral vision. I couldn't breathe,
couldn't lever myself out. I got an arm free to box its
ears, but the blow was weak, ineffective, doomed.

I started to pass out.

Something bright hissed above my head, and
Carrefour screamed. The sound seemed distant. The
weight lifted and I slumped to the ground. I watched
the rider's wide legs stagger backward, my mind
urging my body to function, to rise, to run. Mfume's
voice was calling out, passionate and angry, in a language I didn't know. I rose to my knees, sank back,
then forced myself up again.

Mfume's chain had buried itself deep in the flesh of Carrefour's back, and Mfume stood in the space between house and shed, straining with his one good arm to pull the thing back. Dark blood seeped down the rider's side and it swung its arm wide, its claws raking the metal of the chain but not quite able to grasp it.

Carrefour opened its mouth.

"Joseph!" it howled, its voice deep and masculine and terrible. "Joseph, my love! Stop this. We are so near, so *near*—"

"There is no *we*!" Mfume yelled. "I am my own, and you will release her. Release the woman and go!"

It was a nice thought, but I was pretty sure negotiation wasn't going to work. I gathered myself as Carrefour twisted around to face Mfume. It was as good a chance as any. I ran forward, kicking at its knee. It was like slamming my foot into a rock, but Carrefour stumbled. Mfume shifted to the side, the chain pulling at a slightly different angle. I sidestepped and hammered my foot down on the rider's heel. Carrefour screamed, and it sounded like real pain this time.

For a few seconds, I thought we might win.

Carrefour whipped around, the silver hook in its flesh making a terrible wet sound as it tore free. I saw Mfume stagger and something hit me, lifted me. For an eternal, breathless moment, I was in the air, my arms and legs flailing for anything to grab onto, to find purchase. The ground rose up and hit me like a truck.

Mfume was screaming. I rolled to my side. I didn't think I could stand up, but I could pull myself. If I could crawl into the dark behind the shed, maybe it would ignore me. Maybe it would forget me, give me time to recover. Carrefour bellowed, and I felt the ground beneath me tremble. I dug my fingers into the wet ground and pulled. The grass was cool against my palms.

We couldn't beat it. Not the two of us now, not the whole damned mob of us before. And it had no hesitation in killing us. It was practiced. We were dead.

Sabine's voice came to me like a song being sung in a different room. The words were the same, *Legba louvri le pót,* but there was a depth to them, a seriousness. Worse, a pain. I shifted myself toward the small prison house, the light, the sound of her desperate voice.

Sabine sat on the floor, chains slack on her wrists and neck. Her back was hunched, her face running with sweat as she strained internally. I couldn't help thinking of childbirth. Her eyes were the clear, shining black of river stones. She had too many teeth.

"Louvri mwen, Legba," she said. *"Louvri le pót."*

I pulled myself toward her. Something loud happened outside, sudden and terrible as a cannon. I ignored it. I crawled closer to the girl. The air around her shifted and swirled like water stirred by a thousand writhing tadpoles. I closed my eyes and gathered my qi. I pictured the energy rising through my spine, out my arm, and arcing between my fingertips with a golden light. I held out my hand, and I felt Sabine touch me.

Her flesh was burning hot and sweat-slick. Her fingers clenched mine until my knuckles ached, and I felt something within her pulling at me like a riptide. I wanted to fight it, to pull myself back into myself, but instinct said that withholding now was surrendering to Carrefour. I pressed what little of myself I could focus out, into the girl, feeding the rider within her.

And then she let me go. I rolled onto my back, staring toward the ceiling as in the corner of my vision, Sabine Glapion opened her mouth wide, and then wider. Her jawbone cracked, and the serpent flowed out of her. Sabine's clothing and skin fell to the floor in discarded coils.

The scales shone silver in the bright halogen glow, and the needle-teeth were white as ivory. It wasn't the Legba that had come from Amelie Glapion. This snake was thinner, faster, and brighter. Something about it reminded me of the awkwardness of adolescence, though its motion was perfectly graceful. It turned to me, and I knew that if it lunged for my neck, I wouldn't be able to protect myself. The broad head turned to the darkness and the mist. A black tongue flickered.

"Carrefour!" Legba called, its voice a clatter and a hiss. "You have trespassed!"

The serpent swam through the air like an eel in a drowned city. I forced myself up to sitting and did my best to follow.

Carrefour stood in the pathway between shed and house holding Mfume by his neck in one thick, monstrous hand. The others—Aubrey and Ex, the cultists of Amelie Glapion's congregation—stood still as statues as Carrefour let his once and present victim slide to the ground. I wanted to move forward, to help, but I barely had the strength to keep my eyes open. I wondered almost idly how much granting my will to help Legba's birth had cost me.

"Legba," Carrefour said. "Petit Legba. You are born in time to die. The shortest life. Come to me, Legba the brief."

I propped myself against the doorframe. I couldn't stand. I couldn't fight. Carrefour strode across the night-dark, fog-shrouded space, and I didn't doubt for a second that this new Legba was just as screwed as I was.

The serpent spoke.

"*Louvri,*" it said, and I knew what it meant. *Open.*

I caught my breath. Behind Carrefour, Aubrey lifted his head. The motion was slow, like something happening underwater. Aubrey turned. His face looked wrong; thinner, sharper. He stepped forward, and his shirt and pants hung loose on his body. He was skeletal, and when he spoke, it wasn't with his own voice. It was Marinette's.

"There is no place for you here, brother."

Carrefour spun. Aubrey took two steps forward, and the transformation was complete. The burned flesh, the skeletal thinness, the vicious eyes. But there was something of Aubrey in it too. Marinette's gaze flickered to me and turned back to Carrefour, more angry than before. Man and rider weren't in conflict this time. They had both come to kick some ass, and I found I had the energy left in me for a grin. In the dark air above me, Legba shifted its silver coils, a thousand colors dancing on its scales like a sheen of oil on water.

"Marinette," Carrefour said, its hands out before it, the knifelike claws now pleading. "Please, my love, do not stand with them against me. We are Petro, you and I."

"Your *love*?" Marinette said. The contempt in its voice would have peeled paint. "Radha, Petro, Ghede. What does tribe matter here? I am *loa*. What are you?"

"I will not be stopped," Carrefour said, but it wasn't a threat. If anything, the rider's landslide of a voice sounded sorrowful.

"You will," Marinette said, and Carrefour leaped at her. With a cry like joy, Marinette met its charge, and the impact made the ground shudder. Marinette was thin, but solid as stone. Carrefour didn't treat her gently. It swung its knives, kicked, bit. Marinette blocked the blows with her forearms—with Aubrey's forearms—and Carrefour's claws skittered off them, shredding the sleeves of Aubrey's shirt, but doing no other damage that I could see. On the other hand, I couldn't see that Marinette was doing more than holding Carrefour at bay. It was like watching lions fight. Huge beasts, filled with almost unimaginable violence, inhuman and strong and awful.

A movement caught my eye. One of the cultists—Omar, I thought—bent his arm, pressed his hand against the ground, rose up. Then a woman on the other side of me. And another. Changes were taking them as well as they stood witness to the battle. I saw Aunt Sherrie, but she had also become a horribly scarred woman with a baby in one arm and a wicked knife in the other. One of the men whose name I hadn't known had a wide, jolly face, a tuxedo, and a clay pipe that he was smoking with the bowl turned down. Ex moved, crossed his arms, frowned. His skin was whiter than snow and glittered in light I couldn't see. A fleur-de-lis was on his skin like a tattoo made from light.

As the transformations came, something in me grew very still, like a mouse trying not to be noticed by a gathering of cats. I had felt riders pressing at the fabric of the world, had felt them trying to force their way into my own flesh. I had never felt the raw power that stood around me.

And slowly, Carrefour became aware of it too. Its battle with Marinette became sloppier, more distracted. Marinette pressed its advantage, but it seemed to me it was more proving a point than trying to win. Carrefour broke off, backing away from the thing in Aubrey's flesh. The man with the upside-down pipe shook his head in disgust.

"My brothers!" Carrefour said. "My brothers, I have returned. Rise up! Rise up with me!"

None of the *loa* moved. The expression on the thing's face had gone from glee and killing rage to a mixture of sadness and fear, and I understood what I was seeing.

Carrefour had been sent out, away from its people, away from its family. It had been lost and alone in just the way it had isolated the men and women it rode. And here were its family, its friends, its community arrived together to cast it out again. I almost felt sorry for it.

But not quite.

"You broke faith. You took the part of the Graveyard Child against us," a woman's voice rolled in from my left. "And we cast you away. Now you return as our enemy once more."

"No," Carrefour cried. "No, I have come home."

"You have killed Legba's queen and sought the slaughter of the spirit itself," the woman's voice went on. "We condemn you, Carrefour. You have no place among us."

"Gran Maître!" Carrefour cried, but the words that followed were lost. The roar wasn't sound or vibration, it wasn't the rush of a waterfall or of flame. The unleashed will of the riders filled the crossroads, a maelstrom that tore like winds and pounded like a ship broken free of its mooring slamming itself against the dock. For a moment, I was lifted up on it, carried out of myself by just the backsplash from it. Magic spilled though the cracks between seconds, lit the individual atoms, screamed joy and vengeance and something more primal than either.

And then, from the center of the storm, silence. Or no, not silence, because I could hear the distant chirping of crickets. The battle between the *loa* might still be going on, but it had moved out of the crossroads, out of the world. Out of the thin sphere of human influence.

"Holy shit," someone said from the darkness. The blasphemy had more sense of real awe than anything I'd ever heard in a church. "Oh holy shit."

And then another voice cut through the darkness, high and thin as a violin bowing a single, plaintive note.

"Where am I?" Karen Black said. "Where am I?"

She was standing naked in the fog, her pale hair plastered to her head and neck. Her ice-blue eyes were wide and frightened. Blood was running freely from her shoulder where Mfume's hooked chain had ripped the flesh, and from a dozen other shallow cuts. The red tendrils of it made me think of a dragonfly's wing.

"Karen," I said, levering myself up to squatting. My head swam. Sabine Glapion appeared at my side, free of her chains, and helped me stand. I felt eighteen kinds of damaged, but seeing Karen look at me, seeing her recognize me, seeing her remember was the worst thing that had happened all night.

"No," she said, as if asking me for something. Begging.

I let Sabine walk me forward two exquisitely painful steps. Karen shook her head slowly, the blood draining from her already pale face.

"I'm sorry," I said.

"Karen?"

Ex was behind her, a jacket open in his hands ready to cover her nakedness. Karen jumped away from him like she'd been stung. Ex tried to smile in reassurance, but it didn't reach his eyes. He didn't understand yet that the Karen he'd known was gone, but he suspected. I raised my hand, prepared to wave him back. Karen's voice stopped me.

"I know you," she said.

"Yes," Ex said, holding out the jacket.

"We were lovers."

Ex took a deep breath, maybe at the past tense she used, maybe at something else.

"Yes," he said. "We were."

"Kill me," she said.

I winced. Ex tried again to give her the jacket and she wrenched it out of his hands and threw it into the darkness.

"Kill me," she said, her voice stronger. "Kill me. You have to *kill me*!"

"It's okay," Ex said. "It's over. It's going to be all right."

Karen was plucking unconsciously at her arms, trying to pull the skin off without knowing what she meant by it or why. Her eyes were distant, lost in years of memory that she was seeing with only her own mind for the very first time. Her eyes squeezed closed and she let out a keening wail. Ex looked to me and back at her, as helpless as I was.

"Karen," Mfume said. "Stop this."

He limped out from the fog. One arm still hung limp and dead at his side. He was covered in his own blood. I didn't see any pain in his face, only a hard, insistent compassion. Karen tilted her head, disbelieving.

"You?" she said.

"Me," he said gravely. "Also me. Everything Carrefour did to you, it also did to me. I know what is happening to you now, what it means to be free of it. It is the gift you once gave me."

Aubrey came to my side, helping Sabine support me. I was getting a little light-headed.

"You don't know," Karen said. "You can't. I

laughed. I killed them, and while they died, I laughed. They were my parents."

"You were *forced* to laugh," Mfume said as he slowly, painfully pulled off his own overcoat. "It wasn't your true feeling. It wasn't real. This. Now. These feelings are real."

"I killed them. Oh God, and I killed Michael."

"You did," Mfume said, kneeling beside her and draping the dark, bloody coat over her bare shoulders. "Only it wasn't you. It was the demon that had taken your body and your will. You have done none of this."

"Kill me," Karen said. "Please kill me. You don't understand. If you don't, I'll want it. I'll want it back."

"You will. And then, later, you won't. I have been through all of this, and I can guide you through it too. Stay with me," Mfume said. "If you cannot find peace, I will kill you myself."

The tears streaming down her cheeks looked like gratitude.

"Promise me," she said.

"I promise you," Mfume said.

Karen reached up to him, and he leaned carefully forward, putting his arm around her, cradling her. Her arms lifted up around him, white against the black of his skin and the deep, uncompromising red of his blood-soaked shirt. The rest of us stood silently around them as Karen Black sobbed.

TWENTY-FIVE

How does anyone put a world back together? How does anyone begin again? When everything changes—changes for the better, changes for the worse, a little of both—it isn't just the world that's called into question. It's you too. Who you are, and what that means.

The eight of us sat at the same table Karen had brought us to the first day in New Orleans. The same waiters brought us three huge platters of bright red crawfish. The breeze that stirred the palm fronds was warm, the light pressing down through the hazy late spring sky was probably going to sunburn my nose. If I hadn't been quite so thoroughly bruised and abraded, I'd have been wearing shorts and a halter top. I wore slacks that went down to my ankles and a billowy cotton blouse with long sleeves and a high collar. Getting out of the hotel shower that morning, I'd looked like something from the unpleasant part of a David Lynch film.

Sabine, on the other hand, was wearing shorts and a halter top. She looked beautiful and serene and in command of the table in a way utterly unlike a sixteen-year-old orphan girl who'd lost her grandmother two days before. Daria, sitting to her left, fidgeted and frowned in what I thought of as school-uniform chic. The adults—Chogyi Jake, Aubrey, Ex, Dr. Inondé, and my lawyer—seemed like the disciples here; the city revolved around Sabine Glapion now.

"Well," my lawyer said, scooping the papers out of the way as the third platter of crustacean floated down before her, "I think that puts it all in order. Actually filing will take some time, of course."

"You're sure no one's going to object?" Dr. Inondé said. It turned out he'd grown up in a part of Brooklyn my lawyer knew.

"Emancipation proceedings at Sabine's age aren't at all unusual," my lawyer said. "And with no surviving adult relatives, I can't see anyone raising an objection."

"But it does look awfully strange," Dr. Inondé

said, wringing his hands, "an old man like me being a business partner with, well . . ."

"A little girl?" Sabine said with a grin. She scooped up one of the crawfish, snapped off the head, and sucked at it while Daria made a theatrical gagging sound.

"I'm just saying it looks odd from the outside," Dr. Inondé said.

"However it looks, it will be legal and binding," my lawyer said, "and Jayné here has put aside a little something to cover expenses if anything does come up. You have my number. Only call, and I'll see it's taken care of."

Dr. Inondé nodded, but his brow didn't lose its furrows.

"Something's bothering you about it?" Aubrey asked.

"He doesn't want to fold both businesses together," Sabine said. "Thinks that the Voodoo Heart Temple and the Authentic New Orleans Voodoo Museum ought to stay separate, like two different . . . franchises."

Her use of the last word was careful and not, I thought, entirely correct. For a moment, the persona slipped, and Sabine wasn't the voodoo queen of New Orleans, but a kid thrown into an adult world and doing her best. It was temporary. The lost little girl would appear less and less over time, and before long she'd be gone forever, and some new, still-forming Sabine Glapion would take her place, same as with anyone. Dr. Inondé waved his hands. I picked up a crawfish. Its shell was still hot from the boiler.

"I just think they pull in different types," he said. "My museum's a roadside attraction. Very touristy. The Temple is more local. Part of the community."

"But if you combine those and cut overhead," Ex said with a shrug.

"It will be better as one thing," Daria said solemnly. "Believe me, I *know*."

Dr. Inondé blinked, and Sabine slapped her sister smartly on the shoulder.

"Don't go lying to him, or he's not going to believe you when it's important," Sabine said, and Daria grinned impishly.

"There may be a middle path," Chogyi Jake said, his voice abstracted and thoughtful. The conversation moved on to business planning and maximizing profit, building reputation and reaching out to the tourist trade, what to put on the Web site and whether to advertise outside of the city itself. I let the talk wash over me, a rush of sound and meaning like a wave tugging at the sand.

I was exhausted. My ribs hurt badly. The ACE bandage that I'd wrapped myself with helped some, but it was going to be several deeply uncomfortable weeks before I was whole again.

When our lunch was over, we all walked out to

the street together, Sabine and Dr. Inondé still wrangling about the structure of their new joint business. In truth, it was only the fine points. He would manage and oversee the day-to-day business and draw a salary. Sabine would shoulder the more abstract burden of being the living crossroads, the queen of New Orleans, the avatar of Legba. That and she was going back to finish high school. The combination made my head swim a little.

On the street, a thin white kid was leaning against the wall playing guitar, the case open on the sidewalk with a few crumpled dollars and coins there to confirm its function. Aubrey dropped in a five. We said our good-byes, and as we turned and walked away, Daria ran back, hugging me fiercely around the waist. I held her for a long moment, then let her go pelting after her sister through the narrow, sweating street. My lawyer fell into step beside me.

"That went much better than I'd expected," she said. "I won't lie to you, dear. When you said you were getting involved with the Glapions, I was concerned. They aren't the sort of people you want to be on the wrong side of."

"It took a while, but I figured that part out," I said.

"Your uncle would have been proud," she said. "And about the other matter?"

"I'd like to go too," Ex said, breaking in.

"I said it was just going to be me," I said. "I promised."

Ex's expression hardened, but he didn't push back. Part of him was probably relieved.

I DROVE out alone. The lake was familiar by now, the water greenish-brown in the midafternoon sun. Traffic along I-10 was lighter than I expected, and I got off the highway a couple exits earlier than usual rather than get to Pearl River sooner than I'd meant to. I drove, aiming myself down residential streets, letting the time pass.

The storm damage here wasn't so bad. The bathtub ring wasn't there on the buildings. A few places near the water showed some damage, the searchers' X. And some had new windows. I stopped at a Subway and got a six-inch sub and some salt and vinegar chips that I ate sitting on the curb, watching the traffic and the street life. This wasn't the Vieux Carré. The sense of history and place was less oppressive here. It was only a city, alive and functioning. A little damaged, but growing back. Becoming itself.

How do you put a city back together? One house at a time. One restaurant, one coffee stand. One hospital and one pothole and one cheesy tourist trap voodoo museum at a time. And you try to get ready for the next storm.

The safe house looked the same, but it felt different. It was like the space itself had been altered by what had happened there. I pulled up the drive. The Virgin Mary in front was covered in flowers and burned-out candles studded the lawn before her outstretched arms. Someone had left the Holy Mother a fifth of bourbon as an offering. I wasn't sure what I thought about that, but at least she didn't look like a tombstone anymore. I went to the door of the house I'd bought and knocked tentatively.

Mfume answered it.

He looked rough. Three days' worth of stubble salted his chin and cheeks. He wore a white T-shirt that left visible all the pale pink divots in his arm where the shotgun pellets had been dug out. He smiled when he saw me, the wide, goofy grin I'd first seen in his police record. I smiled back, and he stepped inside, ushering me through. He was still limping pretty bad.

The sunlight in the front room was softened and indirect; shadowy without any actual shadows. It smelled like the chicken noodle soup I'd had when I was sick as a kid. Comfort food.

"She's resting in the back bedroom," he said.

"How's that going?" I asked.

He shook his head and lowered himself to sit on the arm of the couch.

"She sleeps some, and then she doesn't," he said.

"I believe she is still discovering how much has been taken from her. That will go on for some time."

"I'm sorry to hear it," I said.

"It could have been much worse," he said. "It nearly was."

"Yeah, well."

"How are you?"

"I feel like a pit bull's chew toy," I said. "But it'll heal. I'll be fine."

"And the others?"

"Ex is a little screwed up, I think," I said. "I haven't really talked to him yet, but . . . he was sleeping with a possessed woman and didn't notice."

"It isn't obvious," Mfume said. "The rider didn't present itself. How could he be expected to know?"

"He's pretty deeply into the whole self-blame thing anyway," I said. "I'm not sure that being justified in the mistake will really slow him down much."

"That's too bad," Mfume said.

"Yeah. And Aubrey's still processing. But I think he and Marinette sort of made peace with each other during that last fight. He slept through the night last night. No particular nightmares."

I didn't add that I knew that because I'd been sleeping next to him. There hadn't been any sex. Just sleeping. But still.

"And Chogyi?"

"Chogyi Jake's Chogyi Jake," I said. "I have no idea

what happens in his head unless he lets me in on it."

Mfume nodded, started to cross his arms, then winced and put them back down at his sides.

"So," I said, "I've been thinking about it. I don't need this house. I've got a lot of houses and apartments and everything. I'd like you to stay here. Or, you know, if you want to. As long as you and Karen need a place, you can have this one. I'll pop for the utilities and everything. Cable."

"I appreciate what you're trying to do," he said, "but—"

"Here's the thing," I said, not letting him get out a whole objection. "You're dead. I mean, Joseph Mfume's dead, and if he's not, then he's an escaped serial killer. I've got it figured that you're uncomfortable accepting help and all. You spent a bunch of time killing anyone who reached out, and that's got to put a spin on things. Just classical conditioning, like you said. But it's not about you anymore, is it? It's about her now."

Mfume's eyebrows rose and he took a deep breath.

"You were a loner when Carrefour was driving, because that's Carrefour's shtick," I said. "You were solo after that because . . . well, you were doing the fugitive hunter thing. Not really conducive to an active social life. But that's done too. You have to take care of Karen, and I can help with that."

"And why would you?" he asked.

"Because I can. It costs me essentially nothing and it makes me feel better. So, you know. Go me."

The moment was fragile, but it was precious. He nodded.

"Let me think about it," he said.

"Think as long as you want, so long as afterward, you say yes."

He laughed. It was a warm sound, rueful and joyful and cathartic.

"All right," he said. "I don't have the strength to fight with two of you."

"Thank you," I said.

"You're welcome," he replied with a smile that appreciated the irony.

The voice from the kitchen was weak.

"You're Jayné," Karen said.

She walked in wearing a robe. Her eyes were swollen from weeping. Three black scabs on her neck showed where Marinette's fingers had raked Carrefour's flesh. Two riders had fought, and Karen's body had been the battlefield.

The woman I'd known was gone. The self-assured, hyper-competent, kicking ass and taking names occult mistress of darkness had always been a load of crap, whether it was her pretending it or me trying to live up to her.

"Hey," I said.

"I remember you," Karen said. "It hated you a lot. And it was . . . scared of you too."

"I don't know why," I said. "I'm just me."

"Jayné asked us to take care of her house while she is away," Mfume said.

"Like caretakers?" Karen asked.

"Like that, yeah," I said, picking up my cue. "If it's not too much trouble."

"Sure," she said, holding the robe closed at her neck. "I can handle that."

We talked for another few minutes until Karen started wearing out and headed back for another nap. We said our good-byes. Karen hugged me and said how glad she was to meet me.

So here's the thing. Any sufficiently massive change is complicated. It's not just good or just bad. Sabine Glapion lost her grandmother and got possessed by a rider, but she also became the un-disputed voodoo queen of New Orleans with money and property and a congregation of cultists bent on protecting and supporting her. Karen Black escaped years of demonic possession and walked back into a world where she had no job, no family, no friends. New Orleans was broken under the storm, but it re-fused to die, and the city that it became—that it was still becoming—wasn't the one it had been. It was better and worse, lessened and increased, richer and the place where something precious had been lost forever.

Less than a year before, I had known who I was: a failed college student on the outs with her family and estranged from her church and the God she didn't believe in. I had no particular prospects, I had no plans or goals or ambitions more sophisticated than not being homeless. And then I'd been given the world on a plate. Money, power, a secret war against evil that I could champion. But every sufficiently massive change is complicated. Because I'd gotten everything, and I had lost my sense of myself.

The good news was that, just like Sabine and Karen and the city of New Orleans, I could fix that.

When I got back to my room, I showered, changed the dressings on my various cuts and scrapes, and went to Aubrey's room. He was in slacks and a gray T-shirt with a golden fleur-de-lis on it. His smile was warm, but exhausted.

"How'd it go?" he asked.

"Talked them into it," I said, sitting on the bed beside him. He smelled like soap and sandalwood. I leaned against his shoulder. "Karen was easier to convince than Mfume."

"She'll be okay, you think?"

"I think," I said. "Given time. What about you?"

He turned to look at me, his eyebrows raised a millimeter.

"Marinette," I said. "You and her all copacetic now?"

He laughed, then winced. His ribs were a little tender too.

"Better," he said. "Not . . . good, but better."

"So you're not too spun by it showing back up and taking over?"

Aubrey took a long breath, his brow furrowing itself. Slowly, he shook his head.

"No. It was . . . different. When it wanted the same thing I did, it was more like it was on my side. And I cannot tell you how good it felt to kick the shit out of Carrefour."

"Even though it wasn't you in the body?"

"It was, though. It was both of us. Me and Marinette both. When it left . . . Well, I didn't want it to come back, but I could understand why someone would."

I was quiet for a moment.

"But it *is* gone, right?"

"Oh yes," Aubrey said, taking my hand. "It's not subtle. If it were still in me, you'd know."

"Good," I said, and kissed him.

I wanted to push him back on the bed, curl up beside him. Sleep or make out or a little of both. But I had a larger plan to put in motion, and I had one other thing to do before I could.

Ex's hotel room was on the second floor with a balcony that looked out over the street. He'd left the door to the hallway open, and a breeze stirred the curtains. A Bible lay open on the bed. He was sitting at the small, black writing desk, looking into the air with an expression that seemed numb. He had one of his black button-down shirts on, his hair loose and hanging to his shoulders.

"Hey," I said.

He looked up at me, pleasure and dread and the expectation of punishment flickering across him in less than a heartbeat.

"Hey," he said. I sat on the edge of the bed.

"So," I said. "We probably need to talk."

"If you want," he said.

"That stuff you threw at me in Atlanta? The sexuality and failure of leadership thing? You were out of line," I said. "I was down, and I was hurt, and you kind of kicked the shit out of me."

"Yes, I was," he said. "I'm not proud of that."

"Good. Don't be. But here's the thing. I was out of line too."

The confusion in his expression was interesting. He didn't see it. I wondered if he ever really saw anyone's sins besides his own.

"That whole firing you thing was shitty of me," I said. "I was kicking back, and I went too far. I don't get to pull rank on you. Or on Aubrey or Chogyi Jake. I need you guys to be my friends, not my employees. And that means I don't get to go straight to the nuclear option when you piss me off."

"You weren't out of line," Ex said. "I deserved it."

"Doesn't matter. There will be a time when you need to kick my ass and tell me I'm full of shit. And I need to be able to hear that. If we set precedent where I get rid of anyone who confronts me about something, I'm screwed."

"I suppose it's all about setting the right boundaries," he said. There was something wistful in his voice. I hadn't meant to tackle that too, but the issue was right there, and I went for it.

"I'm going to be straight here, okay?"

"You were being crooked before?" he said.

"I may be sleeping with Aubrey," I said. "I'm kind of into him. And if that's a problem for you—"

"It isn't," Ex said.

"You're sure?" I asked.

He was lying, or if he wasn't, he was fooling himself. Ex shook his head, then plucked a black band from his pocket and tied his hair back in a severe ponytail.

"I know what Chogyi Jake told you," he said. "The first thing he did this morning was come to me and confess."

"Yeah, that sounds like him," I said.

Ex held up his hand.

"I wish he hadn't done what he did. I think he's wrong about the motives behind my . . . poor behavior. I don't need you to feel anything in particular about me," he said. "I'm a grown-up. I'll handle it. I only need you to treat me with respect."

"I can do that," I said, then a moment later, tapping on the doorframe, I added, "if you can do the same. The part where you dis me in public for not being able to control my sexuality?"

"I project a little sometimes," Ex said, blushing. "Karen . . . Carrefour messed with my head. I was talking about myself more than you. I just didn't see it at the time. I'm not as good a person as I would like to be. But I'm trying, and I'll get better."

"Pax, then?"

"Pax," Ex said.

A little knot of anxiety I hadn't known was there loosened in my chest. The gang was back together, and all was right with the world.

"Come on down to the coffee shop?" I said. "Planning session."

Aubrey and Chogyi Jake sat at the small table near the street talking passionately about which Stephen Chow movie was better. Bright, complex Dixieland jazz played on the speakers, just the way it had, it seemed, for years. I sat down, and Ex sat across from me. Chogyi Jake's smile passed between us before returning, satisfied, to Aubrey.

"All right," I said. "Carrefour is thwarted. Sabine is . . . well, still possessed, but at least by a demon she knows. Karen Black is being nursed back to health. I declare our work here done."

"About time," Aubrey said with a lopsided grin. "What's next?"

"Portland, Oregon," I said.

Chogyi Jake's eyes narrowed. I could almost hear him thinking.

"Did Eric have property in Oregon?"

"Condo in Eugene," I said. "Nothing in Portland."

"So what's there?" Aubrey said.

"Mfume's history," Ex said, darkly.

"Pink Martini concerts," I said. "Powell's bookstore. It has also been alleged that there are some excellent microbreweries. And most important? Eric didn't have property there. We've been busting hump for months because I was thinking there was somebody I was supposed to be, and you guys were all too polite and supportive to rein me in. Well. I'm reined in now. I've always wanted to go to Portland. I've never been. And I say we're taking some time off."

"Oh thank God," Aubrey said, sagging back in his chair. Ex chuckled, and Chogyi Jake smiled his constant, authentic, gentle smile.

You really *need to find out who you are,* Daria Glapion had said to me once, not very long before. Sitting there with my friends around me, I thought I was making some progress. I wasn't the girl who'd smart-mouthed her father into apoplexy before Sunday services, I wasn't the sad-sack college dropout whose friends had left her behind, I wasn't the demon huntress I'd tried to be with Karen Black. And if I also wasn't sure yet who precisely I was becoming, at least I understood now that the only wrong answer was to hold too tightly to what I thought I was supposed to be. It was a start.

Only it turned out that wasn't what she'd meant at all.